△

CW01113197

CO 2 55 1225

The Killing House

The Killing House
Derek Lambert

DURHAM COUNTY COUNCIL Arts, Libraries & Museums	
5512255	
J M L S	02/04/97
F	£16.99

Copyright © 1997 by Derek Lambert

First published in Great Britain in 1997 by
Judy Piatkus (Publishers) Ltd of
5 Windmill Street, London W1

**The moral right of the author
has been asserted**

*A catalogue record for this book is available
from the British Library*

ISBN 0–7499–0370–8

Set in 11/12 pt Times by
Intype London Ltd
Printed and Bound by Bookcraft (Bath) Ltd.,
Midsomer Norton, Somerset

Whither is fled the visionary gleam?
Where is it now, the glory and the dream?

William Wordsworth, 'Intimations of Immortality from Recollections of Early Childhood'

For Basil Cudlipp-Green
and Paddy Waltham,
good friends

Author's Note

The heart of this novel, a thriller, is the deaths of innocents, in particular children, who die at the hands of terrorists fighting for a cause of which they, the guileless, have no comprehension. I have therefore dedicated this book to FNA, a charity formed 'to rescue, protect, and rehabilitate the lost children of Colombia'. These children live and die long before their time in the streets and sewers of Bogotá, where they are treated as parasites. Victims, in fact, of the worst terrorists of all – grown-ups who betray children's trust. The charity's address, where financial contributions can restore some of that lost faith, is:

>Fundación Niños de los Andes
>Carrera 20 BIS A No. 164–51
>Santafé de Bogotá
>Colombia.

It has a British connection, Children of the Andes, with a registered address at Enterprise House, 59–65 Upper Ground, London SE1 9PQ, and a working address c/o EMA, Flaxman House, Gogmore Lane, Chertsey, Surrey KT16 9SS. The patron is the actress Virginia McKenna.

Part I

Chapter One

Harry Quarrick whimpered in his sleep. Screamed in a nightmare, Helen thought. Where was he in the dream? The fact that two people could lie down close to each other, shut their eyes and take off into different lives had always intrigued her.

She stared out of the window at the fading moon shining through a wound in the clouds. Where, for that matter, had Harry been before he came home and went to sleep? The plane from Paris had been due at Heathrow at 9.55 pm but he hadn't arrived at the house until hours later. Perhaps the flight had been delayed. She would ask him at breakfast. Or would she? Communication between the two of them was now minimal. Sad, because a year ago he would have slipped into her bed – in those days they had shared a double bed – and told her what had happened. And then they would have made love.

His breathing was more rhythmic now, whatever had provoked the whimper dispatched. Helen closed her eyes and drifted away from her husband.

Where Quarrick had been two hours earlier was in a stolen taxi travelling through the rainswept suburbs of west London.

Brady drove at a decorous speed but at a set of traffic lights in Brentford Quarrick noticed the tense hunch of his wrestler's shoulders. He opened the dividing window. 'Don't jump the lights! All we need is to be busted for a traffic offence.'

Brady, one of those who had never totally accepted the authority of an American, grunted.

Rain slanted rose-red in the penumbra of the traffic lights. The streets shone as wet as fish. Clouds sagged from the black sky. Heaps of cardboard, newspapers and rags stirred in shop doorways.

The taxi took off at a gentle speed.

'A little faster,' Quarrick told Brady. 'Cab drivers don't hang around at this time in the morning.'

Brady, who was chewing gum, sighed theatrically.

The idea to use a taxi had been Quarrick's. The police were always on the lookout for Jaguars, Transit vans or clapped-out saloons with souped-up engines, but cabs were as much part of the London scene as red buses and vagrants.

Brady had stolen the taxi from a wooden garage behind a terraced house in Ashford while the owner was at the pub. As an extra precaution, he'd changed the number plates at a work bench in a Feltham warehouse.

Quarrick had arrived on a flight from Paris earlier than the one he had booked in case there were delays, and had landed at 7.50 pm. From Heathrow he took the underground to Hounslow Central and holed up in a dingy flat that smelled of mice and mould.

Brady had picked him up at 4.35 am. Quarrick glanced at the illuminated dial of his watch: it was now 4.50.

He watched the reflection of the cab as it jumped from the window of one shop to another, not as squarely staid as the older models but prim just the same, *What's On* advertised on its black flanks.

A white police car drew alongside. Quarrick leaned forward and touched the suitcase with the green and red straps that he had bought years ago in the now defunct Abercrombie and Fitch store in New York. It contained Semtex plastic explosive, a knife with a serrated edge and, in case he was asked to open it, a Walther automatic.

If they were stopped, Brady's story was that he was taking Quarrick, who was carrying a forged maroon and gold European Community passport number 700481639 in the name of Richard Henry Ziman, to the Royal Lancaster Hotel.

Quarrick opened the zip beneath the straps of the suitcase a few inches. The policeman at the wheel gave a one-fingered salute. We night people, the salute said, we're special. His partner spoke into a handset and the squad car accelerated, tyres hissing.

Brady said over his shoulder: 'Would you have done it?' He had a slight Belfast accent.

'Shot them? Sure: they're the enemy.'

Rain machine-gunned the hood of the cab and wept on the windows. According to the rules, Quarrick thought, I shouldn't be here: a commander jeopardising the power structure by taking part in a mission. But Quarrick believed that an officer should be in the front line, not directing other people's brave deeds from a cosy bunker. His stance had been criticised but he had fought for it and won.

An ambulance squawked past as they plunged under the Chiswick flyover, but traffic was light, most of it travelling in the opposite direction, homeward drivers rehearsing excuses to their partners.

Brady aimed the taxi towards Shepherd's Bush and Bayswater Road. Such evocative names. That was what he liked about London, its enigmatic graces. In fact he liked most of England; what he didn't like was the English.

They turned right from Bayswater Road down Park Lane, Hyde Park on the right, grand vistas of Mayfair, Grosvenor House and Dorchester Hotels to the left. As they neared the target, wingbeats of anticipation grew stronger. These days he even experienced them in his dreams, quickening pulse and respiration, taste of blood in his mouth as he bit the flesh inside his lip. The dreams, usually following a mission, were even worse than reality because children were involved. Often his own.

The taxi turned down Grosvenor Place. At a set of traffic lights a bedraggled man wearing a white scarf offered Brady twenty-five pounds to take him to The Boltons. Brady took off abruptly and the man staggered back, slipped and fell.

'Unnecessary,' Quarrick said.

Brady's shoulders tightened.

Quarrick glanced at his watch again. So far the timing was perfect – the cab would pull up outside Victoria Station just as other cabs arrived to pick up commuters from the first trains of the day. Disruption, not bloodshed, was the objective. If the warnings to the BBC, ITV and Sky were dealt with in time, no innocents would suffer. Incoming trains would be halted, trains from the Channel ferries and Gatwick airport among them. Chaos. Another blow to the hesitant recovery of Britain's economy.

And Buckingham Palace wasn't far away. If the explosive blew, it would disturb royal dreams and you couldn't get your message much closer to the Establishment than that.

Quarrick slipped one hand inside the suitcase, touched the package containing the Semtex and the old-fashioned pencil time fuse, and took out the knife. With four slashes he cut a square in the upholstery of the seat and removed a wad of foam rubber. He placed the bomb on the springs where the rubber had been, tore the package open, squeezed the tip of the acid bulb and replaced the square of seat covering, fastening it with black adhesive tape.

'Nice and easy,' he said to Brady. 'You're just a decent, hard-working cabby with a tatty back seat who's had the good fortune to pick up a fare on the way to the station.'

The taxi turned into Terminus Place outside the big, dozing concourse. There were already two taxis waiting in the covered area at the head of the barriers where, at busier times, passengers were herded and filtered towards the cabs.

As Brady approached the barrier, he cut the engine. The taxi cruised powerless into the area beside the barriers and stopped in front of the entrance to the concourse.

He climbed out. 'Shit!' he said in a loud voice. The drivers of the other two cabs stared stolidly ahead, accustomed to obscenity, deaf to entreaty.

When he opened the hood, Quarrick, carrying the suitcase now containing foam rubber, knife and Walther, joined him studying the engine with the intense interest of an amateur mechanic. He watched as Brady disconnected the battery.

Brady returned to the driver's seat and tried to start the engine. Nothing. He shut the hood. Quarrick paid him and walked towards the concourse, pausing when a policeman approached Brady, fumbling with the catches of his case. Listened.

'What seems to be the trouble?' the policeman asked. He was young with inquisitive eyes.

'Buggered if I know.' Brady had ironed out the Belfast angles from his voice. All he had to do now was curb his temper: always a challenge to Brady, especially in the proximity of the police. Now that he had been seen, he would have to be spirited out of Britain to Ireland.

'Well, you can't leave it here,' the policeman said.

'What do you think I am, a weightlifter?'

Cool it, for Christ's sake!

'What do you normally do if you break down?'

'Normally it doesn't break down.'

'There must be a procedure . . .' The policeman's voice was beginning to harden: stroppy cab drivers pre-dawn on a cold March morning he could do without.

'I'll phone for a breakdown truck.'

'And how long will that take to get here?'

'Your guess is as good as mine.'

The policeman walked round the cab. 'Are you sure this vehicle is roadworthy, sir?' *Sir*: ominous when used by policemen.

Quarrick shook the bag and felt the Walther move inside it. How long since he had primed the bomb? Eight minutes. Thirty-two to go.

'Quite sure, officer.'

'I'm not an officer, *sir*. And I'll ask you again. How long will you take to move this?'

Answer him respectfully, you stupid bastard.

'Half an hour at the most,' Brady said.

The policeman savoured his small victory over the bolshy classes. 'No longer,' he said and, scenting a mug of tea, walked with a jaunty step into the station.

Quarrick followed him, swinging the suitcase. The station was beginning to awaken: bundles of morning papers thumping down beside the newsstands, cleaners on the move, destinations rippling on the arrival and departure screens.

He made a detour and joined the first crop of commuters, striding with feigned vigour across the concourse, and walked out of the station. The taxi was still there; Brady wasn't. He would now be in a call box in Victoria Street telephoning the warnings to the TV stations, three of them just to make sure. Quarrick would have made the calls himself except that these days they were recorded and voice sensors would pick up his American background.

He hoped as he left the station that he looked like an ordinarily successful businessman, crisply barbered and confident of step. Who at this time of the morning would notice the shadows of fatigue below his eyes? Who but an insomniac shrink would perceive the purpose beyond the limits of ordinary men?

He walked down Buckingham Palace Road and picked up his black Mercedes 190 SE from a parking lot in Belgravia, locked the suitcase in the trunk and drove home to the genteel old house in Chelsea between Cheyne Walk and King's Road.

He left the Mercedes in the garage, slotted his key into the front door and climbed the stairs, taking care to avoid the one that creaked. He could hear the boys breathing; the house breathed with them.

He undressed in the spare room and, naked, crept into the bedroom and climbed into his celibate bed. Eight minutes until the bomb was due to explode ... What if the forecourt hadn't been cleared in time? What if commuters stood waiting for cabs as the life of the time fuse ran out?

He swallowed two sleeping tablets one after the other with mouthfuls of water. Closing his eyes, he saw the bodies of his children, Ben and Jaime, catapulted into the sky as the bomb exploded. In the dream he screamed.

Helen Quarrick awoke sexually aroused from a dream of intense eroticism in which a man with a muscular body and snakes tattooed on his thighs made love to her beside a lake. Swans watched incuriously as, having brought her to the brink of an orgasm, he thrust into her; such was the depth and intensity of his drive that she awoke.

She peered across the no-man's-land between the two beds. Harry's was uninhabited. She remembered the whimpering in his sleep; remembered that he had come home very late.

She tried to return to her dream but it had vanished to wherever dreams went. She got out of bed, put a robe over her nightdress and peeped into the children's room; Ben and Jaime were still asleep.

A slat of light showed beneath the kitchen door at the bottom of the stairs. She heard the clink of a cup on saucer. She went to the bathroom, ran a bath, stripped and examined herself critically in the long steamy mirror on the wall. Thirty-four years old, blondish, full breasted, Caesarean scar (Jaime), no serious stretch marks, mature – sexy, according to a huntsman scenting a broken marriage – and yet somehow incomplete. Her eyes were sea green – impenetrable, according to the huntsman – her lips full.

She squirted a cachet of liquid bath salts, silvery yellow and smelling of lemon, into the water, stepped into the bath and slid into its shallows, temporarily drowning the memory of the man with the snakes on his thighs. Another man took his place.

A young man, not quite as muscular, but spruce with watchful brown eyes, crisp hair and a tan. He was wearing a red ski suit and he was sitting at the twenty-two-foot long bar made from a single log in the Inn at Long Trail at Killington in central Vermont. He was drinking a beer and, without introducing himself, he bought her one.

'I don't like beer,' she said.

'No problem, I'll drink it.'

'You would have ordered it anyway?'

'I'm a two-beer man.'

A too-sure-of-yourself man, she decided.

'Can I get you something else? A Coke?'

This wasn't a pick-up: it was an assumption.

'Beer will be fine,' she said.

'Are you always perverse?'

'According to my mother.' She sat on a bar stool beside him; skiers wearing bright suits drifted in, bringing with them gusts of winter.

'Have you been skiing today?' he asked.

'I don't ski.'

'Boy, you *are* perverse.'

'I just happened to live here. In Plymouth, that is. Calvin Coolidge territory. Born 1872, woken at 2 am or thereabouts to take the presidential oath at the age of fifty-two.'

'A conversationalist too!'

'I grew up with Calvin,' she said. 'Everywhere I went, there was Silent Cal. His ghost, at any rate,' she said, in case he lacked a sense of humour.

' "There is no right to strike against the public safety by anybody, anywhere, at any time." '

She regarded him more closely. 'Don't say you're a Calvin buff! I couldn't take it.'

'I'm studying American history at Columbia. Coolidge was a good president – he couldn't be anything else after Harding. Do you know what Teddy Roosevelt's daughter said about Harding?'

Nettled – Cal was her visiting card to respect – Helen said she didn't.

' "He was not a bad man, he was a slob." '

She honked with laughter.

'What are you doing in Killington if you aren't skiing?'

'Can't you guess?'

'Calv?'

'My father's giving a talk about him: I drove him here.'

'You never ski?'

'I skate,' she said.

'You eat?'

'When I'm hungry.'

'OK,' he said. 'Country French at the Red Clover. I'll see you there at seven.'

But Harry Quarrick didn't see her there because that afternoon he broke his leg skiing. She hadn't seen him again until the autumn of that year when the leaves of the deciduous trees were the colour of embers and the conifers were as dark as unlit coals. On Columbus Day they found a motel near a sugar house in the St Johnsbury area and made love for the first time. They were married the following year in Boston and spent their honeymoon on Nantucket Island.

That same year Harry got a job with the State Department in Washington. They rented a small house in Alexandria and Helen gave birth to the two boys. Ben, who was now ten, and Jaime, two years younger. Then Harry, who had been hustling for it, got a posting to the United States embassy in London.

'The luck of the Irish,' he said at the time.

'Funny,' Helen said, 'I never think of you as Irish.'

'As Irish as Honey Fitz,' Harry said, smiling.

And they had been happy in the rented house in Chelsea, its inner warmth and graces belied by its austere lines and privet hedges, until about a year ago.

Helen searched for the soap, found it with one foot and trawled it upstream. She sat up and soaped her breasts. Where had Harry been? It must have been 5 am at least before he got in. And what had made him whimper in his sleep?

What had happened to him? The brooding. The snap in his voice. Disappearances sketchily explained – when you were a public servant you could tuck anything away in the diplomatic bag. Dreams. Night sweats. Sexual withdrawal. The quarrel when she had suggested that the prize-giving ceremony at the boys' school might be more important than any professional obligation.

Is it my fault? She had asked the question many times. And had always come up with the same answer: *Not guilty.*

So was there another woman? And did she still love him? When they had walked out of the Inn at Long Trail together, she had thought the snow would taste of sugar.

The lemon-scented bath water gurgled down the drain. She finished drying herself and applied body lotion. Then she put on her white towelling robe and went downstairs to the kitchen.

Harry was gazing into his mug of coffee. He looked up, eyes so bloodshot that she could feel their soreness. 'Hi,' he said. 'I tried not to wake you.'

'Very considerate.'

'I'm a very considerate guy.' He poured her coffee from the percolator.

She poured milk on muesli and slotted slices of wholemeal bread into the toaster. Outside pale sunshine lit the small dripping garden and a starling perched on the bough of a rowan tree. She liked the kitchen better than any other room in the house because it was the forum where the day ahead was orchestrated. A psychotherapist would have read a lot into her purring gadgets.

The kitchen, though modernised, retained the set of numbered bells on the wall which had once summoned servants to the room where their services were required. Number five rang, the children's room. 'Ben's up,' she said. It rang again. 'And Jaime. They're probably fighting.'

Harry didn't take any notice. The toast sprang out of its trap and she retrieved two slices, buttered them, spread honey. The newspaper dropped into the hall; Harry collected it from the doormat. She noticed that his hands were shaking as he scanned the headlines.

She waited five minutes before asking: 'How was Paris?'

'Paris was fine.' He turned a page and studied it intently. She tried to read a headline upside down: PARIS ... EURO MPS ... Perhaps that was the clue to his visit to Paris.

'What time did you get in?'

'I don't know the exact time. About five, I guess. Maybe earlier, maybe later. The flight was delayed, then I had to deliver documents to the ambassador.'

'He was up at that time in the morning?'

'His sidekick was,' Harry said. 'Those guys never sleep.'

She touched the black windbreaker hanging from the back of a chair; it was damp. 'You bought that in Paris?'

'Yep. And no, it isn't what you'd expect a diplomat to wear, and you'll find my Crombie in the back of the Mercedes. Anything else?'

'What woke you? I heard you take a sleeping pill.'

'Two, as a matter of fact. Too tired to sleep, I guess. It happens.'

'Or did the dreams wake you?'

'How did you know I was dreaming?'

'You whimpered in your sleep. What were you dreaming about, Harry?'

'I dreamed I was being interrogated by a beautiful, nosy woman.'

Another bell rang and bobbed on its spring. Number four: the bathroom. 'They won't stay there long,' she said.

She prepared their cereal, poured orange juice from a carton into two glasses and boiled the water for their eggs.

Harry switched on the small television stationed in the middle of a row of cook books. It flickered energetically – it was the oldest gadget in the house – before the picture settled. Police cars, ambulances, photographers ... a reporter standing in a courtyard of some sort.

Helen said: 'Not the City again.'

'Victoria Station,' the reporter said. 'Just before dawn. The bomb is thought to have been left in a taxi parked in the rank outside the station concourse.'

Cut to what had been a London cab and was now a mangled wreck. Behind it police in orange vests were still cordoning off the area.

'Maybe no one was hurt,' Helen said. 'There wouldn't have been many people around, not at that time of day.'

The reporter was telling them that the blast had been heard for miles around. Not in Chelsea, Helen thought, not as she lay in the arms of the young man with the snakes on his thighs.

'A warning was telephoned to TV stations but it came too late and was apparently vague about the exact location of the bomb.'

She glanced at Harry. His hands had stopped shaking but his knuckles were shining bone white.

The reporter recalled that another bomb had exploded at Victoria in 1991. 'Two people are believed to have been killed in today's blast and five injured, two of them seriously. One of the injured was a child, an eight-year-old boy. Most of the victims were waiting for taxis—'

Ben, blazer wrongly buttoned, tie askew, arrived in the kitchen. 'Who killed them?'

'A murderer,' Harry said.

'Just one?'

'Who knows?'

He switched off the TV. Its dead grey eye stared at them from among the cook books.

When she was twenty, Helen had been taken on vacation by her parents to Colombia. They had stayed in the old fortress town of Cartagena on the Caribbean coast. They had spent two days in Bogotá, where her father had bought a few emeralds and she had found a hero. His name was Jaime Jaramillo, hence the name of her younger son and he was a crusader who rescued abandoned children from the scrap heaps and sewers of the capital. The children lived by theft and scavenging; the boys sniffed glue and cocaine, the girls sold their bodies in the streets above the sewers, many becoming pregnant at the age of twelve or thirteen; both sexes were occasionally gunned down by police like rats exterminated by rat-catchers.

She had been introduced to a girl named Luz Rosa who had given birth to a baby girl at the age of fourteen. She had once lived in a sewer; Helen met her with her baby in a room painted in pastel shades, mobile suspended from one wall, in one of Papa Jaime's homes run by his charity, Fundación Niños. Although Luz Rosa couldn't yet read, Helen had written to her from Vermont; later, when she could read, from Washington. When the Quarricks moved again, Helen had intended to contact the British branch of the fund but they had found her first. Now she was a formidable fund raiser, making strikes on the diplomatic circuit.

She had asked the American ambassador's wife at a cocktail party: 'Do you have a sewer under your house?'

A glass of champagne stopped en route to her mouth. 'I don't know. Why?'

'In Bogotá you might have a child living under you. Several children.'

'Oh, really?' She raised her glass to the French minister-counsellor in London, but he was short-sighted. 'Why would I?'

And Helen had manoeuvred her into a corner of the chandelier-hung room and told her about the street children and exacted a promise of a $1,000 annual subscription to the Children of the Andes.

On the morning of the bomb at Victoria Station, Helen deposited Ben and Jaime with other parents waiting for the school bus and set out in her blue Fiesta for the charity's registered address near the National Theatre on the south bank of the Thames.

At traffic lights in Pimlico she glanced at other drivers sitting behind the wheels of company cars, like statues except for fingers drumming, lips following a tune on the radio, eyes glancing in the rear-view mirror in case there was a pretty woman in the car behind. If it took a commuter one hour to get to work and one hour to drive home, that was ten hours a week sitting in a car – say 500 hours a year, three weeks or so, longer than the holiday that many of them took. She was into statistics these days, compulsion born of stress.

She opened the window and smelled the mossy scents of the Thames. The sun shone luminously from above watercolour clouds. The line of traffic jolted and began to move lugubriously towards the heart of London.

She made her call, then crossed the river and bought an early edition of the *Evening Standard* outside Charing Cross Station.

The front-page lead was, of course, the explosion at Victoria Station complete with photographs of the concourse damaged by the blast and the tangle of metal that had been a taxi. One column concerned the fight to save the life of the injured boy in Charing Cross Hospital. His name was Peter Tuchman, he was eight years old and he had been on his way to Cuckfield to surprise his grandfather on his seventieth birthday. He should have been chirruping around waiting to present Grandpa Pete with a pipe or a tin of tooth-wrenching toffees or a scrapbook full of memories... Instead Grandpa Pete was waiting to see if his grandchild would live.

She parked the Fiesta and had lunch in an Italian restaurant in the complex where Covent Garden market used to be. Sipping her cappuccino, she finally allowed herself to dwell on the thoughts she had been suppressing all morning.

Why had Harry's windbreaker still been damp at eight in the morning if he had driven home from the covered car park at the airport more than three hours earlier? Where had he been to get soaking wet?

Had his flight been delayed?

Why buy a windbreaker to wear over an expensive suit at all? Why not wear his smarter Crombie? Because the Crombie was expensive and therefore conspicuous?

On the way back to Chelsea she switched on the radio. The boy's condition was 'critical but stable'. Stable was an additional qualification and it would reassure the boy's parents and Grandpa Pete. She wondered what terrorists thought when they viewed innocent victims of their aggression on television. Did they regard eight-year-old Peter as an unavoidable casualty of war? She remembered the shine on Harry's knuckles as he watched the reportage on TV. Remembered the scene in the kitchen, the shock-horror on Harry's face. She relaxed her grip on the steering wheel.

Back home she did some housework. The tall, thin house was old and needed a lot of attention; like a querulous patient, it sighed as she spruced it up, cleaning the leaded windows, dusting the awkward alcoves, washing the paintwork, which was chipped in places like nail varnish on an old duchess. Her feelings towards the house were ambivalent: she loved its dignity but deplored its angular inconveniences.

She went into the kitchen and washed up; the waste disposal growled, the refrigerator hummed, the coffee percolator bubbled. She relaxed, switched on the radio and heard 'not yet off the danger list'. But the implication was that he might be soon.

She returned to the living room, dusted pollen from beneath a vase of daffodils on the mahogany table and then did what she had been trying not to do ever since she got back – try to enter Harry's study. But the door was locked, as she had guessed it would be.

She sat in front of the empty grate longing for a cigarette but she had given up six months ago because, with the stress, she had been getting through a couple of packs a day. She imagined the first catch of smoke in her throat, remembered a pack of Marlboros in the drawer of her bedside table. She stood up and called British Airways information.

'Was BA325 from Paris on time last night? It was due at Heathrow, Terminal four, at 21.55,' she added.

'I don't have that information,' the woman on the other end of the line said. Her life was governed by the uncertain future, not the resolved past.

'But your computer does.'

The woman sighed. 'I'll see what I can do.'

Helen imagined her fingers conjuring facts from the keyboard as she consulted her surrogate brain.

'It was delayed, madam.'

'By how much?'

An impatient intake of breath. 'Exactly two hours, madam.'

'Thank you.' Smiling at the receiver. 'Thank you very much.'

'You're welcome.'

Helen hung up. So he hadn't been lying. She switched on the radio again: Peter Tuchman was 'out of danger'. She blew a kiss at the radio and went out to pick up the children.

Quarrick tried to contact Brady in his flat in Kilburn twice that morning but it wasn't until 3.30 pm that he finally made contact from a call box in Mayfair, a few hundred yards from the embassy in Grosvenor Square.

Brady's voice was sleepy, Belfast vowels stretched. 'Who wants him?'

'You know who wants him, Brady. Where the hell have you been?'

'Having a bit of a kip.'

'What went wrong?'

'What do you mean, what went wrong?'

'Innocent people died.'

A woman with a blue rinse and a miniature poodle under one arm stationed herself outside the call box.

'If you plant bombs, people get hurt,' Brady said.

'You were supposed to phone warnings as soon as you left the station.'

'The boxes were vandalised.' A yawn.

'All the way from Victoria to Kilburn?'

'I made the calls from Trafalgar Square.' A pause. 'And I don't like being interrogated.'

The woman glanced at her watch; the poodle curled its lip and sneered.

'What's your problem?' Brady said. 'The fucking bomb went off on time. We made our point.'

'Why were the warnings vague?'

'Who says they were?'

'The police.'

'Since when did you start believing them?'

The woman placed the poodle gently on the ground; it cocked its leg against the call box.

'An eight-year-old boy's on the critical list,' Quarrick said.

'A casualty of war.'

'If he dies, you murdered him.'

'And you didn't?'

'You're being shipped back to Ireland,' Quarrick said.

'On whose say-so?'

'Mine.'

'The word of a Yank? I could never understand why you were in charge in the first place.'

'You're on the first Dublin ferry out of Liverpool.' The woman tapped her jewelled wristwatch with one finger. 'Pick up your papers from this address.' He gave Brady the number of a street behind King's Cross Station. 'The name on the doorbell is Andrews. Your name is Moore. You're an electrical engineer visiting your old mother.'

'And if I don't choose to take the ferry?'

'I'll book you a slot in Highgate Cemetery.'

Quarrick replaced the receiver and opened the door of the call box. Outside he felt dizzy, the two sleeping pills still affecting him. He leaned against the call box as the woman picked up the poodle and murmured into its ear before brushing past him to make her call.

In his flat Brady swigged from a bottle of Bushmills and considered his options. Defy Quarrick and stay in London or return to Ireland still in good odour with the high command.

In truth there were no options. Quarrick was an executive appointment. An American! Christ, what had happened to the identity of the fight?

He packed his belongings in a punished suitcase, gave the keys to the torpid landlord in the basement, waved aside a vague offer to refund a week's rent and made his way to the address behind King's Cross Station. His destination was a terrace of Victorian houses, each with a different-coloured door.

He pressed the buzzer marked *Andrews, Second Floor.* A scratchy voice emerged from a small grill beside it. 'Who is it?'

'Moore.'

'Occupation?'

'Electrical engineer.'

A click. He pushed the blue door. It opened. Ahead a flight of stairs ascended into the gloom that was an integral part of the fixtures and fittings.

He paused on the first landing. Listened. Tensed his wrestler's shoulders. Realised too late that the Bushmills had slowed down his reactions.

He tore at his throat with both hands. But they were no match for the wire cutting through his windpipe.

Chapter Two

After the rain, spring arrived in Kensington Gardens and Hyde Park. Courting couples spread their coats on the wet grass; office workers nibbled their sandwiches; lonely men walked exuberant dogs beneath dripping trees; rowing boats scattered the waters of the Serpentine into jostling coins of sunlight.

The man in the brown blazer shared this awakening with the lunchtime celebrants. His name was Toland; he was Irish, fifty-two years old with crisp grey hair and a sun-lamp tan, and he believed he was still attractive to women of a certain age. He wore faded jeans and white trainers to give a bounce to his years. He was by profession a talker – double glazing, time-share – and a police informer earning as much as a hundred pounds a squeal.

Crossing the Ring, he walked along the path beside the Long Water in Kensington Gardens towards the statue of Peter Pan. He walked jauntily, offering smiles to women by themselves, casting wistful glances at couples sighing on the grass. It wasn't until he reached the statue of the boy who never grew up that he sensed someone might be following him: a flickering movement behind him when he turned, a lingering image of a camel-hair topcoat, a bird flapping peevishly from a tree. Imagination perhaps, but over the years he had become sensitive to furtive pursuit. He quickened his step.

When he reached the fountains in front of Marlborough Gate, he took evasive action. He strode onto the pavement and darted across the street, leaving behind him a wake of braying horns and bunched fists. Once across, he dived into a triangle of streets and squares bearing county names – Gloucester, Cambridge, Norfolk – pausing momentarily in Sussex Square, where Churchill had once lived. A Great Dane taking its owner for a walk strode majestically past; apart from that, nothing. Maybe it *had* been his imagination. He turned a corner and shrunk into a doorway; no one followed.

Relaxing, he crossed Sussex Gardens and made his way to his bedsit in a terrace of sagging houses near Paddington Station. He stopped outside a newsagent's on the corner and used the window as a mirror to see if he was under surveillance. A fatigued whore with streaked make-up, a black man on a bicycle with a drunken front wheel, a wino clutching a betting slip.

Toland walked on. The front door of the house had once been primrose yellow; now it was soiled and splintered by kicks. Used tea bags, a dirty nappy and a couple of condoms lay in the area beneath blunted railings; buzzers dared callers to press them. Toland unlocked the door. A bicycle stood in the hallway, which smelled of pot and cabbage. There was a slogan in black aerosol on the wall: PEDRO IS A DICK-HEAD.

He opened the door of the bedsit on the first floor. Dishevelled bed, abbreviated gas cooker, rented TV, Wilton carpet showing its tendons, photograph on the wall of Brendan Behan looking implausibly sober, a cupboard hung with neatly pressed clothes, a washbasin below a mirror spattered with toothpaste, a rheumy window with a view of a brick wall. Home.

Toland opened a can of Guinness, boiled up some baked beans, slotted two slices of Mother's Pride into a toaster. Crumbs from yesterday's meal flamed and glowed on the grill. He switched on the TV: snooker.

He was holding the saucepan of baked beans poised above his plate when the door flew open and a man wearing a camel-hair coat burst into the room, gun in hand.

Although he hadn't realised it at the time, Collins had rehearsed the forced entry into Toland's bedsit fourteen years earlier. At The Killing House.

Kicked open a door, heel of boot on the handle, hurled a stun grenade into the room – a precaution that Toland didn't merit – and charged the swinging door, 9-mm Browning pistol in his hand. Instead of a camel-hair coat he wore a black flak vest, respirator and anti-flash hood.

The room was sparsely furnished with a table and chairs, two armchairs and a TV set. None of the men sitting there offered any resistance but Collins and his companion shot them just the same, hitting the ground and rolling as they fired the first shots, thirteen to each gun. Unlucky thirteen.

'I think we'll try that again, gentlemen,' the sergeant said. 'A little slow, weren't we? They' – pointing at the dummies – 'could have had a shit, shave and a shampoo in the time it took you to shoot them. And *he* – ' pointing at the 'hostage' – 'would have been as dead as a stuffed penguin.'

Six more times that day Collins and his partner shot the bullet-riddled dummies in The Killing House, officially known as the Close Quarter Battle House, at the Special Air Service's home base at Hereford. When Collins went to bed at 10.30 it wasn't the gunfire that lodged in his skull, it was the scorn of the instructor. He awoke at 2 am, the hour of doubt.

He had passed the selection course and continuation training. Completed a forty-mile footslog carrying a fifty-five-pound Bergen rucksack and a rifle in nineteen and a half hours, enduring buckshot rain and sleet on the Brecon Beacons. Defied interrogators who kept him hooded for twenty-four hours and immersed him in water for twenty-second periods. Eaten hedgehogs and fungi on a three-week survival course on Exmoor. Resisted the most cunning of all blandishments: 'If you want to quit, no one will think any the worse of you.' Except yourself.

Out of the hundred volunteers from conventional regiments only twelve had passed and been presented with the beige SAS beret, the badge bearing the winged dagger and the words WHO DARES WINS. Well, he had dared but he wasn't convinced that he had won.

His early career had been conformist. Left right, left right, in his father's footsteps. Marlborough, Sandhurst, Green Jackets.

From the beginning, his adolescence had been dunked in the leftovers of the military career of his father, a retired brigadier. Medals jingling at reunions, the aroma of cigars and the hiss of the soda syphon, bellicose reminiscences.

It wasn't army life that he disliked – in fact, he wore it as smartly as a British warm. What he resented was the assumption that he was part of the regiment from conception to expiry. That any initiative outside the battlefield was insubordination. His decision to chance his arm with the SAS had been seen as an act of rebellion with undertones of disloyalty.

He broke the news to his father after dinner one evening in the old country house between Winchester and Salisbury, after his mother had retired to bed with a copy of *Country Life* and an infusion of camomile. It was as if he had been cashiered.

His father swirled brandy round his balloon glass and sniffed it as though it were discharging gunsmoke. Finally he had said: 'Are you drunk, Jack?'

'Never more sober, sir.'

'How can you even contemplate leaving the regiment? It's your life, your birthright.' A nerve in the parchment skin below one eye twitched; one hand sought his white moustache.

'I don't think anything should be preordained. Just because I'm in the army doesn't mean to say that I don't have a mind of my own. I read other books apart from the Queen's Regulations.'

'The Green Jackets are the finest regiment in the army! You can't betray them.'

'Frankly, I don't think they'd miss me all that much.'

'What about your duty to them?' He waved his glass at the warrior ancestors bristling on the walls of the dining room.

Collins met their reproving gaze, seeing himself framed up there one day. He didn't sport a moustache but he wouldn't look out of place. The same grey eyes warily hooded at the corners, high cheekbones, a cleft in the chin which he sawed at with one finger at times of stress. There was one major difference between him and his forebears: whereas their features were stamped with resolution, his also posed questions.

His father swallowed more brandy; two spots of red burned on his cheeks. 'The SAS isn't a proper regiment. They're adventurers, a bunch of cowboys, no better than terrorists.'

Collins felt an acid wash of anger. 'You have to have a declaration of war to protect innocent people?'

'If you're a soldier, yes.'

'Bullshit!'

'Don't talk to me like that or—'

'You'll have me court-martialled? I may be your son but you're not my commanding officer.'

His father didn't seem to hear him. 'You will not join the SAS and that's an order.'

Collins resorted to reason – a mistake. 'Look, Father, I want to join one of the finest fighting forces the world has ever known. How can that bring disgrace to the family – or the regiment?' It can if I fail, he thought.

'I utterly forbid it,' his father said. 'Have you thought how this will upset your mother?'

'Maybe it won't. Maybe she wants what's best for her son.'

'I know what's best!'

'Anyway,' Collins said, 'it's too late.' He was gripping the edge of the dining table.

'Too late?' His father's breathing was swift and shallow. 'What do you mean, too late?'

'I've been accepted for a selection course.'

His father stood up, accidentally sideswiping the brandy glass with his hand; it smashed on the floor. The red spots had spread across his cheeks, heightening the white of his moustache. 'You had no right—' He staggered, leaning on the table, fingers of one liver-spotted hand splayed.

'Are you all right?'

'Of course I'm bloody well all right.' He began to walk unsteadily towards the door.

'Look, I'm sorry—'

'You could have become a general! Instead you want to be John Wayne. I'm ashamed to call you my son.'

The door closed behind him. Collins listened to his retreating footsteps, heard a muffled crash and the sound of a gong. When he reached the hall his father was lying on a tiger skin on the polished floorboards, one outstretched hand on the tiger's impotent snarl, the other beneath the swinging gong that normally summoned them to dinner.

The stroke slowed movement on one side of the Brigadier's body; when he spoke he chewed his words. According to the doctor the blood clot had been a time bomb waiting to explode; but Collins, lying awake at the SAS base in Hereford, still felt guilty.

He finished the free-fall parachute course – jumping from 25,000 feet with a rifle and Bergen pack – and the crash course at the Royal Army Education Corps School at Beaconsfield. Many of the recruits studied Russian and Arabic; he studied Gaelic. He served in Ulster, fought in the Persian Gulf, returned to the Green Jackets and then to the SAS.

Back in Britain he met a model with heartbreaking legs named Judy at a party thrown by a fellow officer in deepest Berkshire. He loved her instantly and, he assumed, hopelessly. How could a girl from the catwalk, who commuted between London, Paris, Rome and New York, be attracted to a soldier?

Who Dares Wins ... He asked her to lunch at Rules the following day and to his astonishment she accepted. Blonde, blue-eyed, icily Nordic, she arrived wearing a silk blouse, a cashmere sweater over her shoulders and faded jeans. Beneath prints and paintings and playbills where, as Prince of Wales, Edward VII had once dined with Lillie Langtry, they ate steak and salad and drank white wine, and she told him that she was sick to the back of her sharp white teeth with jet lag, dieting, and temperament.

Suddenly, after the strawberries – 'No cream,' with a sigh – she touched his chin and said: 'Cleft chin, devil within. True or false?'

'False,' he said, sensing that she was only too conversant with the male ego.

He waited for her to ask him about the SAS – 'How many men have you killed?' – but instead she told him about her childhood in a gentrified Georgian house in Canonbury. Her widowed mother, an East End dressmaker, had saved enough money to buy the house before it was tarted up and in 1953 had posed for a picture for *Good Housekeeping* about the emergent inner-London suburb. After that she had done a bit of modelling.

'She then married my father, her agent, so what chance did I stand? She looked a bit like the Queen,' she added.

'*You* don't.'

Judy glanced at the Swatch, dial bright with hearts and flowers, on her wrist. 'I've got to go and catch a taxi.'

'The waiter will call you one if—'

'A water taxi, on the Grand Canal in Venice. A picture stepping off it onto the quay in stiletto heels, everyone hoping I'll fall in. And then those damn pigeons in St Mark's Square. I swear I know every one by name.'

He met her when she returned from Venice. Still daring, but with little hope, he proposed to her beneath the plane trees in Sloane Square – near the Duke of York's Headquarters in King's Road, which housed Group HQ of the SAS. To his amazement she accepted and kissed him passionately; he led her to an old pub winking with ornate mirrors where she drank a pint of bitter and ate a steak and kidney pudding. As she walked out ahead of him, men raised their heads from their drinks. Collins smiled at them. 'She's mine,' the smile said.

After their marriage and honeymoon in Scotland, away from war and fashion, they settled in Hereford. While Collins took his turn interrogating recruits, mostly from the Brigade of Guards and the Parachute Regiment, Judy became a housewife and set about trying to charm the wives of other officers. The vain entreaties from her agency to return to the catwalk stopped when she became pregnant a year after their marriage.

Their daughter Jane was four when Collins was sent to Northern Ireland on a special assignment. If he hadn't been sent, his life would have been entirely different.

The ambush was set up on two gentle hills on either side of a farmhouse in southern Armagh, on the border with the Irish Republic.

Collins did not enjoy southern Armagh, not just because it was the heartland of the IRA but because it confused his values. Its allegiance had never been to the Protestant North, certainly not to the United Kingdom, and ever since 1921 it had been a green and bloodstained reproach to those who framed Partition. Here IRA guerrillas swanned around with impunity, melting across the border into the Republic when pursued.

His disenchantment on this warm, moonlight night was compounded by the lament of many British soldiers in Northern Ireland: they were not allowed to shoot armed terrorists unless their own lives were endangered. Which was why his troop was ambushing ideas instead of bodies.

'It's a bloody disgrace,' said Sergeant Lloyd Hood, crouching beside Collins in a copse of oak trees on the hill to the west of the farmhouse. 'Six commanders down there any minute now. Take them out, I say, and smash the Provos for ever.'

Hood was a Welshman, the son of a miner who had lost his pride when his pit was closed down. Hood, recruited from the Welsh Guards, consequently carried a heavy sense of injustice. On the grounds of emotional instability he might have been rejected by the SAS if Collins who had interrogated him at Hereford, hadn't believed that a strong sense of what was right was preferable to a blind acceptance of authority.

Hood was young and dark, a scar cradled in his cropped hair, with a taut, muscular body. Like Collins, he wore camouflaged combat gear.

'We can't kill them,' Collins whispered, 'we aren't at war with them.'

'They're at war with us!'

'Commit an act of war and you're playing into their hands. That's what they want – war. They want to be heroes.' Collins hoped that Hood would be more convinced than he was.

'What I'll never understand,' Hood said, 'is why they can kill us and we can't kill them. You know what happened in Belfast.'

Collins knew well enough. Taffy Hood had recognised the gunman who had killed his friend, Bomber Mitchell, near the Lower Falls but had been ordered not to retaliate. Bomber had died in agony, eyes wide with terror as his fingers found the gaping wound in his belly.

Collins said: 'Not for us—'

'To reason why? Do you really believe that? Eye for an eye, tooth for a tooth... It's in the Bible, isn't it?' His voice rose and fell in furious Welsh cadences.

Collins put one finger to his lips and raised the other arm; the troop froze. Below, a jeep stopped and three men climbed out, clearly defined on the visual display unit, cameras and bugs having been installed the previous day.

He stared at the three men through infrared field glasses: no doubt about it. One was the regional commander of the Provos, another his second in command. So it looked as though the intelligence communicated by the informant, a barman in Crossmaglen, had been accurate: the hierarchy of the IRA was assembling within their gunsights.

The three disappeared into a barn. Out of vision but into the range of the bugs that he had secreted, disguised as a Gaelic-speaking farm worker.

The receiver of the headset to his ear, Collins listened.

'Where are the rest of them? They're late.' Mid-Ulster accent – the regional commander.

'No, Declan, we're early.' His deputy.

On the VDU, the third man appeared, leaving the barn – the driver, probably, doubling as minder.

'Let's be having a jar then.'

Sound of liquid being poured.

'Mud in your eye.' The second voice.

'Death to the Brits.'

His voice had an edge to it, as hard as his face, which, Collins remembered from photographs, bore a scar from forehead to jaw.

Hood cuddled the butt of his Heckler and Koch. 'When they all get there we should take them.'

'It's information we want. Not bodies.'

'Is there anything wrong with getting both?'

'They're not endangering us.'

'They're alive! Of course they're endangering us!'

'Don't do anything stupid,' Collins said.

A Land-Rover drew up outside the barn; chickens jumped and squawked. Collins stared at the VDU screen, then peered through his infrared field glasses. Concentrating on one image, he shivered.

He touched Hood's shoulder and pointed at the screen. 'Recognise him?'

Hood stared, blinked, rubbed his eyes with thumb and forefinger. 'Shit!' he said. 'It can't be.'

The limp, the broken nose – a British rifle butt, according to him. The trenchcoat... It was him, all right. The commander in chief of the Provos.

'And we're going to let the bastard walk?'

'Listen!'

'Good evening, Liam.' The voice of the regional commander.

'Evening to you, Declan.' A cultured Dublin brogue as soft as the waters of the Liffey. 'A fine night for a killing.'

'A killing, Liam?'

'In the financial sense. I'll take a wee drop.' Liquid splashed. 'Is everyone here?'

'Risteard sends his apologies. The RUC are staking out his house. Everyone else present and correct.'

'Well, gentlemen,' the commander said, 'let's get down to business. We're running out of time – and funds.' A pause. 'We need cash to pay for the arms coming into the Republic on the *Gresham*.'

'*Gresham*?' Another voice, Cork by the sound of it.

'The cargo ship which is going to break down in the Atlantic four miles off Slyne Head. The ship we're going to *rescue*.'

Collins imagined the wink. He wrote rapidly with a ballpoint in a ruled exercise book.

'And who's going to provide us with the cash? The Brits, of course. Who else?'

'So what are we going to do?' the regional commander asked. 'Rob a bank?'

'Exactly, Declan. Barclays in Chancery Lane. In the heart of London. More publicity than you'll get robbing some piggybank of a place in the suburbs. And not so far from our own clearing banks in Camden Town and points north.'

Collins's ballpoint raced across the page of the exercise book.

'Who's organising it?' The third voice.

'Our man in London.'

Name, Collins pleaded.

'You mean—'

'No names, no pack drill.'

Date, Collins implored.

A rustle of papers.

'Here's all you need to know.'

Silence. The copse was suddenly full of nocturnal noise. An aircraft passed overhead, lights winking.

The commander's voice. 'No time for debate, gentlemen. We'll meet again in two days' time.'

Where?

'Not here, of course. Just in case . . .'

Collins felt his gaze laser through the wall of the barn.

'I think you all know where.'

I don't!

Subdued noise as they shook hands on it. A rectangle of light appeared in the wall and, one by one, leaders and lieutenants walked into the VDU screen.

The commander came out last.

'All right,' Collins whispered. 'Let them go, then we'll get the hell out of it.'

Hood didn't reply. He was kneeling, H and K rigid in his hands.

'No!'

He could feel Hood's concentration, see the target through Hood's eye.

The commander was halfway between the door and the Land-Rover. The engine of the Land-Rover fired.

As Hood's finger tightened on the trigger of the H and K, Collins jumped him. They sprawled together in wet leaves left over from last autumn. Collins smelled them, felt their dampness against his cheek. Anticipating a knee in the groin, he rolled clear, hand bladed for the chop across the throat; but Hood's body was motionless.

'You should have let me do it,' Hood said softly. 'For all of us.'

Collins stood up, aware that he was under scrutiny from other members of the troop. 'We are not like them,' he said. *Unless we are authorised*, he thought. 'We obey orders. We are not terrorists.'

Moonlight glinted in Hood's eyes. 'Am I under arrest?'

'Our first priority is to get out of here.'

The Land-Rover took off, followed by the jeep. An owl hooted; a cloud passed over the moon.

Collins said: 'Pack up the VDU.' He spoke into a handset to the men on the other hill.

In units of four they made their way to a pick-up point at Keady on the road to the city of Armagh, where they were to disperse and regroup at the SAS base at Newtownards, east of Belfast.

Hood was waiting when Collins arrived at Newtownards at 4.30 am.

'What am I going to be charged with? Attempting to shoot the enemy?'

'The enemy? Who *is* the enemy? Know something, Hood? The British Army was welcomed here by the Catholics. Back then, we were their saviours from the Protestant assassins. Now we, the saviours, are the enemy.'

'You're not putting me on a charge?'

Collins thought about it. Then he said: 'Not this time. After all, we aren't a conventional force, are we? We're SAS.'

The following month, July, the IRA suffered two serious setbacks.

On Tuesday 5 July, four gunmen gained entry to Barclays Bank in Chancery Lane in London. They were met inside by officers of PT17, the armed section of the Metropolitan Police, carrying Browning pistols and pump-action shotguns. They were disarmed and arrested.

On 7 July five members of the IRA set out in a motor launch from Killary harbour on the Atlantic coast of the Irish Republic to go to the aid of a cargo ship, the *Gresham*, which had broken down in rough weather. They were met on deck by a unit of the Royal Marine Commandos from Mount Wise, Plymouth. The arms and explosives on board were confiscated and handed to customs officers from the Republic.

Sergeant Lloyd Hood, at the end of his second term of service, decided not to re-enlist in the SAS. He joined the Metropolitan Police and, because of his SAS training, was swiftly channelled into Scotland Yard's Anti-Terrorist Squad.

Collins was highly commended for masterminding the intelligence coup and one year later was assigned to the Counter-Revolutionary Warfare Team of the SAS in London.

In the same year the fate of the police informer Toland was sealed.

Collins and his wife bought an Edwardian semi in Clapham near the Common and Judy set about rehabilitating its morose rectitude. She went hay-making in the overgrown garden where nettles and goldenrod flourished; painted the front door blue and the portico white; ripped up old carpets which smelled of cats; bared woodwork lurking beneath half a dozen coats of paint; took a hammer and chisel to the ancient kitchen; painted Jane's room in creamy pastels and stuck a Winnie-the-Pooh frieze on the walls.

She left their own bedroom and the sitting room to the last. So, while Jane, now six, lived as cosily as a small animal in its nest, her parents were still eating takeaways on a camping table and making love on a lumpy mattress on the floor.

Collins went to work in his black Volvo, sometimes to the Duke of York's barracks in Chelsea, sometimes to the new headquarters of the Secret Intelligence Service on the south bank of the Thames where MI5 and MI6 were supposed to liaise with the Counter-Revolutionary Warfare Team of the SAS.

From time to time he went away, returning several days, maybe weeks, later. Judy never asked where he had been, what he had done, and he never volunteered the information. But mostly it was nine to five and he enjoyed the regimen – a Scotch with ice and water at 5.50 pm, a Chinese or Indian takeaway or a pizza at 7.30, a quick burst of television, then early to bed on the mattress. It was a far cry from soldiering with the elite – but what was better, living with a beautiful, loving wife and daughter, or rampaging round an assault course bayoneting sacks that bled with straw?

Twice he flew to Madrid at the request of the Guardia Civil fighting the Basque separatists ETA – Spain's IRA; once to Rome where arms were finally being taken up against the Mafia in Sicily; a couple of times to Germany to help police infiltrate the neo-Nazis. Several times he went to Belfast and Dublin. On each occasion he went strictly under cover discarding his very English camel-hair coat.

On Judy's thirtieth birthday, with the house taking shape around her, he gave her a white Renault Clio, second-hand. She drove it around south London with elaborate care. On the following day, a wistful September Sunday, she drove them to Richmond Park, where they watched deer running free and knocked chestnuts from the trees, prising the polished conkers from their nests.

They ate lunch in Richmond and strolled beside the Thames, throwing bread to the swans and ducks. Judy took his arm, Jane ran ahead, and he felt very uxorious and respectable.

Judy, bleached hair bright in the pale sunshine, pressed herself close to him. 'I love you,' she said.

Jane, supposedly out of earshot, turned. 'What about me?'

'I love you too,' Judy said, adjusting the tartan-lined hood of Jane's navy coat.

'And you?' Jane pointed an accusing finger at Collins.

'I love both of you,' he said.

'That's all right then.' Jane, who possessed his dark hair and a handful of freckles, skipped a few steps, then turned again. 'What do you do in London, Daddy?'

'This and that. Why do you want to know?'

'Miss Morgan asked me.'

'Tell her to mind her own business.' He held up one hand. 'No, don't. Tell her I'm Something in the City.'

'That's silly,' Jane said, throwing a stick into the mud-coloured water and watching it drift towards the sea. 'She says you look like a soldier.'

'Retired,' he said.

'Retarded?'

'Close,' Judy said.

Togetherness, he thought. That's everything. Looking at the night sky and seeing the same star. He wondered if they should have another child.

When Jane was again presumed out of earshot, he said to Judy: 'I was wondering...'

'I know you were.'

'Good God, has it come to this, reading each other's thoughts?' He paused. 'What was I wondering?'

'Whether we should have another child.'

'Well?'

'It's just possible,' she said carefully, 'that your wish might come true.'

He stopped. 'Good grief!'

'Watch it, Jack! We don't want a scene from a black-and-white movie. You know, the one where hubby suddenly realises how babies are made.'

'Are you sure?'

'Near as damnit.'

He bent his head and kissed her; her lips were warm and dry. Noticing them, Jane pulled a face.

'I don't think we should tell her just yet,' Collins said.

'Of course not.'

'Tell her what?' Jane ran up to them.

'It doesn't matter,' Judy said.

'Secrets?'

'Right,' Collins said.

Jane turned to her mother. 'Are you going to have a baby?'

'I might be.'

'Don't you know?'

'Not yet.'

'Why not yet?'

'She's going to be a QC,' Collins said.

Jane said: 'I hope it's a boy.'

'Why?'

'So you *are* going to have one!'

'George Carman, step aside,' Collins said.

They reached the lawns sweeping up to Richmond Hill, turned and retraced their footsteps towards Richmond Bridge. Oncoming promenaders passed them at a sedate pace. The afternoon was beginning to beckon winter.

Collins laughed. 'I always liked those movies where the doctor emerged from the bedroom, nodded at the distraught father and said, "It's a boy!" Pause. "And they're both doing fine." '

'Accompanied by a squawk from behind the closed door.'

'Cut to mother smiling weakly.'
'I really do love you,' she said.
'Did you ever dream you'd marry a soldier?'
She shook her head. 'I thought I would marry a tree surgeon.'

She drove the Clio north from Richmond with theatrical nonchalance, tapping her fingers on the steering wheel at traffic lights.

The red Mazda hit them at the junction of Richmond Road, Roehampton Lane and Rocks Lane: not a hard knock but enough to push them to the side of the road. Judy put on the hand brake, switched off the engine and covered her face with her hands.

The Mazda accelerated towards Roehampton. Collins made a note of the registration number, but he knew there was little point. There were four youths inside it – joyriders. The Mazda had almost certainly been stolen.

He touched Judy on the nape of her neck. 'It's all right, love.' He turned to Jane in the back seat. 'Just a scratch. No harm done. Stay there while I have a look.'

But it was more than a scratch. The lights on the front off-side were smashed and the wing was touching the tyre. Red paint gashed the white as bright as blood.

He spoke through the open window. 'I'll find a phone, call the police and the AA.' Judy nodded, tears beginning to gather in her eyes.

He found a call box, reported the accident to the police and gave a description of the Mazda knowing as he did so that by now it would have been dumped with the doors wide open, its occupants long gone.

A breakdown truck towed the Clio to a garage in Wandsworth and the AA dropped the three of them at their house, its blue door welcoming.

After he had made tea and poured oranged juice for Jane, they settled down to an inquest around the camping table.

'It wasn't your fault,' he said, loading his tea with sugar.

'It doesn't matter whose fault it was: it's my beautiful Clio that got hurt.'

'It will be as good as new.'

'I was going to see my mother tomorrow,' she said. 'I'll have to ring and cancel.'

'Take my car,' Collins said. 'I'll take the Underground.'

'Are you sure?'

'Nothing much doing in the City tomorrow,' he said, looking at Jane. 'Is Miss Morgan the one with the sniff?'

'As a matter of fact,' Judy said, 'I was thinking of taking Jane with me. One day off from school can't make that much difference at this stage in her career.'

Much later, when Jane was in bed and the TV news had come and gone, Judy, wearing a short black nightdress, beckoned him to the lumpy mattress. She took the pins out of her fine blonde hair and it fell around her face like a silken veil.

Her parents had bought a second home in Dorchester and she and Jane left early the following morning. Rain was falling from a luminous sky and they dashed to the black Volvo beneath a rainbow-coloured umbrella.

The Volvo started first time. It always did. Collins, standing at the doorway, watched as Judy executed a perfect three-point turn. They both waved, then the Volvo accelerated along the decent little street of semi-detached houses and sentinel plane trees.

It exploded at the T-junction 300 yards away. Even as he ran, shoes slipping on wet leaves, rain splashing into his eyes, Collins knew that his life would never be the same again.

Chapter Three

Toland rotated in his swivel chair. He had bought it, only slightly damaged, at a knock-down price and now wished he hadn't. As he turned, first one way, then the other, it seemed to him that his brain stayed still, floating and aching inside his skull. Lights flashed dimly through the sack covering his head; the voice came at him like a mosquito diving at night.

'Names, boyo, that's what I want.' A very English voice despite the boyo.

'Jesus, I keep telling you I don't know any!'

'They'll come to you – I've got all the time in the world.'

'If I knew, I'd be telling you.'

'You know all right, Toland. You've made a few bob in your time betraying your countrymen.'

'Gossip picked up in boozers before chucking-out time. Honest, Mr—'

The chair spun violently in the opposite direction, severing his voice. The unspoken words fluttered inside his head. A bone clicked in his neck. Lights flashed and fused into colours like petrol on water.

'Names, Toland.'

They spilled from his lips. Callaghan, O'Leary, Brady, Moore, Donegan . . . every Irish name his tongue could find.

'Good lad. Now you've spewed up the Irish telephone directory, let's get down to basics. Not all micks these days, are they? The last two lads caught were as English as bangers and mash, weren't they? One had been in the Army, Royal Signals. Got a UN peace medal in Cyprus! I wonder if he wore it when he planted the bomb? Any other fine upstanding Brits working for you?'

'Me? I'm nothing to do with the Provos.'

'What I really want is the name of the head man, the big wheel who authorises the hits. Harrods, the Baltic Exchange, Woodside Park tube station, Victoria...' A pause. Then, his voice like a switchblade: 'The car bomb at Clapham...'

Silence. Worse than the interrogation. The lights stopped flashing. Footsteps. Door of the bedsit opening.

Toland screamed. 'Please don't leave me alone!'

The door shut. The chair rotated slowly a few more times, then came to a halt. Below, the front door slammed.

Collins blundered through the streets like a blind man without a stick, tripping over a child beggar, cannoning into commuters scurrying for the Underground. He was running from the wreckage of the Volvo, the Volvo that he should have been driving that day. Running from the shredded rainbow umbrella, from the melted Smarties, from the scorched fragments of a tan trenchcoat... all that was left of the only two lives he had ever really shared.

The IRA had admitted responsibility for the bomb and regretted the deaths of Judy and Jane. An accident, unavoidable in war. They had assumed that Collins, recently appointed deputy commander of the SAS Counter-Revolutionary Warfare Team in London, formerly engaged in anti-Republican activities in Ireland, would have been driving the Volvo.

Lying on the mattress where, the night before, he and Judy had made love, Collins made his own declaration of war. He sold the house in Clapham, taking all Judy's and Jane's possessions to his in-laws. They were part of another man's life, the man he had once been. He kept only photographs – Jane on a swing, Judy pushing – Jane's first school report and a Swatch with hearts and flowers on the dial. During his compassionate leave he found an apartment off the Fulham Road, near the Queen's Elm pub, within walking distance of the Duke of York's headquarters. And, anticipating the official response to his bereavement, he prepared to raid the electronic brains of the SIS, the Secret Intelligence Service, and his own unit, the Counter-Revolutionary Warfare Team.

First came the obligatory interview with the commanding officer of the CRWT at the Duke of York's.

The CO, formerly with the Royal Horse Guards, was an affable major with soft hair and a hard edge to his voice. His campaign tan would never leave him, and the lines on his forehead sprang to attention when he perceived a strategy. His name was Ferris.

He stared at Collins from across his desk, hands clasped in prayer. 'I don't have to tell you how I feel.'

'I appreciate your sympathy.'

But Collins was impervious to condolence. Apart from the occasional rapier thrust he was detached from bereavement, a mercenary dedicated to vengeance.

Ferris fingered the lapels of his grey suit which he wore with military panache. 'Certain decisions have to be made.'

Have *been* made, Collins thought.

Ferris launched into a short recitation. The 'terrible tragedy' he had endured... In CRWT officers should not be emotionally involved – although that wasn't the main consideration...

So why mention it?

'What concerns everyone from the head of SIS downwards is that your cover has been blown. The IRA has openly admitted that the bomb was intended for you. In other words, they know your name, your face, your previous involvement with Ireland.'

'And we know theirs.'

The lines on Ferris's forehead tightened. 'That isn't the point. Their brief is to kill; ours isn't.'

'Why not?'

'You know why. We don't go to war with a bunch of desperadoes.'

'But they're at war with us. They can murder and maim women and children as the fancy takes them, but we can't lay a hand on them.'

'The deaths of your wife and daughter were a tragedy. But they were not the intended victims.'

Collins, still standing, placed both hands on Ferris's desk. 'Are you apologising for them, sir?'

'Don't be a bloody fool, Collins! Of course I'm not. I'm just pointing out that we can't operate on their level. Our brief is to control them, not annihilate them.' Ferris glanced at his watch. 'I've got an appointment at the ministry. What I wanted to tell you was that you've been posted back to Hereford.' He reached for his battered suitcase: the interview was over.

'Admin?'

'Temporarily.'

'When do I leave?'

'You'll be given a couple of days to clear your desk.'

'One question, sir. What do you think a terrorist feels when he switches on the television and sees the faces of kids he has maimed or murdered?'

'How the hell should I know?'

'I didn't think you would.' He strode out of the office to wage his private war.

*

35

In his apartment he had installed the latest IBM hardware. As soon as he got back from the interview with Ferris, he went to work.

He locked himself in the spare room with a glass of milk and a cheese sandwich. The wallpaper in the room was mauve, covered with pink roses; it had been badly hung and at the seams roses failed to connect with their stems. The occupant of the apartment above him clomped around in lead boots.

He switched on the IBM; the screen glowed frostily. He sat in front of it, hands raised like a pianist posed to embark on a concerto. Not that it would be a milestone in the history of hacking – he already had the access codes to both the CRWT and the SIS computers. If they had been changed, which they routinely were, then he would help himself to the replacements while clearing his desk.

His fingers fluttered over the keyboard. One by one, classified secrets flickered on the screen: passwords, cells in London, Liverpool and Manchester, names, addresses, specialities . . .

Brady, Liam, deceased. Resident of Kilburn, getaway driver. DNA tests on samples from saliva in chewing gum found in call box from which warnings were phoned and from body indicate possible involvement in taxi-bomb outrage at Victoria Station. Murdered, in all likelihood by the Provos because he was unreliable, a weak link in their structure in Britain.

Collins's fingers paused over the keyboard, then hurried on.

When, on the second day, the microchips had yielded the last dregs of esoteric information, Collins asked the IBM to suggest the identity of the leader of the IRA in Britain. The computer was very coy: probably Irish but not necessarily, possibly resident in the UK as a sleeper before being activated . . . The IBM struggled on but its conclusions were fading dreams.

Collins stared across the narrow garden at a lighted window. It was dusk, except in the room beyond the window where, watched by a boy in a wheelchair, a man and a woman were putting up Christmas decorations. Pockets of plastic snow lodged in the corners of the windows, lights stuttered into life on a small tree . . . Collins averted his gaze, turned back to the IBM. A factor was missing. There had to be something, some vital piece of evidence, that had so far eluded him and his electronic accomplice.

He went to the kitchen to get a clean glass. He poured a Black Label and fired soda into it from a syphon. He took a gulp, felt the whisky warm his stomach. In the Christmas tableau in the lighted room, the boy in the wheelchair clapped his hands.

He looked at his watch: 5.35 pm. By now the minders had gone home, leaving computers to process lives through Visa and Access, driving and TV licences, tax returns, CVs, hospital records, criminal convictions, not so secret vices...

But there were more basic sources of information which were fed into the maw that made privacy as quaint as chivalry on an underground train. Facts obtained by interrogation, burglary, blackmail... Tips supplied by informers!

Collins' fingers danced over the keyboard and up they came, the snouts, the grasses, the ferrets who, for the price of a week's rent, a fix, a debt to a bookie, had betrayed casual intimacies, blood oaths and family understandings. Jones, Regan, O'Hara, Heald, Flannigan, Toland, Clancy...

Christmas and New Year had come and gone before Collins applied himself to Toland. Daffodils were nodding in the parks and even in the precincts of Paddington Station spring had touched a few window boxes leaving behind orange and mauve crocuses.

When Collins re-entered the bedsit, Toland's head, still hooded, jerked up. 'Who's that?' A shred of hope in his voice.

'It's me,' Collins said. He took off the jacket of his navy suit and threw it beside the camel-hair coat on the put-U-up. 'Now let's get down to business again.' He picked up a flashlight and beamed it at Toland's shrouded head, switching it on and off. 'You've had a good rest, time to think. Come up with anything?'

'Ask me questions and I'll try to answer them.'

'Where are these pubs where all the big mouths hang out?'

Toland named pubs in Hackney and Stoke Newington – strongholds of Red Action which was sympathetic to the IRA – Kentish Town, Camden Town and Lisson Grove.

'I'm glad you're cooperating.' Collins made notes, fodder for his IBM. 'Any minute now we can take that hood off.'

'I've always helped you people.'

'You're very highly thought of.'

'Then why are you treating me like shit?'

'Because you're lying?'

'Those pubs exist all right.'

'Lying by omission,' Collins said.

He paced the grubby room, stepping over the detritus of Toland's life. Pages from yesterday's *Sporting Life*, a half-empty packet of Jacob's water biscuits, library book – men like Toland spent long hours in public libraries when they weren't in the pub or betting shop – a blow heater, its vents powdered with dust. How could someone so fastidious about his appearance live in a sty?

He picked up Toland's sun lamp. 'Quite a tan you've got.'

Toland didn't reply.

'The ladies like it, do they?'

'They might.' The chair had stopped spinning and Toland's head was lolling.

'I want names, Toland.'

'I've given you names.'

'Not the chorus of *Finnegan's Rainbow*. Real names. One name in particular. Because, you see, I don't believe you get your info from pubs: I think you work for the boyos.' The IBM had come up with that: 'believed to be casually employed to case targets'. 'You must know who employs you when you sell time-share or double glazing. When, generous soul that you are, you give an old lady a fiver for an heirloom which you flog in the Portobello Road for a hundred quid and tell the boyos about the lodger who just happens to work at the Ministry of Defence.'

'Phone calls mostly,' Toland said.

'You get paid over the phone?'

'Envelopes left in certain pubs.'

Collins pulled the hood off Toland's head. He blinked bloodshot eyes like an animal emerging from hibernation.

'Time to start work on that tan of yours.'

'What the hell are you talking about?'

'It's fading. So, off with your shirt!' Collins gave a savage tug and it ripped. He placed the old-fashioned sun lamp on a rickety coffee table and aimed it at Toland's now exposed chest. 'How long do you usually give yourself?'

Toland stared at him, comprehension beginning to dawn. 'Five minutes max. You wouldn't—'

'We'll start with ten,' Collins said. 'That should do you to a turn.'

'Jesus!'

'And if you haven't remembered anything by then, I'll give you another five while I telephone the Provos and tell them they've got a grass on their payroll.'

'They'd kill me.'

'Without a doubt.'

Collins switched on the lamp. Its single tube flickered, then found strength, ultraviolet giving off an odour like an indoor swimming pool.

Collins settled himself on the put-U-up. 'So, who tells you where to employ your talents?'

'I told you, a voice on the phone.'

'Sometimes person to person?'

'A couple of times. On the footpath beside Regent's Canal by the goods depot. The lamp, it's too close. Move it a little, please.'

'Name?'

'Smith.'

'Pull the other leg,' Collins said. 'It's got bells on it.'

'Honest, that was your man's name. I know because we had a couple of jars in a pub and the barman called him Smithy.'

'Describe him.'

Medium height, Toland said. Thinning sandy hair. Scuffed bomber jacket, jeans, soiled training shoes... Toland glanced at his own pristine pair.

'Irish?'

'Ulster.'

'The last time you met him, what did he tell you to do?'

'Time-share,' Toland said, trying to angle his face away from the glare of the lamp. 'A house in West Kensington. Home of an MP who comes on strong about the Provos in the Commons...'

Collins frowned. A memory was trying to surface.

' "Find out where he garages his car," Smithy said.'

'And did you?'

'Sure I did. But nothing was ever done about it. And the funny thing was that his missus bought time-share! A week in Majorca. How big a fool can you be? Now, please, switch that fucking thing off.'

The memory had a sharp edge and it was scratching at the inside of his skull. He glanced at his watch again. Toland had been cooking for four minutes.

'Did he ever say who briefed him?'

'Not in as many words.'

'What do you mean "not in as many words"?'

'He didn't name him. Now if you'll turn that thing off I'll tell you everything I know. Not that it's much.'

Collins hesitated. There was a point in an interrogation, he had learned at Hereford, where you became Mr Nice. The memory scratched again.

He switched off the lamp and leaned forward, elbows on his knees. 'So?'

'He didn't get his orders from the top.'

'How far down the chain?'

'The man he got his orders from knew the commander here.'

'And?'

'We were drinking Bushmills, me and Smithy. In this pub in Camden. Smithy said he'd heard, from this other body, that the headman went on most hits himself, and that he spoke with an American accent.'

'Are you sure?'

'That's what your man said.'

Collins leaned back on the put-U-up. No one that he could recall had even floated the proposition that an American could be working for the IRA in Britain. Contributing to NORAID funds in the United States, certainly, but not taking the fight abroad.

'Anything else?'

'Reckoned he lives in Chelsea. Family man, he said. Father of two kids.'

He might have garnered further intelligence, Collins later admitted to himself if, at that moment, the memory hadn't finally surfaced. *Time-share.* Judy had told him a few days before her death that a time-share salesman had called at their house in Clapham. Irish, full of blarney, she had said. 'Asked what sort of car you had and where you kept it and when I said a Volvo he said that if you could afford one of those you could afford a holiday home for a week or a fortnight... Bargain of the century, he said. Your *own* holiday haven instead of some package deal rip-off. I told him we always spent the summer vacation with Prince Rainier and he made a hasty retreat, pulling at his forelock.'

Collins hit Toland on the left side of his face with the back of his right hand. Toland's head jerked to one side. His eye began to close immediately. 'What the fuck was that for?'

'Did you ever try the time-share crap in Clapham?'

'Not that I—'

Collins hit him on the other cheek with the flat of his hand. 'Did you?'

'No!'

'You're a liar.'

Seeing the melting Smarties, the shredded umbrella, the fragment of the tan trenchcoat, Collins hit him full in the face with his fist. He heard Toland's nose snap.

'No, I swear.' Toland spat out a tooth. Blood flowed from his bent nose and his split upper lip.

Collins saw Jane wave goodbye.

He hit Toland again and again. Heard his frantic voice clotted with blood. Saw his eyes roll.

Then he heard Judy's voice again, describing the time-share rep. 'Tall and thin and pale, not my idea of an Irishman. Looked as if he needed a time-share vacation himself.'

He stopped a sideswipe in mid-flight. Toland slumped forward and remained still.

Collins picked up the torso of his cream shirt, held it under the tap beneath the spattered mirror and wiped blood from beneath his crushed nose. Then he opened his mouth and with his little finger hooked out broken teeth and his tongue from the back of his throat.

A bubble appeared from one of his nostrils and slowly inflated. He saw a pulse in his neck where blood flowed through the carotid artery on its way to the brain. He untied him, laid him on the put-U-up and puffed a cushion behind him.

He bent and spoke into his ear. 'Can you hear me?'

A slight nod of the bloodied head.

'I'm going to call an ambulance. But before I go I want you to remember this: if you ever try to identify me or tell anyone what questions I asked, then I'll come back and finish the job. Do you understand that?'

Another nod before the head lolled again.

Collins let himself out of the bedsit, went to a call box in Paddington Station and dialled 999.

Chapter Four

Four weeks before Judy Collins and her daughter Jane died in the car-bomb explosion, Helen Quarrick received a letter from Colombia. She slit the envelope over a mid-morning coffee in her well-appointed kitchen. It was written on lined paper, a's, e's and o's like small balloons on the ends of tangled lengths of string, and it was signed Electra, daughter of Luz Rosa. Since it was in Spanish, she took it to a Spanish restaurant off the King's Road and asked a sad-eyed waiter to translate.

The letter said that she, Electra, was very well, that her mother, Luz Rosa, was very well and that she hoped Helen was very well. Was there any probability that Helen would be able to visit Bogotá and could she become her Mother of God?

Helen thanked the waiter and rose to leave.

'Now perhaps you can be helping me,' he said. 'I want to know what this means. I hear it often.' He wrote on a paper napkin: 'FUCK.'

'You're right,' Helen said, 'it is used a lot. It's a very useful word because it sums up three words.'

'And what are they, señora?'

'Get lost, buster,' Helen said and walked out of the restaurant into the sunshine.

Why not? she thought, considering Electra's request. The children were going to summer camp for two weeks, Harry was as distant as ever, except when he was with the boys, and she wanted to visit her father in Vermont. A round trip before the snow settled there and the Calvin Coolidge winter season began. She wondered how Harry would react. With relief, probably.

But he didn't respond with relief; worse – with indifference. He was sitting at the kitchen table beside the Aga, jacket off, loosening his tie, like any other sleek young executive, to release the burdens of the day. He had been looking more relaxed recently. Ever since their vacation in Scotland, where he and the boys had flown kites with whipping tails on Highlands covered with gorse and heather which, in the distance, looked like lichen. As the breeze found its way through the valleys, taking the kites with it, his wary, once boyish features had softened. When they got back to London, she noticed that he had left some of the premature creases in the Highlands. It was always like that with the kids. They're better for him than I am, she thought: he is a father, not a husband.

'So I thought I'd plan an itinerary returning from Bogotá via New York.'

'That travel agency we use in King's Road will work out the details.' He picked up the evening newspaper.

'And you don't mind the expense?'

'We can afford it. Did I tell you there's talk of me becoming the first secretary for politico-military affairs?'

No, she said, he hadn't.

'We're flying high,' he said, scanning a report in which the legal rights of a bank to take over a building society were challenged.

'Will you miss me?'

'Of course I'll miss you.' He turned a page of the newspaper.

Two weeks later Helen, carrying an updated health certificate, a tourist card and traveller's cheques, landed at Bogotá's El Dorado airport, where she was met by Jaime Jaramillo.

Jaime, still youngish with luxuriant black hair and matching moustache, didn't take her straight to the house. First he took her to the rioting slums to the south of the city, to garbage tips and shanty towns and sewers. After that he allowed her a glimpse of the grand, guarded mansions to the north. He then took her to the Zone of Martyrs and pointed at a poster on a peeling wall. A little dizzy from altitude sickness, she tried to read it, gave up and asked Jaime to translate.

'It's an invitation,' he said. 'To a funeral.' Finger following the black words, he read slowly: "The industrialists, businessmen, civic groups and community at large invite you to the funerals of the delinquents of this sector, events that will commence immediately and will continue until they are exterminated." He pulled at his moustache as though he wanted to remove it. 'The milk of human kindness, huh?'

'The community at large ... They're inviting street kids to their own funerals?'

'Making sure they attend by gunning them down. You can hire a hit squad here for the equivalent of three thousand pounds. Did you know Colombia has the worst murder rate in the world? Thirty thousand a year. Everyone jumps to the conclusion that they're drug-related but in one year 2,800 children were murdered. Easy targets, too, when they're stoned on glue or *basuco*, our version of crack.'

Three waifs had gathered behind them in the square. Their faces were sharp with precocious knowledge, their stomachs swollen with hunger; one sucked his thumb as though it contained sustenance.

'Typical candidates for what they call a social clean-up operation,' Jaime said.

'But why?'

Jaime shrugged. 'They're blamed for the rise in crime. Break-ins, mugging. Dangerous criminals, aren't they?' He stabbed a finger at a barefoot girl of five or so with smudged cheeks and ringlets of hair falling in her eyes; a smile grew around the thumb in her mouth. 'Developers reckon they bring down the price of property.'

Helen found a bar of fruit-and-nut chocolate in her bag and handed it to the children. It was unwrapped, divided and disposed of in a flurry of small fingers. The children chewed and stared at her seriously.

'How do they live?'

'Begging, scavenging, picking pockets, selling their bodies – like Luz Rosa. Many of them won't see out their teens. The cutest ones take to the sewers. Want to see them?'

It was dusk, mountains advancing from the daylight. The children coming out of the hole in the wall beside a plot of waste land reminded her of ants emerging from a nest after rain. As they jumped onto the balding grass they looked around cautiously before hurrying away on their desperate errands.

'We'll come back later,' Jaime said.

She glanced behind her. The three gamins from the Zone of the Martyrs were still with them. 'Can we do anything about them?'

'We've only got so much accommodation. However... It's your lucky day,' he told them in Spanish, or that was what she thought he said. Whatever it was, the thumbs came out of their mouths like corks out of bottles and they piled into the back of his Range Rover.

He drove to one of the four homes of the Niños de los Andes. It was half hostel, half school, full of young noise. Noise that became more exuberant when Papa Jaime was spotted. The three urchins in the back of the Range Rover shrank, scared of so much happiness.

A tall, graceful woman in her twenties came out to greet them.

Luz Rosa, a mother from the age of fourteen. With her came a girl of thirteen or so, Electra. Sired by an emerald dealer or an orchid grower or a drug baron. She bowed her head and studied her feet as though she had never noticed them before.

Helen embraced Luz Rosa. Her hair was reddish in the fading light, lips full as though they had never quite recovered from a beating long ago. And she was beautiful in the way of the *mestizo*, with Indian and European blood in her veins. She said she now worked in the home. She had a boyfriend, she said, and pointed at a young man wearing a baseball cap, who grinned ferociously.

In the room occupied by Luz Rosa and her daughter, mobile still attached to the wall, Helen took her presents from her bag. One remaining bar of fruit and nut, clothes from Marks and Spencer, Scrabble in Spanish, make-up from Boots, perfume.

Electra touched the gifts with her fingertips as if they were alive and might make a run for it.

Luz Rosa nudged her daughter. Her daughter said in English: 'It is very good of you to come. Will you be my Mother of God?'

'Godmother,' Luz Rosa said.

'Of course I will,' Helen said. 'I am honoured.'

Electra reverted to Spanish.

'What did she say?' Helen asked Jaime.

'She wants to know if she can visit you in England.'

'I will look forward to it.' Odd how collaboration with an interpreter dipped your words in starch. 'Tell her it's a godmother's duty to send lots of presents,' she added. And to look after a child if anything happens to its parents!

They drank *ajicao*, thick chicken soup served with corn on the cob and capers, in the dining hall, mopping it up with hunks of bread. Jaime, Helen and Luz Rosa shared a bottle of red wine which would have stripped paint.

Helen slept in a bare, whitewashed room. Jaime woke her just before dawn and drove her to the entrance to the sewer. As the street children returned, one by one, Jaime gave them bowls of *ajicao* and bread and vitamin tablets, making sure they swallowed the pills instead of saving them to resell.

One boy was missing. Hit by a police car, the others said. As a tourist shouting '*Ladrón*, thief!' chased him across the Plaza de Bolívar. 'A good night,' Jaime said. 'Only one missing is a good night.'

But the following night was a bad one.

Word reached the headquarters of the Niños de los Andes that guerrillas were planning a hit in the centre of Bogotá and volunteers were dispatched to get the waifs off the streets.

Helen volunteered to accompany them. She was advised not to but went just the same, striding along the dark streets beside a thin young man with a poet's face named Quico.

Quico was a naturalised American from Medellín, city of orchids, the tango and cocaine. Its citizens, he told her, were descended from persecuted Jews. Quico, she understood, embraced suffering.

'Every June the first I return to Medellín to dance at the Festival of the Tango in memory of Carlos Gardel.'

'Gardel?'

'The world's greatest tango singer in the 1930s. He was scared of flying but friends persuaded him to tour South America by plane. The aircraft crashed outside Medellín and he was killed,' Quico said with melancholy satisfaction.

They stopped while he told three children with starved faces to get back to the sewers. One was drinking from a bottle of Poker beer. He offered it to Helen. 'No,' she said, waving it aside, 'you get home . . .' Home, a sewer?

'Where did he get the beer?' she asked Quico.

'From a bar, I guess. In exchange for *basuco*.'

'You're very cool about drugs . . .'

'Sure, cool. For hundreds of thousands of Colombians it's life, you know. They grow it, pamper it, process it. Without coca they would die.'

'Coke kills too.'

'So don't take it,' Quico said. 'Users have a choice: growers none. And, you know, it's a safe local anaesthetic. Have a nose job and they'll freeze it with cocaine.'

'You seem to know a lot about it,' Helen said as they passed the Dorantes Hotel on Calle 13.

'Sure. I've been to San José de Guaviare on the plains of Los Llanos, cowboy country. There's a river there the colour of chocolate. Alongside they grow coca and process it. You should see them slopping around in coca leaves knee deep in water – and a little sulphuric acid. Then lime, gasoline, potassium, ammonia . . . From there it's shipped to laboratories to be refined. Things have got better, but when I was there it was no-man's-land. FARC guerrillas sworn to overthrow government by privilege, M-19 guerrillas who figured the elections were rigged, *sicarios*, hired guns, paid to kill guerrillas.'

'So who's planning the hit tonight?'

'The Colombian Revolutionary Armed Forces – FARC. They work

together, these international revolutionary groups. Not so long ago they had an IRA guy training them. An American, would you believe?'

They made their way south down Carrera 7 in the direction of the Plaza de Bolívar, the square flanked by the Palace of Justice, a church, La Capilla del Sagrario, and other grand bastions of authority.

The street was deserted and the breeze flowing from the mountains smelled clean.

The bomb left in the street cleaner's cart exploded near the statue of Bolívar the Liberator in the middle of the square.

Helen and Quico arrived as a police car skidded to a halt. Two policemen leaped out and together they stared at the three victims. All dead. All small. One clutching a bottle of Poker beer which had somehow remained intact. Helen took it from his hand and placed it beside Bolívar the Liberator.

Her father was pleased to see her, not overwhelmed but willing to give up a little time from his latest researches into Silent Cal. He was working on a thesis suggesting that the Norman Rockwell values of the Coolidge era should be resuscitated in the 1990s. He did not dwell, Helen noted, on the fact that the stock-market crash and the Depression had followed hard on the heels of the Coolidge administration.

After four days her father, who was showing increasing signs of taking up residence in the past, indicated, although not in so many words, that it was time for the visit to end.

Helen boarded a coach to New York City and booked into the St Regis for two days. The next morning she read in the *New York Times* that a mother and her daughter had been blown up and killed by an IRA car bomb in London.

She got back to the house in Chelsea a day early. It was empty, the kitchen spotless and humming, Harry's bed made up. She wondered when he had last slept in it. There were letters on the front doormat and the morning newspapers.

She sat in the living room, kicked off her shoes and switched on the television. The car bombing was the third item on the news. A former major in the SAS was being interviewed.

'Do you think, major, that the SAS will retaliate in any way?'

'Not the slightest chance of it,' the major said in a crisp voice. 'SAS, like any other regiment, obeys orders.'

'More's the pity, major?'

'You said that, young lady, I didn't.'

The interviewer, a woman, hating him, said: 'There is widespread feeling that, given the opportunity, the SAS could wipe out the IRA tomorrow.'

'Statement or question?'

'Could they? Wipe them out, that is?'

'Purely a matter of speculation. I am a retired soldier: I cannot comment on the present-day potential of my old regiment.'

'Do you not believe – and I'm only asking for your opinion – that it's time for retaliatory action? I mean why, in your opinion, should terrorists be allowed to get away with murder time after time?'

'Afraid I can't comment on that.'

'Why not, major?'

'That would be a political decision and I, thank God, am not a politician.'

'But the SAS does have a go-it-alone reputation, doesn't it? Don't mess with the SAS—'

'SAS,' the major said, 'does what it has to do.'

'Thank you for finding the time to appear on this programme,' the interviewer said.

Helen put a pizza in the microwave. She wasn't hungry – unlike most seasoned travellers, she enjoyed in-flight meals – but it was something to do. It was 9.15 pm. While the pizza cooked, she made another inspection prowl of the house.

When had Harry last been here? She fancied she could smell cigarette smoke; Harry didn't smoke. She examined the ashtrays. Pristine. It must be a yearning, not an actual odour.

On the mantelpiece she found the postcard she had sent from Vermont. Killington, where they had met. On the back her scrawl: *Silent Cal sends best.*

She wondered how he had reacted to the car-bomb explosion in Clapham. Now why had she invoked that? Because, she supposed, he had been away just before the last atrocity at Victoria Station. And was away now. Stupid!

Certainly Harry had Irish ancestry – parents killed in a road accident in Ulster, brought up by second-generation Irish foster parents in New York – but he was as American as apple pie. Lawyer, diplomat, Mets fanatic.

She took the pizza out of the microwave. Cardboard with a Pear's soap topping! She consigned it to the waste-disposal grinder; even that tried to regurgitate it. She poured herself a glass of claret posed to degenerate into vinegar and tried not to think about the pack of Marlboros still calling her.

She switched on the central heating. Where was he? Paris again? She checked the clothes rack in the hall. The black windbreaker was there. Guiltily, she dug her hands into the pockets. A crumpled five-pound note and a packet of Kleenex.

She checked the answering machine; it had nothing to say. He could have left a message somewhere, on the blackboard in the kitchen . . . Why should he? I'm not expected home until tomorrow.

She stopped beside the door to his study, struggling with her conscience. She tried the handle; it moved easily. A click. She pulled, and the door opened.

She angled her hand round the door frame, fingers searching for the light switch. She found it and entered.

The room had a neglected intensity about it, trapped breath stale. Law certificates on the walls, a picture of JFK, a photograph of the incumbent president smiling boyishly, law books on shelves, leather-topped desk with her and the boys smiling from within silver frames, drawers of the desk locked. No, not locked. As she pulled it, the top left-hand drawer opened. Snoop! I will confess. 'Figured you might have some cigarettes in there.' Pathetic.

Letters, bills, a prescription for hay-fever tablets, packet of Tipp-Ex, ballpoint refill for a Cross pen, visiting cards, at the bottom the protruding corner of a colour photograph.

She was about to extract it when she heard a car pull up outside. She closed the drawer, snapped out the light, shut the door and ran upstairs to the bedroom.

He was a little drunk. Had, in fact, been drinking too much ever since, while he was in Dublin, he had heard about the car bomb in Clapham.

He sat for a moment in the Mercedes outside the house, resting trembling hands on the steering wheel. Had he imagined it or had he seen a light in his study? The light came on in their bedroom. Helen wasn't due back from New York until tomorrow!

He opened the front door and stood in the hall. Felt her presence, smelled her perfume. He walked into the living room. A flight bag lay on the chesterfield in front of the television.

He strode, stumbling on a rug, to the door of his study which, not expecting her back for another day, he had left unlocked. Left the drawers of the desk unlocked too.

He opened the door and switched on the light. The air was thick and undisturbed, a tableau waiting to be animated. He must have been mistaken about the light.

He opened the top left-hand drawer. From beneath the detritus of his privacy he extricated the colour photograph of his parents aiming toothpaste smiles at the photographer. Himself. Across the photograph, long ago, he had scrawled in ink: 'Victims of War.'

Chapter Five

The British Army Lynx helicopter on the other side of the border hovered like a predatory insect. Above the clatter of its wings Harry heard gunfire.

He put down his glass of warm lemonade, picked up his father's binoculars and peered through them. He could just make out the face of the pilot and a soldier aiming a gun. At what?

This was the bonus of his visits to the pub with his father: there was always a possibility that, from a safe distance, he would be able to witness some action. Besides, there was the pig.

There were two pubs in the village, one Catholic and one Protestant, and their regulars were as faithful to each as worshippers to their respective churches. Once, Harry had been told, a Prod fuddled with drink had strayed into the Catholic pub and the barman had spiked his pint of Guinness with powdered glass. So drunk had he been, so the story went, that he had poured the stout down his throat, ordered another pint, raised it to heaven and shouted: 'Down with popery!'

Harry occasionally peered into the pub; a dismal place, he thought. Wallpaper with a stone-wall design peeling at the extremities, a long bar furrowed with cigarette burns. He much preferred the garden on summer days such as this drinking lemonade, sharing his potato crisps with the pig – a sow, in fact, named Samantha – and peering into Northern Ireland through a line of sunflowers with drooping blossoms as big as plates. Into south Armagh, land of trout lakes, apple orchards and gunmen, across the border from the Republic.

The helicopter banked. More gunfire. From the ground, Harry fancied. A battle, probably, between Prods and Provos because today was 12 July, when Prods wearing bowler hats celebrated a historic victory over the Catholics.

But Catholics would have to be pretty stupid to show themselves on such a day. In south Armagh? Maybe not. At the age of seven Harry was still not sure why two religions worshipping the same god should wage war against each other.

One thing he did know: the Protestants were the enemy. That he had heard from the crib. He sipped his lemonade and fed Samantha more crisps.

He peered again through the binoculars. The helicopter was low over the ditches and green pastures beyond. It was following someone, something. The soldier was aiming his gun, finger tight on the trigger – but that, of course, was his imagination.

The barman, wearing flared black trousers and a white shirt, walked across the balding grass carrying a tray as though he were dancing with it. On the tray was a pint of Guinness and another glass of lemonade with a bent straw protruding from it.

'Your man sent it,' the waiter said. 'Your da.'

'Tell him thank you,' Harry said. 'And tell him about that.' He pointed at the helicopter.

'I'll tell him,' the waiter said, waltzing back to the bar even though he now held the tray at his side.

A few moments later his father emerged from the snug. He wasn't drunk but he wasn't entirely sober. He carried his jacket over his arm, shirt open-necked above a green and gold brocade waistcoat; that was how Harry would always remember him, big and kind, restless and half-dressed.

He sat opposite Harry and scratched Samantha's hair, as strong as needles on her pink skin.

'Look, Da.' Harry aimed the straw across the border. 'Trouble.'

'Was it ever any other way, son?'

'Is it like that all over Ireland?'

His father wiped a moustache of foam from his upper lip. 'Only in the North, Belfast and Derry ... and here along the border. The Republic itself is as safe as a sanctuary.'

Harry, who had heard furtive noises inside and outside their house at night, said nothing.

'The Catholics in the North are only fighting for what is theirs, never forget that, son.'

'But who was here first, in the whole of Ireland, I mean?'

'We were. The Irish – Celts, Picts, Gaels ... Then the Vikings had a bite until Brian Boru sent them packing in 1014. Then the Normans, then the bloody British ... Don't they teach you any of this at school?'

'They make it boring,' Harry said.

'The history of Ireland – boring? You might as well say a rose is ugly.' He drank more stout. 'But we sent the British packing after the First World War. The Black and Tans – you've heard of them?'

'British soldiers?'

'That's right, Tommies. They shot my brother in Dublin. Outside the post office in O'Connell Street. All he was doing was minding his own business.'

'I know,' Harry said. 'And your father made bombs in your kitchen and threw them at the Tommies when they were raiding the Sinn Fein office in Harcourt Street.'

His father smiled. 'Am I becoming a bore, son?'

'Never,' Harry said.

'And after the fighting we got Home Rule in the South while the Prods in the six counties in the North stayed with the British.'

'Whey were there so many Prods in the North?'

'A lot of them came from Scotland in the seventeenth century to cultivate plantations. They brought with them oatcakes and their religion. That's why they have a different voice to us, a bit of Irish and a bit of Scots.'

Harry fed Samantha the last of the crisps. 'If the Prods in the North want to stay with the British, isn't that their business, Da?'

'No, son. Ireland is one country. It should be united and independent. Partition was a mistake. An excuse for the Prods in the north to victimise the Catholics there.'

More shooting could he heard from across the border. The helicopter settled lower. Harry and his father stared at it from behind their raised glasses.

'Do you know what started the Troubles again in 1969?' his father asked.

Harry said he didn't: dates, those were what made history boring. Neither the shooting nor the helicopter was boring.

'The Catholics in Derry finally hit back at the Prods. And what happened then? The Prods in Belfast went crazy and burned dozens of Catholic homes.'

Harry spoke even more cautiously. 'Isn't it true then that the British soldiers went there to protect the Catholics?'

'And stayed, didn't they? To look after their own. British soldiers still in Ireland: it's obscene.'

More shooting, closer this time. Dust rose from beneath the helicopter's blades. A small blue saloon car materialised heading for the Republic at speed, skidding round a bend in the thin road where in the summer road bowls was played. Harry saw soldiers at the checkpoint raise their rifles and fire. The car bounced off a stone wall, then it was across the border. The soldiers lowered their guns; the helicopter banked and flew north. Like a dragonfly, Harry thought.

'Good luck, lads,' his father whispered as the blue car disappeared. He sighed. 'What a lot we are, eh, Harry? Why, even St Patrick was a Frenchman. Or was he a Welshman?'

They walked home through the village, its two terraces of cottages taking the sun, skirting the ruined castle which, like the rest of Ireland, was haunted. A sheep peered at them over a wall between two bursts of yellow gorse. In the distance the bog languished beneath a wig of cotton grass. Even in their home, the Big House, turf was burned in the winter and the tall chimneys spouted smoke that smelled of autumn.

The table was laid, stew steaming in an earthenware dish just as Harry knew it would be. His father was a little scared of his mother and always timed his return from the pub to perfection.

His mother smiled patiently at her family and spooned stew onto their plates. Often, it seemed to Harry, her mind was elsewhere, somewhere in the mist in the mountains, perhaps. She came from Cork – her maiden name was Roche – and at school Harry had overheard one teacher telling another that she could speak Béarlagair na Sier, the secret language of the tinkers, once the tongue of high-caste priests. He had asked her about it and she had put her finger to her lips, drawing him into an undefined conspiracy.

Although she sometimes looked wistful when a tinker's barrel-shaped caravan passed by, she only descended from her peaks of detachment when two subjects were raised – the British, who had burned her parents' house in Cork, and Harry's education.

Cutting soda bread, she told her husband, who was already deep into the stew, that she had found a fine school for Harry in Dundalk. 'Later, of course, he will go to Trinity in Dublin.'

'Not University College, Cork?' He glanced up slyly from his stew.

'Trinity,' she said firmly, putting Harry in the queue behind Swift, Goldsmith, Burke, Oscar Wilde, Synge . . .

'I'm only asking, woman.'

That night Harry heard sounds again, but there was nothing furtive about them. The screech of brakes, thudding footsteps, shouting, gunshots.

Shivering, he climbed out of bed and peered down into the moonlit courtyard. Men wearing hoods, eyes glittering behind them, were running from a jeep towards the outhouse on the far side of the yard.

The door opened and he saw his father silhouetted in the frame, a pistol in his hand. Another vehicle, a Land-Rover, skidded to a halt in the yard; soldiers piled out.

He heard one of them shout: 'Halt or we shoot!'

'You're in the Republic,' his father replied, 'get back where you belong.'

The hooded men, three of them, were almost at the doorway.

A shot. Harry didn't know who fired it. He slipped his hands inside his pyjama jacket and hugged his chest.

A cloud passed over the moon. In the darkness his father, framed in the doorway, was now a perfect target.

'No!' Harry shouted and punched out the window with his fist. 'Don't shoot!'

The burst of gunfire ripped the night.

The hooded men fell.

At first, his father remained upright. Impervious to British bullets! Then he pitched forward and, as he fell Harry noticed that one side of his brocade waistcoat was wet with blood.

Harry gave evidence at the inquest and the courts martial of the lieutenant in charge of the troops who had crossed the border from Northern Ireland and the soldier who had wounded three Provos and killed his father. In their defence they claimed that the Provos had ambushed and killed three British soldiers at Crossmaglen in Northern Ireland; that, in giving chase, they hadn't realised they had crossed the border; and that, in any case, Quarrick's house was a notorious haven for IRA fugitives.

Harry was asked by the officer defending the soldier if his father had aimed a pistol at the British soldiers.

'No, sir – they just gunned him down.'

'Was it dark at the time?' His accentless words snapped out as if they were on elastic.

'Very, sir. A cloud had passed over the moon.'

'So your vision was impaired?'

'No, sir. It made it better. You see, my da was framed in the doorway and there was a light behind him.'

'I put it to you, young man, that all you could see was a silhouette.'

'You can put it to me if you wish.'

The officer raised his eyebrows to the ceiling; he had a postage-stamp moustache the same colour as the hair on Samantha's back. 'Then I do put it to you.'

'I could see he wasn't aiming a pistol.'

'Did your father harbour strong feelings about the British?'

'He did, sir. They shot his brother outside the post office in O'Connell Street. They also burned my mother's house in Cork.'

'Was your house often used as a bolt hole for fleeing IRA terrorists?'

'I'm sorry, I don't understand the question.'

'What don't you understand?' Once again seeking guidance from the ceiling.

'What is a bolt hole?'

'Did terrorists hide in your house?'

'If they did, sir, they didn't bring any terror with them.'

'Are you being impudent, young man?'

'With respect, sir, my da is dead.'

'Do you realise that a young man's future depends on your recollection of that terrible night?'

Harry thought about the question. Stared at the accused soldier, young with a chipped tooth and gingery hair. He said: 'My da doesn't have any future at all, does he?'

The defending officer sat down.

The officer commanding the pursuers was sentenced to three years, the soldier who fired the shots that killed Harry's father to eighteen months.

After the sentences had been announced, a young man with cropped hair came up to Harry outside the barracks.

'You're Harry, right?'

'I'm Harry, to be sure.'

'The soldier who's just gone down for eighteen months, he was my mate.' He spoke with an accent that Harry identified from television as Cockney.

'He killed my father,' Harry said.

'And you're a lying little bastard. Know why we were sent to Northern Ireland? To protect little shits like you.'

'He wasn't in Northern Ireland when he shot my father,' Harry said.

The soldier bent down and spoke softly. 'He's SAS, Harry. Undercover. One day you'll get yours.'

After her husband's death, Harry's mother retreated more often into the mist-shrouded peaks where Harry had always believed she found sanctuary. When she died fourteen months later she spoke on her deathbed in a language no one there understood.

Harry became a terrorist at the age of eight. Although he didn't realise it at the time.

The recruitment occurred in a first-floor room in a Georgian terraced house with a fanlight above the front door near St Stephen's Green in Dublin.

The recruiting officer was one of his father's four brothers, the youngest. He wore his hair cut so short that you weren't sure where the baldness began, and he prowled in tight circles as he talked.

Harry sat opposite him eating Kerry Creams washed down with Lucozade while his uncle Padraig asked him about his reactions to the killing of his father – 'poisoned with British bullets' – and the death of his mother.

'I saw my da killed. Isn't that enough?'

'Of course.' He took a sip of Powers whiskey – Jamesons was the Prod brand, Harry remembered. 'What did you think about the soldiers who killed your da?'

'Hated them, what else?'

His uncle, wearing a suit as dark as a funeral, patrolled the high-ceilinged room. 'Of course you did. What else?' He clasped his hands behind his back and knitted his fingers. 'Do you want to revenge your da's death?'

'Of course.'

'Good boy.' He stopped prowling and turned suddenly. 'How would you like to go to America?'

'America?'

'New York.'

Harry's mind filled with images from the movies: skyscrapers, crowds and traffic.

'Would you like to live there for a long time? Several years?'

'*Live* there?'

'With a family. In a place called Queens, one of the boroughs of New York City.'

'What would I be doing there?'

'Sleeping,' his uncle said. Then, inadequately, he explained.

Harry *slept* for eight years. He was adopted by the Quarricks, second-generation Irish who had just moved to a decent-sized house in Forest Hills, and became a naturalised American attending high school, supporting the Mets and the Jets, playing tennis, winning cups at a shooting range and exercising Irish charm. He was assumed to be the Quarricks' natural son – a NORAID agent within the adoption society had supplied a birth certificate and other documents – but at regular intervals he was reminded by Joe Quarrick of the tragedy of Ireland, the tragedy being the presence of the British on territory foreign to them. But despite such tutelage the Quarricks were at pains to mould Harry as all-American rather than shamrock Irish and he never attended the St Patrick's Day parade on Fifth Avenue.

He was *woken* on 27 October 1980, the day seven Republican prisoners in the Maze prison in Belfast began a hunger strike, eight days before Ronald Reagan won the US presidential election for his first term.

The awakening took place in Fragrance Garden, a haven for the blind, in Brooklyn Botanic Garden.

With Joe Quarrick was a lean man with brown eyes and an air of enduring patience; he wore a tan topcoat and kept his hands deep in its pockets as though he might be holding a gun in one of them.

Joe said he was the leader of the Cause in New York, in the United States for that matter, and they shook hands with watchful formality. The leader's name was Tully.

They walked past a bed of faded roses. Harry couldn't smell them; maybe the blind could.

Tully said: 'You must have been wondering, all these years.'

'And guessing,' Harry said. He wore a black rollneck sweater and a tweed jacket, grey scarf whipping in the chill breeze.

'So you guessed you were chosen a long time ago for an important job. You probably guessed New York. Wrong.'

'Ireland?'

'Wrong.' Tully closed his eyes for a moment as though searching for a fragrance left over from summer. 'Britain. London, in fact. You see, we're looking to the future and we want to establish the structure of a new cell there. With you at its head.'

'How far into the future?'

'Ten years,' Tully said. He turned to Joe Quarrick. 'Why don't you get yourself a coffee? We'll meet in half an hour in the Japanese garden.'

'You don't trust me?'

'You know how it is, Joe. Too many ears... You've done a wonderful job.'

'We always wanted a son,' Joe Quarrick said. He strode away, grey curls bobbing in the breeze.

'Was he paid?' Harry asked.

'Sure he was paid.' Tully put his arm round Harry's shoulders as they walked along the footpath. 'How old are you, Harry? Sixteen?'

'Going on seventeen,' Harry said.

'We've been watching you. You're our man. Are you game?'

'I figure it was written,' Harry said.

'We think so, too. And that's why we're establishing you in the enemy capital. The Brits spend their time rounding up Paddies or turncoats: they'll never suspect an American. And a diplomat at that.'

'Diplomat?'

'We want you to go to university here – you're a bright boy. Study law. Then we want you to get a job in the State Department in Washington.'

'Just like that?'

'We have contacts,' Tully said. 'And then apply for a posting to the US embassy in London. Believe me, you'll get the job.'

'Contacts?'

'It's not what you know...'

A cold excitement settled on Harry like a flurry of snow on a winter day. He imagined himself mingling in London with the people who had burned the house of his mother's parents, shot his father's brother, killed his father and, indirectly, his mother.

'Are you game?' Tully repeated.

'I'm game,' Harry said.

They walked briskly round the lake, past rows of crab apples to the Japanese garden, where Joe Quarrick was waiting.

During his spell in Washington with the State Department, Harry twice visited Europe on 'official business' while Helen took the two children to Vermont. On both occasions he flew to London, picked up on-flight tickets at Heathrow and took Iberian flights to Bilbao, the gritty industrial city in the Basque region of northern Spain. There he picked up a waiting black Renault and drove into the mountains on the road to Vitoria. He stopped at the end of a dirt road beside a *baserri*, a Basque farmhouse with an alpine roof. On his first visit an ETA terrorist leader was waiting for him at the door.

His name was Joxe – 'Better you call me Joe' – and he had once been renowned in the field of wood chopping, a Basque national sport. He sat Quarrick in front of an open fire, poured them both beers and pointed out of the window at mountains winged with snow. 'So how do you like our country?' Quarrick knew he meant the Basque provinces bounded in the north by the Bay of Biscay and southwest France, which also had a Basque population.

'Almost as beautiful as Ireland,' Quarrick said.

Joxe grinned and a gold tooth fielded the firelight. 'We have a lot in common,' he said. 'For Gaelic read Euskera, the oldest language in Europe, possibly the world, so different that a sixteenth-century author thought we used it to communicate with the monsters of the deep. For London read Madrid – the seats of foreign rule. For Celts read tribes – Vascones, Vardulos, Caristios and Autrigones. For hurling read pelota. For IRA read ETA.'

Quarrick drank beer and stared at the sparks chasing each other up the chimney. 'I appreciate what you're doing for me,' he said.

'Injustice should be shared, my friend. Like a handshake in which hands become fists.' He poured more beer. 'Here's to Euskadi, our land, and Eire, yours.'

Gazing out of the window at the mountains, Quarrick fancied for a moment that they were the Mountains of Mourne in Northern Ireland.

The following day he was introduced to one of the ETA military's *liberados legales*, an active militant unknown to the police of the Guardia Civil. He was a garage owner who had lived in Chicago, and he instructed Quarrick in the art of keeping up a front. 'Pursue your profession energetically. A diplomat with immunity? Shit, how lucky can you get?' He punched Quarrick in the arm. 'Always have a reason for an absence. Never confide in your wife or your mistress. Are you married?'

Quarrick said he was. Happily, he added.

'Good – it helps. Kids?'

'Two.'

'Even better, a family man. Hobby?'

'The kids,' Quarrick said. 'I fly kites with them.'

'Keep 'em flying. Make sure your soldiers do most of the dirty work. The hits . . .'

Quarrick made a blade of his hand and sliced the air with it – the language of the hands was catching and easier than Euskera. No, said his hand, I'll be there in the front line.

'Stupid, but suit yourself.'

'An American giving orders to the Irish in London? If I'm going to survive I've got to be where the action is.'

'Then don't blow yourself up; it's been known.'

The following day Quarrick returned to the mountains to learn how to blow up people other than himself.

The course started with lessons in handling terrorists' bread and butter, the Czech-made plastic explosive Semtex. It handled beautifully, Quarrick thought, like Plasticine. Safe, too, his instructor told him – until you inserted a detonator with an old-fashioned time fuse or one that with the assistance of a lithium battery, could be activated by remote control. The latter combination, said the instructor – an amiable young man with a butcher's hands – was by far the most popular instrument of mass execution.

He learned how to send clandestine messages with quartz crystals

– just as British Special Operations Executive agents had done in World War II; he practised with an Armalite rifle, managing to cut out a cardboard man's heart on the fourth day; he learned how to use a one-time pad, the venerable but unbreakable cipher system; he learned how to spike bullets with mercury in case he failed to carry out a clean assassination; he struck up a tentative friendship with a razor-sharp commando knife.

He was told after his second visit that he had graduated with honours. 'Even though you're a lawyer,' the instructor said.

Later he trained guerrillas of the Revolutionary Armed Force in Colombia.

He was awakened the second time after he had been living in London for two years. Three meetings in suburban parks – where would terrorists and saboteurs convene if these lonely pastures had never been landscaped? – with the retiring head of the London-based operation, a saturnine Provo who worked for the Catholic Herald.

Reluctantly the Provo handed over the reins – code names, informers, north London arsenals in semidetacheds, blown British agents – and, after the third meeting, took a flight to Belfast, where he abandoned journalism and became a political strategist with Sinn Féin.

Quarrick worked assiduously for the first secretary for politico-military affairs in the US embassy in Grosvenor Square and for the IRA. Until a boy lost an eye in an explosion in Liverpool. That was when the nightmares began. So vivid were they that often, on waking, he couldn't distinguish dream from recent reality.

The dreams got worse after the bomb at Victoria Station.

Far worse when he was in Dublin, but culpable just the same, when a car bomb exploded in Clapham killing the wife and daughter of an SAS officer.

Victims of War. He replaced the photograph in the drawer of his desk and locked it. Locked the door of the study.

He undressed on the landing, washed, brushed his teeth and opened the door of their bedroom. Helen was breathing rhythmically.

He climbed into bed, pulled the duvet round his shoulders and waited for the curtain to go up on his dreams.

A mother and daughter in a small white car. An explosion which he heard in colour, blood red. He opened his eyes. The mother and the little girl were peering reproachfully through the window.

He was still dreaming. Wasn't he?

Part II

Chapter Six

The headquarters of British intelligence is housed in a stylish new building, not unlike the bridge of a giant ocean-going liner, on the south bank of the Thames not far from St Thomas's Hospital, Waterloo Station and Lambeth Palace.

On 6 June 1994, the fiftieth anniversary of the Allies' D-day landings in France in World War II, the head of MI5, Mrs Susan Norton, sat in her office on the fourth floor of the block studying a report about a murder.

Susan Norton was fifty-two years old, her short black hair only just beginning to frost. She had two children and three grandchildren, and every time she read about a terrorist outrage, Republican or Loyalist, she momentarily imagined that the victims were members of her family. She didn't consider that emotional involvement was a handicap in her job; indeed, as the first woman to hold the appointment, she felt that she had more to offer than her male predecessors, whose attitudes had been rooted in the archives of conventional treachery.

She averted her eyes from the sparkle of the Thames, forced herself to forget the festivities in Henley, and reread the word-processed report from the head of Scotland Yard's Anti-Terrorist Squad, Superintendent Bernard Davis.

An Englishman named Ronald Secker, an electrician from Kennington in south London, had been murdered, his body dumped outside the Harrods store in Knightsbridge, scene of two bomb explosions. It was believed that Secker had been recruited by the IRA. In fact, he had been under investigation for his part in two explosions that had twice devastated parts of the City of London.

Explosives had played no part in his death. His neck had been almost severed, probably by cheese-cutting wire with handles at each extremity.

It was the second such murder. And both victims had been IRA terrorists. Susan Norton picked up one of the telephones on her desk and summoned Bernard Davis.

Davis sat on the other side of her desk. He was lean and frowning, black hair needled with bright strands of silver, and he did not look like a policeman, more like a barrister. He wore a grey suit, slightly crumpled, and sported a gold chain looped across his waistcoat and a red rose in his lapel.

'Sorry to disturb you on a day like this,' she said.

'No trouble, Mrs Norton. I always knew I'd have to work overtime today – perfect day for the Provos to let off a big one with London lost in red, white and blue nostalgia.' He was a Mancunian and he had brought some of his Manchester vowels with him to London. 'Mind if I smoke?'

'As a matter of fact, I do.'

'Ah, well.' He slapped his pocket, beating his cigarettes into submission. 'You're right, of course. Filthy habit. The wife says I smell like an ashtray.'

'I've read your report about Secker,' she said. 'Someone doing your job for you?'

'Looks that way. But we can't have it, can we? Human rights will be at our throats.' He almost smiled. 'Sorry, slip of the tongue. They'll accuse us of operating outside the law, pursuing a private vendetta, stooping to tactics as reprehensible as the terrorists... They'll throw the book at us. And arouse sympathy in America.'

'Have you got any theories?' She sometimes wished she had a regional accent: they were important in a country that would remain class-conscious until the Day of Judgement.

Davis stood up like an eloquent barrister addressing the jury. 'When Brady was killed, we thought the killer might have been a Provo because he was unstable, a weak link in the structure. He was involved in the Victoria Station bomb. We thought they might have taken him out because he would reveal who came up with the taxi angle. Clever, that. Rumour has it that the head of the cell goes on the hits himself. Action man, not just desk man.'

Susan Norton placed her hands flat on the desk.

'No offence, Mrs Norton. Someone has to sit behind one. At the Yard, too.' He cleared his throat and faced the jury once more, hand to his invisible wig. 'We stayed with that theory for a while. But now it looks as though someone is taking vengeance into their own hands. Why else would they dump the body outside Harrods?

And it looks like an inside job, doesn't it? Someone inside the Provos or someone inside the security forces.'

'So we have several thousand suspects?'

'Not quite. It's either a closet nut or someone with a score to settle.'

'Nuts apart, that narrows it down a little.'

'Yes, we're—'

'Pursuing your inquiries?'

'I've got a good man on the job. Inspector Lloyd Hood, formerly a sergeant in the SAS.'

'Another assassin, chief inspector?'

'Takes one to spot one. Is anyone else involved?'

'Anyone else?'

'Special Branch, MI6?'

'Involved, of course. But not closely. I should like to meet this Inspector Hood.'

'Of course. A tough nut. Son of a Welsh miner. Legs bent as though he has a sack of coal on his shoulders.'

'Does he sing as well?'

'Not in our line of business.' This time a smile did twitch in one corner of his mouth. 'He had a good record in the SAS.'

'Gibraltar?'

'No, no.'

'Because that we can do without.'

'Do you think there's a connection with someone hurt or killed in the Harrods atrocities?'

'It's a possibility.'

'Or could it be a diversion? To make us concentrate on the Harrods victims?'

'That's possible too.'

'Is Inspector Hood bright as well as tough?'

'Tough as a nut, bright as a button.'

'When can I see him?'

'He's waiting outside.'

On Hampstead Heath in the north of London the kites were flying high. Diamond-shaped kites, box kites, Chinese kites with beaks and wings and trailing legs . . . riding the thermals, straining for the blue between swift white clouds, diving for land.

Watching Harry urging a red, white and blue box kite into the sky, watching Jaime and Ben take their turns at the helm, Helen reprimanded herself for her absurd suspicions. Harry a terrorist! He was a family man. She remembered how horrified he had been when she had told him about the deaths of the three children in Bogotá.

She spread two tartan blankets on the grass on Parliament Hill Fields, from which you were supposed to be able to see across London to the Surrey hills, and, feeling very Edwardian, began to unpack a hamper. Tupperware jars of Russian salad and potato salad, pork pies, Cornish pasties, Branston pickle, Golden Delicious apples and overripe bananas ...

Family man and devoted father. But not such a devoted husband. It was as though he gave all his affection to Jaime and Ben. Another woman? Stress at work? Covert work, for the CIA perhaps? She would tackle him soon. But not this buoyant Sunday.

The box kite wheeled and plunged. Ben tugged desperately on the nylon thread. Harry shouted instructions. But nothing could stop the kite's crash dive.

'I'll fix it,' Harry said to the boys. 'After lunch.' He uncorked a bottle of Chablis and unscrewed a Pepsi. 'Do you want to hear some history?'

'History's boring,' Ben said. He had Harry's watchful eyes and brown hair.

'I used to think that. Is the end of the world boring?'

'It hasn't happened yet,' Ben said, 'so how can it be history?'

'In the eighteenth century the end of the world was forecast and crowds gathered here to wait for it.'

'What happened?'

'Not a lot,' Harry said. 'Do you know why this part of the Heath is called Parliament Hill Fields? Because Guy Fawkes and a lot of other guys – ' he paused to see if they got the joke – 'tried to blow up the Houses of Parliament in 1605.'

'The seventeenth century,' Jaime said.

'Don't interrupt,' Ben said.

'After they had lit the fuses to the gunpowder barrels, they came up here to watch the explosion.'

'Except that there wasn't one,' Helen said.

'Just like the world not coming to an end,' Jaime said.

'A famous highwayman, Dick Turpin, used to drink in an inn here, the Spaniards,' Harry went on. 'And the mantel over the fireplace in another pub, Jack Straw's Castle, is supposed to have been made from the gallows on which another highwayman, called Jackson, was hanged.'

'Harry,' Helen said, 'let's talk about the fauna and flora.'

'Another time,' Harry said. 'Know what we're going to do when we've finished lunch?'

'Fly the kite, of course,' Jaime said.

'And then?'

They bit into their apples and waited.

'We're going to the pond to watch the radio-controlled model boats. Some of them are ten feet long.'

'Can we have one?' Ben asked.

'Maybe.' Harry grinned at the children.

'Provided the world doesn't come to an end before then,' Jaime said.

Collins read about the murder of Ronald Secker, the English IRA operative, in his quarters – his private battle HQ – at the SAS camp at Hereford in the West Midlands.

According to the newspaper report, Secker had been responsible for planting the car bomb that had killed Judy and Jane. The ballpoint pen he was holding snapped in his fingers.

Still in his dressing gown, he leaned back in the stiff-backed chair in front of a small desk and surveyed his spartan room. Photographs of Judy and Jane on the desk, sturdy bed, number two dress uniform with black buttons hanging in the open wardrobe, sand-coloured beret hanging from a hook on the door. It was as he wanted it, unforgiving.

So now two Provos operating in Britain were dead. First Brady, linked by genetic fingerprinting to the explosion at Victoria Station, and now Secker, linked... Collins stood up abruptly and stared out of the window, seeing nothing.

It was the commander of the cell he wanted, the man who authorised the atrocities. American accent, living in Chelsea, two children... Part of his duties, now that he had been assigned to admin, was liaising with the 21st SAS at the Duke of York barracks. That, too, was in Chelsea. *Who dares wins*!

He dressed in a pinstripe, slipped a 9-mm Browning pistol into his briefcase, let himself out and walked briskly to his second-hand silver Jaguar XJ6 – no more Volvos, ever. He drove south through Herefordshire, land of orchards, hopfields and the dreaming river Wye, until he picked up the M4 south of Chepstow, and headed east to London.

As he drove, he planned. He would get his official business completed as quickly as possible, then call at the US embassy brandishing one of his newly printed visiting cards: *John Raymond Melrose, Chief Statistician, Office of Population Censuses and Surveys*. With forged ID to back it up if necessary. 'We want to ascertain how many American nationals are living in London. We also want to know how they adapt to the, ah, English way of life. You know, social customs, et cetera. In particular, our educational system – if, that is, the children don't attend an American school.' Very casually: 'Are there any particular schools that Americans favour in Chelsea? We're carrying out a concentrated survey there.'

He drove past the exit to Swindon. To the south lay Winchester, his old HQ, and Salisbury Plain where he had carried out many a tedious manoeuvre beneath leaking clouds.

He put his foot down and the Jaguar surged past a battered white Transit van emblazoned with the name of a pop group, the Bovver Boys. In the rear-view mirror he caught a glimpse of a young man with a shaven head thumb-nosing him.

If the Americans didn't come across, then he would make inquiries at private schools in Chelsea and its environs. Same visiting card, same ID. 'Any American children studying here? It must be interesting watching how American kids adapt. Accent is everything, do you agree?'

Collins urged the Jaguar through the western approaches to London, past the exit to Heathrow airport, abandoned the M4 a little later and parked the car outside his flat off the Fulham Road.

His business at the Duke of York barracks completed, John Raymond Melrose took a cab to the embassy.

The US embassy, all six hundred rooms of it, stands magnificently in Grosvenor Square, surmounted by a gilded aluminium eagle with a thirty-five-foot wingspan. John Adams lived in the square before he became president of the United States; Walter Hines Page, US ambassador from 1913 to 1918, lived there; so did the American financier John Pierpoint Morgan; in World War II, when the elegant buildings were occupied by the US military hierarchy in Europe, it was known as Eisenhower Platz. A statue of Franklin D. Roosevelt stands in the middle of the square.

Collins was received by a junior diplomat in a small room built around a green-topped desk that would not have brought cheer to the heart of the architect, Eero Saarinen. The incumbent president smiled down upon the two of them from the wall.

The blond-haired diplomat sat behind the desk, asserting territorial rights, and, holding the visiting card between two powerful fingers, said: 'So what can we do for you, Mr Melrose?', reading the name as though he had just mastered a code.

Sawing at the cleft in his chin with one finger, Collins told him.

'Now that's really interesting,' said the diplomat as though he actually thought it was. 'No, I mean it.'

'Do *you* have any ideas? About adapting, that is.' Collins took a pen from the inside pocket of his jacket.

The diplomat sought presidential approval from the portrait on the wall before speaking. 'As a matter of fact, I do. All Americans should visit the pubs. As long as they don't drink the draught beer.' He offered Collins a chip-toothed smile.

'You have family here?'

'No, sir.'

'So how do you relax?'

'I don't go to cricket games.'

'Your loss,' Collins said, smiling.

'No disrespect, sir, but to me it looks like a video on pause.'

'We have difficulty understanding baseball.'

'That's your loss.'

Collins made a few sprawling notes. 'Do you mix a lot with the Brits?'

'I've got an English girlfriend. Sally. Great girl. We're going to get married.'

'What does she do?' Collins asked.

'She's a model.'

Collins froze.

The diplomat said: 'Are you OK?'

'I'm fine. It's just that I knew a model once.'

'Not as cool as they make out, are they? Not when they get off the catwalk.'

'No,' Collins said, 'they're not. When are you getting married?'

'Soon, I guess.'

'Not too soon. Make sure you're right for each other. Marriage is a precious commitment.'

'I'll remember that, sir.' The young diplomat stared curiously at Collins. 'Is this all part of your survey?'

'No.' Collins cleared his throat. 'We're carrying out a concentrate' – he was proud of that, the sort of term statisticians would use – 'in Chelsea. Do you know Chelsea?'

'Sally and I go there a lot. She lives in Kensington.'

'Many Americans there?'

'We're everywhere. Highgate, Hampstead, Swiss Cottage, Kensington, Knightsbridge, Chiswick, Wimbledon . . .' He was obviously proud of what he had learned from Sally.

'Does she like steak-and-kidney pudding?'

'Sir?'

'Sally. The model I knew loved it but she never put on weight.'

'She likes spaghetti with clams,' the diplomat said cautiously.
'Why Chelsea?'
'Ideal location for a clash of cultures.'
'Maybe you're right. So what do you want?'
'A list of names of American business people living there. Your commercial attaché should be able to help.'
'I'll see what I can do.'
'In particular, families with kids. We want to find out how Americans adapt to the British educational system – provided they don't go to an American school.'
'That shouldn't be too difficult,' the diplomat said. He clicked the back of his chipped tooth with his thumbnail. 'As a matter of fact, some of the people working here live in Chelsea.'
'Really? With kids?'
'One for sure. I knew him back in Washington. We both worked in the State Department. He's got two kids. Boys. And they go to school some place in Chelsea.'
'Name?'
'Sorry, no can do.'
'Why not?'
'Protocol,' the diplomat said, savouring the word.
'I understand.' He wanted to karate-chop his neck. 'You've been very helpful. Get me a list of those business people and I'll call round in a couple of days.'

The following morning Collins went to Chelsea public library and checked out the private schools in the area.
The first one he visited was a cosy, gabled building out of sympathy with its grey neighbours. Its asphalt playground was whooping with children and two mothers were waving through the railings at offspring who refused to acknowledge them.
The deputy headmaster was crumpled and chalky and smelled of cough sweets. A lifetime of asking questions seemed to have stunted his ability to answer them.
'Americans,' Collins repeated as they walked along a parquet-floored corridor. 'Do you have any American children here?'
'I'm not sure. Americans?' He frowned.
'With respect, you must know.'
'We've got so many pupils. Too many, really. I keep telling—'
'I really need to know,' Collins said. He pointed at the visiting card in the deputy's hand. 'We're a government body.'
'I think you'd better see the head. She's not available at the moment. She's—'

'At a meeting?'

'In Putney,' the deputy said.

A girl in uniform thundered past, steadying herself with the corner of the deputy's jacket.

Collins, going for the jugular, said: 'I must insist otherwise I shall have to make a report to the Ministry.'

A bell shrilled.

'Classes,' the deputy said. 'If you could come back tomorrow.'

Collins, dodging waves of Fisherman's Friend, said: 'Now.'

Bowed by an authority which he had never mastered, the deputy led Collins to an office and pulled out the drawer of a filing cabinet. Outside children stampeded.

'Well yes,' he said.

'Yes what?'

'We do have three American children here. One from Boston, one from Denver and one from Philadelphia.'

'Boys?'

'All girls.'

Collins said: 'Thank you, Mr Chips.'

'But—'

Dodging a panting boy who was chasing a girl who didn't display any urgency to escape, Collins made his way into the street of parked cars, terrace houses waiting behind them.

The second school was near the Chelsea Physic Garden, as quiet and well-mannered as the other had been rowdy. He was ushered into a cramped office, the lair of the bursar, who looked as though he yearned for distant parade grounds.

It takes one to recognise one and, as soon as they were seated, he said to Collins: 'What mob were you in, Melrose?'

'The Blues,' Collins told him.

'Were you? Were you indeed?' Collins feared he might salute. 'Signals myself—'

'Where would we be without them?'

'Where indeed?' He narrowed his eyes conspiratorially. 'What can I do for you?' *Send an illicit signal?*

Collins told him and within a couple of minutes the bursar had produced the embryonic CVs of four American children at the school. Collins scanned them. One family in Oakley Street, one across the river in Battersea. But no brothers.

The bursar leaned across the desk and said: 'Fancy a drink down the road?' making a clandestine mission of it.

'Another time,' Collins said.

'Of course.' The bursar understood: he had been presumptuous.

The third school was further west. More of an academy than a school. High grey walls trapping knowledge and discipline inside them. On the outside an aerosol legend: PROTECT THE WHALES.

The headmistress received him sternly. Snooping, she implied, was not part of the curriculum. 'I can't imagine who would be interested in how Americans adapt to living here,' she said.

'Americans?'

'Surely they know already?'

'Am I right in assuming you teach logic?'

She took off her spectacles and went over to the window. 'Come here.' She beckoned him and then pointed in the direction of a horse-chestnut tree in the corner of the playground. Underneath its white candles stood two boys, one fair, one dark.

'Those two are the sons of a diplomat at the American embassy. But I can't give you the names and addresses,' she said. 'Not until I've been in touch with the parents.'

'I understand,' he said, knowing what he had to do.

Helen was supposed to pick up the boys from the school bus at 4.15 pm. She glanced at her watch. 3.30. In the smoothly humming kitchen she picked up the letter that had arrived that morning from Electra in Colombia and reread it.

She hoped Helen didn't mind her writing but her mother was ill. A pain in her chest. She thought Helen should know. *She loves you too much.* A postscript. *What is the weather like in Inglaterra now?*

Helen picked up the telephone and punched out the number of Jaime Jaramillo in Bogotá.

'I think I know why you've called,' he said immediately.

'Luz Rosa?'

'Is she very bad?'

'We don't know yet. She's having tests. Sewer kids sometimes pick up bugs that don't show themselves until they're much older.'

'Can I speak to her?'

'She's in hospital. The tests . . .'

'Electra?'

'She's with her.'

'Give them both my love. Tell them I'll be in touch. How are things, Jaime?'

'Not too bad,' he said. 'Only one kid killed last night.'

She replaced the receiver. It was 3.40. She decided to walk to the corner where the boys disembarked from the bus.

The sunshine was warm and gentle and the leaves on the trees were expanding. She could smell the muddy breath of the Thames nearby.

A young man in a denim jacket winked at her and she smiled at him; disconcerted, he crossed the street. A wino with a gooseberry chin asked her for the price of a cup of tea and she gave him 50p.

She arrived at the corner of the street five minutes early. A silver Jaguar turned the corner and headed for the Embankment.

Other mothers congregated, acknowledging each other but scarcely speaking. The bus drew up one minute late, air brakes whooshing.

Ben walked beside her at a distance but she hung onto Jaime.

As they neared the house, Ben said: 'We met a nice man outside the school when we were walking to the bus.'

'What did he want? I told you—'

'He wasn't a strange man,' Jaime said. 'He just wanted to know where a street was.'

'What street?'

'I forget.'

'Mulberry Walk, I think,' Ben said. 'I said we'd never heard of it. Mulberries, isn't that what silkworms eat?'

'Is that all he said?'

'No, first he asked us, "Do you live round here?"'

'And what did you tell him?'

'I told him the name of the street, and Jaime gave him the number. Does it matter?'

'He didn't give us any candy,' Jaime said. 'That's what you warned us about.'

'What did this man look like?'

'Big,' Ben said.

'Not too big,' Jaime said.

'Dark,' Ben said.

'With a sort of dent in his chin,' Jaime said. 'What's for supper?'

'Pizzas,' Helen said.

Midway through supper she thought she heard a knock on the front door, but when she opened it there was no one there.

Chapter Seven

Lloyd Hood collected postcards. Plain postcards from the nineteenth century; picture postcards from the golden age, 1895–1915, when 880 million were dispatched in one year, 1914; humorous postcards by Donald McGill; a dirty postcard or two.

His hobby had been inspired by his father, who had once said: 'The postcard was man's greatest invention, greater even than the wheel.' Over the years friends and relatives had received hundreds of picture postcards from Idris Hood, from Tenby and Porthcawl and Colwyn Bay, favoured resorts for their annual fortnight's holiday, and once when, daringly, they crossed the border into England, from Minehead in Somerset. *Wish you were here* – 'The most popular lie in the world,' according to his father.

He had stopped sending postcards when the pit in the Rhondda valley where he had hewn coal for thirty years had been closed down and there was no longer anything to celebrate in Tenby or Porthcawl or Colwyn Bay. When Lloyd joined the Welsh Guards, his father said: 'Send us a postcard, son,' but by the time the postcard, Queen Elizabeth side-saddle on horseback, arrived, he had died.

He had joined the SAS because it seemed the best weapon Britain possessed to fight injustice. But not, it turned out, in Northern Ireland, where tactics were drawn up by strategists in Whitehall. Decent chaps who insisted that, because they were not at war, British soldiers could not shoot armed terrorists unless they were in imminent danger. Which was how Bomber bought it.

Instead of re-enlisting, Hood, disillusioned by the mandate of the SAS, joined the Met police; his application to work with the Anti-Terrorist Squad was granted almost immediately and he was promoted to inspector.

He bought a terraced house with a bay window in Muswell Hill, near the elephantine hulk of Alexandra Palace, and in the evenings drank a pint or two in his Edwardian local. This spring evening, with the scent of privet blossom on the air, he went straight home, preoccupied with the brief presented to him by the head of MI5 – the apprehension of the killer who had so far murdered two Provos in London.

Tricky. Hood walked into the living room and spread out the computer print-out he had brought back from Scotland Yard.

Toland. Three times the name had appeared in the context of violence, fatal or otherwise, directed at members of the IRA on mainland Britain. Hood knew him well: a grass. One of several who repeatedly betrayed the shamrock to the Anti-Terrorist Squad, Special Branch or MI5. Sometimes such info was genuine; sometimes it was disinformation leaked by the IRA; often it was twenty-two carat bullshit.

Toland's tip-offs had usually been genuine. Which presumably was why he had been beaten to a pulp. By the Provos? Hood wasn't convinced: they would have killed him. What he suspected was that someone had been trying to extract specific information. Something more important than routine intelligence. What?

Hood looked up from the print-out at a set of framed photographs: his parents, his sister in Toronto, and Bomber horsing around, presenting arms with a broom. A few days later he had been killed in the Falls Road area of Belfast.

Certainly Toland's interrogation hadn't been professional. You don't knock suspects around until they are incapable of responding. Not in the SAS anyway, where interrogation was a fine art, both resisting and applying refined brutality. What could the interrogator have been after? The next hit, so he could anticipate it? A bomb-making factory – astonishing how fertiliser could both encourage growth and kill? What was it that was more important than routine intelligence?

What *I* would most like to know is the identity of the commander of the terrorists in Britain. Eliminate him and his lieutenants, and the IRA would be broken on the mainland.

Bingo!

That was what Toland's interrogator had been seeking. Had discovered? So what I have to do is extract the intelligence from the same snout. Professionally. Before the heavy-fisted amateur has time to act on what he may have discovered. Pay a call on Toland, who had been discharged from hospital and deposited in his bedsit.

Just as there were divisions between the agencies fighting terrorism

– MI5, MI6, Special Branch, the CRW unit of the SAS, Scotland Yard's Anti-Terrorist Squad – so there were differences within each agency.

Superintendent Bernard Davis, chief of the Anti-Terrorist Squad, was not over the moon about Inspector Lloyd Hood. Orthodox by nature, Davis regarded unconventional attitudes as a threat. And the SAS, Hood's former regiment, was a law unto itself. So the Welshman had to be controlled.

Hood was well aware of Davis's reservations. After all he had encountered them before – from some members of the regular forces who regarded the SAS as a bunch of tearaways, and from civvy snoops – though often the criticisms were accompanied by a grudging admiration.

Davis was standing in front of a window in his office at New Scotland Yard. He did not relish trying to find out what the head of another department, a woman at that, had told his junior officer.

'Glad you could make it, Hood.' As if he had any choice. 'I thought we should discuss your brief.'

'Sir.'

'Do you feel like a bevvy?'

'Sir?'

'A drink,' said Davis, who was never at home with vernacular. 'I thought we might go down to the pub.'

'In working hours?'

'Don't be pompous, Hood.'

They walked along Victoria Street, turned into Francis Street not far from Westminster Cathedral, and went into the Cardinal. Davis stationed himself beside a red-curtained window and ordered a pint of bitter. 'You?'

Hood said he would like a ginger ale with ice. Davis looked at him with distaste.

'So,' Davis said, thumbs seeking the pockets of his charcoal-grey waistcoat, 'what do you think?'

'About what, sir?'

'Your brief.'

Hood sipped his ginger ale. 'It seems reasonable, sir.'

'Reasonable? Is that all you can come up with?'

'I assume you know what she wants. After all, you put me up for the job.' He exaggerated the hills and valleys of his accent because he suspected they irritated Davis.

'I thought your knowledge of Northern Ireland would come in handy. Who were you attached to there?'

'The Sappers,' Hood told him. 'Undercover, of course.'

'Of course,' Davis said, wiping a moustache of foam from his upper lip.

'We also worked with the Special Boat Service, Paddy Ashdown's mob, and Customs and Excise to try and stop arms being smuggled into Northern Ireland. Fat chance,' he added.

'Race apart, the SAS?'

'Yes, sir, you could say that. Can I ask you a question?'

'Go ahead.' Davis drank more beer.

'You don't seem to be very fond of SAS.'

'That's a statement, not a question.'

'So why have you put me in charge of this investigation?'

'Because,' Davis said, 'it's at the bottom of my list of priorities. Whoever killed those two Provos is doing our job for us.'

'Dangerous thinking, sir. I thought you did everything by the book.'

Davis sighed. 'I'm not saying we mustn't get a result. If we don't, human rights and every MP who hasn't made it to the tabloids by screwing his secretary will be on our backs.'

Hood sipped his dry ginger, ice clicking against his teeth. 'Is that why you brought me here, sir? To tell me that my investigation is bottom of your list?'

'Not quite.' Davis paused while a priest ordered a large whisky. 'I have a few ideas I want you to follow up.'

'Sir?'

'If it isn't the IRA executing informers, if it isn't the Loyalists bringing their war to London, then it's someone with a personal score to settle.'

'Collins? A possibility. But when Brady was killed, he didn't have the motive.'

'Innocent bystanders killed at Victoria Station? He had *a* motive. And, working with the CRW mob inside the SAS he may have had Brady's name and address.'

'At the time the Provo who was dumped outside Harrods was killed, Collins was tucked away in Hereford.'

'Doesn't take long to drive from Hereford to London once you've hit the motorway. Check him out. If your wife and child had been blown to bits—'

'I'm a bachelor, sir.'

'Your attitude leaves a lot to be desired, Hood. Do they call you Robin?'

'In SAS, sir.'

'I thought as much,' Davis said.

He took a gold hunter from a waistcoat pocket, considered it carefully and rose. Hood followed him the door.

Outside the pub a group of tourists hesitated. French, by the look of them; if they had been Irish, they would have been in the pub by now. When they had passed the group, Davis said: 'I read that some members of the SAS have their own special weapons.'

'Sir?'

'Find out if Collins had one. A wire cheese cutter, for instance.'

They walked through a patch of sunlight and back into shadow.

'Keep in touch,' Davis said. He turned on his heel and walked briskly in the direction of New Scotland Yard.

Hood dodged a beggar with bloodshot eyes and made his way to Victoria tube station. Toland, he thought.

There was a notice in the second-floor window; BED SIT VAC. A woman's voice through the intercom. 'Who is it?'

'I've come about the room.'

Footsteps. The door opened and a woman with a small mouth enlarged by lipstick and red hair in heated rollers said: 'Welsh, is it?'

'Welsh it is, girl. Where are you from, then?'

'Cardiff,' she said. 'Tiger Bay.'

'Shirley Bassey country.'

'Lived in the next street.' Her hand strayed to her rollers. 'Come in. It's a nice little room.'

Hood surveyed the room – cane furniture, washbasin, cooker ... Little, certainly; nice, no.

'Make yourself at home,' she said. 'I'll be back in a jiffy.'

When she returned, the curlers had gone and the lipstick had been renewed.

'Where are you from then, Mr—?'

'Jones. Rhondda Valley.'

'Pit closed, father out of work?' She sat opposite him.

'You've got it.'

'Working?'

'Oh, yes,' Hood said, 'I'm working all right.'

'Week's rent in advance. Seventy pounds—'

'I've got a confession.'

'Skint, is it?'

'Not exactly. How about a drink in your local, a snack maybe?' She placed one hand on his knee. 'Confession first.'

'You're an attractive woman,' he said, looking at the chipped lacquer on her fingernails.

'Not so bad yourself. What have you done wrong?'

'Misled you,' he said, wondering what the interrogator had extracted from Toland in this room as he beat him into a pulp. Hadn't anyone heard anything? Probably, but in tenements like this the sound of violence was common enough.

'You don't want the room?'

'It's a nice enough room.'

'It's the pits,' she said.

'Where shall we have a drink?'

'What *do* you want?'

'Information,' Hood said.

'Ah. What are you, a debt collector? A hit man? I never trusted that Toland. Too smarmy.'

'Do you know where he is?'

She shook her head. 'He just upped and left. He'd been beaten up, you know. Scared out of his wits when he got back.'

'Didn't give you a forwarding address?'

'No.'

'Pity.'

'Are you sure you wouldn't like the room? Fifty pounds to a fellow Taffy.'

'I have been looking for somewhere to put my feet up,' Hood lied.

'I could tart it up a bit for you.'

'Let's have that drink first,' Hood said. 'And then a Welsh rarebit maybe?'

'Are you married?'

'A long time ago. Once caught, twice shy.'

'I know the feeling,' she said.

'When he first came here, Toland, that is, didn't he give you an address? A reference?'

'Cash in the hand is all I ask. No point in references. As reliable as a Coal Board promise.' Looking at her fingernails, she folded her arms, tucking them out of sight. 'I could do with a man here to help out. Get a lot of aggro here. You strike me as someone who can look after himself.'

'Did a bit of boxing when I was a boy. Won a few gongs.'

'There you are then.' She squeezed his knee. 'What about it?'

'Let's have a wet first. Talk about it.' He placed his hand over hers. 'First I've got to know where I can find Toland.'

'Business?'

'You could say that.'

'I wish I could help you . . .'

'Think,' he said. 'Think hard.'

'I'm thinking.' She looked at him, head to one side, lit a cigarette and blew a jet of smoke towards the ceiling as though she were eager to get rid of it. 'You might stay here?'

'I might,' Hood said.

'You and me both being Welsh.'

'Taffies together,' he said.

'Better than being Irish.'

'We burned down a few English homes, don't forget.'

'Stupid?'

'I think so.'

'We could get together, you and I. Know what makes the perfect partnership?' He shook his head. 'Sex' and the same sense of humour.'

'Didn't he ever mention anywhere? From his past, that is.'

'Persistent, aren't you?'

'My job.'

'Which is?'

'Doesn't matter. Welsh rarebit?'

'He said he had a sister in Streatham.'

'Unmarried?'

'Does it matter?'

'Same name?'

'Spinster, I think.'

'Where in Streatham?'

'If I tell you, are you going to walk out of here and I'll never see you again?'

'Of course not.'

'Near Streatham Common.'

'Rookery?'

'Gardens in the Common, so he told me.'

'So he did talk about his past?'

'He talked about a lot of things. Thought he was full of the Irish blarney.'

'The Rookery.' Hood wrote it down. 'Street number?'

'No street, no number. A flat, I think. You're not going to kill him, are you?'

'I'm going to talk to him,' Hood said. 'Now how about that drink?'

'Have you got a hobby? I like a man who's got a hobby. Pigeon racing, something like that.'

'I collect postcards,' Hood said.

Chapter Eight

Alfred Hitchcock, wearing a blue suit, was standing beside potted plants emanating menace. Below him, wearing a mauve dress and a string of pearls, sat Agatha Christie.

Quarrick loitered in front of them, pondering the degree of tension the two of them had generated. He glanced at his watch. Butler was already three minutes late, a privilege to which an IRA big shot in Ireland was entitled. A precaution, too.

According to the catalogue, Hitchcock hadn't been able to attend the unveiling of his waxwork duplicate here at Madame Tussaud's in Marylebone Road. He had sent a cable: 'From the flesh to the wax – Good luck.'

'Sorry I'm late,' Butler said in a tone that said he wasn't. He spoke with a faint brogue and looked more like a monk than a terrorist.

'Let's have a look around,' he said, taking Quarrick's arm.

They drifted round the exhibition, and came upon a display called Garden Party, set beneath an evening sky in an English country house.

'Some setting for a few pounds of Semtex,' Butler said. 'If they were real. Three things I want to talk about,' he said, taking his hand from Quarrick's arm. 'One, the Collins job.'

'While I was in Dublin, you know that. That stupid bastard Secker.'

'Dead stupid bastard. An accident, Harry. They happen. All right, Secker was out of order – he shouldn't have authorised the bomb under Collins's car without your authority. A glory seeker, that's all he was. Look where it got him.'

'Look what happened to Collins's wife and kid.'

'Collins ambushed our boys in the Republic. Had you forgotten?'

Quarrick was silent for a moment. Then he whispered: 'No, I hadn't forgotten.'

'Not going soft on us, are you, Harry?'

They passed Nigel Mansell, Boris Becker and Paul Gascoigne.

'No,' Quarrick said, 'I'm not going soft.'

'You must never forget the Cause.'

'I understand that.'

'It's not just Catholics versus Prods. They're merely badges. The whole country belongs to us, none of it to the British and their lackeys in Ulster.'

'The Cause... Was it worth the deaths of an innocent woman and child?'

'Was the war against the Nazis worth the death of all those innocents in the Blitz?'

They descended into the Grand Hall where Henry VIII stood surrounded by his six wives.

'What you must have,' Butler said, 'is belief. Especially now.'

'Why now?'

'Because the fainthearts are trying to take over. Renounce violence. Negotiate. Crawl. That was the second reason I came to see you.' He nodded at Churchill, hands on the lapels of his jacket, jaw thrust forward. 'If he had been Irish, he would have understood.'

'What?'

'That even if a cease-fire is announced, some of us will have to continue the fight. But no more random blood-letting. What we have to do now,' Butler said, 'is wage war. For a united, independent Ireland.'

Sipping tea in the Pier Café below the Grand Hall, Butler, pale skin taut across his cheekbones, talked about provocation. Acts so intimidatory that they would lead to a state of war, declared or otherwise, despite any renunciation of violence. 'Hawks win fights, doves just flap their wings.'

At a nearby table a group of Japanese were discussing the waxwork of the Sumo wrestler Mitsugu Akimo, known as the Wolf; at another, two children pleaded to be allowed to visit the Chamber of Horrors.

Butler said he was taking over the Hawks. No more random soft targets; no more mortar attacks such as those at London airport. 'Jesus, supposing the stupid bastards had hit an American jet?' He paused. 'Are you with us?'

Quarrick saw his father silhouetted in the doorway in the courtyard; saw him fall. 'I'm with you,' he said.

'Right. Ideas are what we want – your department. That taxi bomb, a grand idea. Myself, I thought about the Channel Tunnel. Then I realised it would be just as stupid as mortaring Heathrow. Suppose we killed French, Germans, Dutch, Belgians... It's sympathy we want, not hostility. And in any case we might make Britain an island again. Give it back its balls. No, leave the Chunnel alone: it's like a haemorrhaging artery.'

'I'll work on it,' Quarrick said.

'I thought about the Thames Barrier at Woolwich, too. As high as a five-storey apartment block with its gates raised. Took eight years to build and cost the Brits £500 million. Get the winds and the tides right and you could flood London. But all the tourists... You'd have the world at your throat.'

A small freckled boy eating a chocolate bar, chocolate mingling with his freckles, stopped at the table and stared at them.

'Let's walk,' Butler said. As they headed for the ground floor he said: 'Who's killing our boys, Harry?'

'Brady and Secker?'

'Both fucked up. And paid the penalty?'

'We're investigating,' Quarrick said.

'To be sure you are. You're a family man, Harry... Must have upset you, that kid injured at Victoria Station, the mother and daughter at Clapham...'

'I don't like kids getting hurt.'

'Who does?'

'Casualties of war?'

'At least we're going to have a war – if you can pull it off. But don't ever take the law into your hands, Harry.'

They reached the exit to Marylebone Road. A group of tourists wearing name tags and I LOVE WINNIPEG badges came in.

Quarrick said: 'It will take time. We've got to make a hit that'll keep us in the public eye until then.'

'You'll think of something,' Butler said.

Quarrick, who already had, said: 'I guess so.'

'Meanwhile we've got to beef up your cover. What's your next job with the embassy?'

'Lobbying a meeting of the Anglo-Irish interparliamentary body in London. Tomorrow,' he added.

'Good. You'll pick up some useful intelligence for the Americans.'

Butler put an arm round Quarrick's shoulders. 'Take good care, Harry. I'll be in touch.'

Quarrick lingered for a while, drawn to the Chamber of Horrors. Murderers were on show here, exciting the public's curiosity about what it felt like to kill. Quarrick wondered if one day he would be among them.

In his shared office overlooking Grosvenor Square, Quarrick mentally composed a list of political targets that would goad Britain into retaliation.

One was obvious. In central London, on the banks of the Thames. Security would be formidable but not insuperable. Ideas were his strength.

And then... The idea came to him so abruptly that he felt the surge of adrenalin. The ultimate provocation: one that would not be ignored whatever the pacifists said.

He left the embassy five minutes early and drove to a small shop called the Kite Store in Neal Street, where he bought a new bird kite, an American bald eagle, for Ben and Jaime. Thought about it and bought two.

Chapter Nine

'Good morning, Mrs Quarrick. My name is Collins and I believe your husband was responsible for the deaths of my wife and daughter.'

Indisputably that was not the way to make the approach. She would pick up the phone and dial 999. Yet he had to recruit her as an accomplice, to persuade her to find out if Quarrick was truly the commander of the IRA in London. Because the word of a terrified, half-conscious grass could not be trusted.

Collins was back in combat uniform, seconded from admin to interrogation for two weeks. He turned to the weary young soldier tied to a chair in front of him. 'I didn't hear you. What did you say the name of your regiment was?'

The soldier's name was Mackay and he had volunteered for the SAS from the Scots Guards. He had been told that his mission was to locate heavy artillery in an imaginary war in Oman.

The guardsman, muscular but innocent-looking, gave his name, rank and number.

'You can quit now; no one will think any the worse of you.'

'I think they will.'

'Why do you want to join SAS, Mackay?'

'Because they're the best.'

'Nothing to do with secrecy, the private ego?'

'If I was to try and put a word to it. Two words—'

'Go ahead.'

'I'd say self-respect.'

Good boy, Collins thought. 'I'm going to leave you here for another few hours. Wearing the hood. It really doesn't matter if you change your mind.'

'I'll stay,' Mackay said.

'Your regiment would be very proud of you if you named them.'

'I don't think so. Did you go through this?'

'I ask the questions.' Much worse, Collins remembered; strapped to a board and submersed in water for up to twenty seconds – they didn't intend to kill you but they could make errors of judgement.

He pulled down the blinds and switched on a swivelling strobe light. Every five seconds the beam penetrated the hood covering Mackay's head.

'I'll be back,' he said. 'Are you sure—'

'Quite sure.'

Collins returned to his room, sat down on his bed and stared at his hands. How could he intrude into her life? The first step would be to follow her, he supposed. Like a love-sick swain. Except that she wouldn't be aware of his presence: he had been trained to be invisible.

Four hours later he returned to The Killing House in temporary use as an interrogation centre. Mackay was sitting quite still. Collins raised the blinds and pulled the hood off his head. Mackay squeezed his eyes shut, then opened them like a patient surfacing from anaesthesia.

Collins said: 'It was the Irish Guards, wasn't it?'

Mackay cleared his throat. Gave his name, rank and number. Blinking, he reminded Collins of Toland.

'I want names.'

Mackay's head jerked up. He frowned. 'Names?'

'Smith, wasn't it?'

'I don't know what you're talking about. Is this some kind of trick?'

'Time-share . . .' Today would have been Jane's seventh birthday. Collins bunched his fist and raised it.

Mackay ducked his head to avoid the blow.

Collins heard a voice from long ago, a lecturer in interrogation. 'Brutality is counter-productive.'

He unclenched his fist, lowering his arm.

'You did well,' he said, and untied the rope strapping Mackay to the chair.

'For one minute I—' Mackay hesitated.

'Thought I was going to hit you?' Collins summoned a smile. 'You forget, I'm an officer and a gentleman.'

He strode out of The Killing House. Rain, was falling lightly, releasing summer scents from the earth. Ducking his head into it, he tried to remember what else the instructor had taught him. And what advice he would have given on the interrogation of a woman.

*

Mindy Rivers was an understudy. 'Always the bridesmaid, never the bride,' she was fond of saying. She had a modest but adaptable singing voice and had understudied in *Phantom* and *Miss Saigon*; she was currently second string for a new Tom Stoppard at the Haymarket and *Pygmalion* at Chichester – a potential mind-over-matter feat of which neither producer was aware. On one occasion she had been acclaimed by a critic who had taken his son to a matinee of a Noël Coward revival – matinees were Mindy's prime time – and pronounced her performance better than the star's, a threat which the star had remedied by never again succumbing to an attack of nervous exhaustion. She had once stood in for an American star who had lost her voice on the opening night of a West End musical but, through no fault of hers, the show had folded two nights later. Recently she had auditioned for a role in a television soap, but she did not expect to get it even though she had slept with the director.

She came from Dorset but could switch on almost any dialect within the British Isles. Beneath her curly, finger-combed hair, she looked a bit like Emma Thompson, whom she was convinced she would one day understudy. Helen Quarrick met Mindy twice a week, Tuesdays and Thursdays, in the coffee bar where they had first met in Fulham.

On this morning, in the first week of August, Helen left her Fiesta parked outside the house and walked to Fulham Broadway, skirting Brompton Cemetery and Stamford Bridge football stadium. As she walked, she became aware of her sixth sense slipping into gear. It told her that she was being watched.

Slowing her pace, she used shop windows as mirrors, just as they did in chase movies. Swung round abruptly and found herself facing a huge, bespectacled West Indian. 'Wanna dance?' he said.

She darted down a side street and waited behind a tree. No one followed. She returned to Fulham Broadway at a dignified pace.

She stopped outside a butcher's shop. Steaks for dinner? Fillet? The meat looked cold and pink. A butcher sharpening a knife winked at her. She started walking again, turned suddenly and saw a man in a dark suit shrink into a doorway. She retraced her footsteps. A chemist's. She went in. The man in the dark suit was buying a bottle of Grecian 2000. He looked at her guiltily. No, the sixth sense told her. The man you're looking for has a 'sort of a dent in his chin' . . .

She returned to the sunlight. An airliner chalked a line across the blue sky. She noticed a display of melons. What she wanted more than anything was a slice of honeydew melon, but it was 11.03 and she went into the coffee bar.

No sign of Mindy, who reserved punctuality for the theatre. Helen sat down opposite a painted beach scene and took off her shades and the brown scarf imprisoning her blonde hair. She ordered coffee and a slice of melon. The waiter, staring at the beach mural as though he had left his heart there long ago, said there was no melon. Could he get one? The waiter shook his head. Helen placed a five-pound note on the table. Anything was possible, he said.

Mindy swept in, bringing a swirl of vitality with her. She sat down, cupped her chin in her hands and examined Helen. 'So, how's it going?' Mindy believed that she understood Helen's problems better than Helen; that she was her understudy.

'OK, I guess.'

'So how's Harry?'

'As well as can be expected.'

'Still broody?'

'He's got a lot on his mind.'

'No sex?'

Helen shrugged.

'Then he's got a lot on someone else's mind.'

'I don't think there's another woman.'

'No?' Mindy put a few more curls into her hair with her fingertips. 'Maybe he's just a serial killer.'

The waiter brought a whole melon on a plate with a small kitchen knife. Helen asked him to slice it but he was on the beach contemplating the frozen waves. 'Why the hell do we come here?' she asked.

'Habit,' Mindy said, reaching for the knife. She halved the melon, cut a slice and bit deep into a half-moon of flesh.

Helen cut her half into cubes and speared one with a fork. 'Any word on the soap?'

'The director's still trying to make out who performs best on the casting couch.'

Helen ate another cube of melon.

'Was Harry the first?' Mindy asked. 'You know, not *the* first. The first one you really loved?'

'I guess so. Even though he was arrogant.' She thought about it. 'Maybe not arrogant; maybe he just knew—'

'That you were meant for each other?' Mindy did a Bette Davis voice.

'Something like that. Then he broke his leg.'

Mindy laughed her vulgar laugh. 'Doing what?'

'Skiing.'

'A lonely sport,' Mindy said. 'Beautifully lonely. That's why skiers make such a row at their après-ski parties, because they're ashamed of what they've discovered. Were you lonely as a kid, Helen?'

'Not as a kid. Not as a teenager, either. Later, a little . . .'

She told Mindy about her mother's slow and painful death. About her father's dependence on her – and Silent Cal. How, after college, she had tried to escape from the Switzerland of North America, but each time her father had nearly drowned her in tears of self-pity so that she had stayed. Although she loved the pastoral majesty of Vermont, she had felt she was being left on a grassy shelf remote from reality. Harry had provided not only love and security but a justification for escape. And when she had finally made the break, her father had proved remarkably resilient.

'For the first ten years or so it was perfect. You know, courtship and marriage, no different. Not even when the kids came. And then . . . It was as if someone had woken another Harry Quarrick. The Harry Quarrick I met on the ski slopes isn't living with me any more. I don't know where he's gone.'

'Do you care?'

'I did. Not so much now. The stranger I'm living with . . . Hell, we wouldn't have got together in the first place.'

'So if you slept with him you'd be cheating on the first Harry Quarrick.'

'Chance would be a fine thing.' Helen sank her teeth into the last cube of melon.

'What about Harry Quarrick, father?'

'He's still around,' Helen said, dabbing juice from her lips with a paper napkin. She remembered the kites trying to pull the boys into the sky over Hampstead Heath. Considered telling Mindy about her suspicions; decided against it – treachery. Instead she said, 'Stupid, I guess, but this morning I felt as if I was being followed.'

'Felt?'

'I said it was stupid.' To give the stupidity some credibility, she told Mindy about the man who had approached Jaime and Ben outside the school.

'What did he want?'

'An address.'

'Yours?'

'He got that as well.'

'A long time ago?'

'A few weeks.'

'And you only decided you were being followed this morning? What did he look like, this man who spoke to the boys?'

'Medium height, dark-haired.'

'Any distinguishing marks?'

'A cleft chin,' Helen told her.

'Very interesting,' Mindy said in her beautiful-spy voice.

'What's so interesting about that?'

'I just saw a man with a cleft in his chin as big as Kirk Douglas's. He went into the pub across the road. As a matter of fact, I can still see him. At the window, looking this way.'

Collins had intended to infiltrate Helen Quarrick's life much earlier but, instead of being returned to admin from interrogation, he had been dispatched to the United States to lecture to elite forces there about the Falkland Islands. As if they wanted advice from a limey, their expressions said as they sat yawning in ranks in front of him.

He had now been following her for three days. To Holland Park, where in rain as fine as mist she had paused for five minutes to admire the Caroline Testout roses. To the Prospect of Whitby, still in the rain, on the banks of the Thames at Wapping – low tide, mud glistening in the hesitant light – for lunch with a woman friend. To a cocktail party at the Japanese embassy, not far from the US embassy, with her husband. To Marks and Spencer in Oxford Street to buy clothes for the kids. To Sainsbury's and Chelsea public library and an electrician across the river at Battersea and now this grotty coffee bar in Fulham.

He knew her gestures, her athletic stride, the sudden smile that began in the right-hand corner of her mouth when she remembered some shiny moment in the past. Not many shiny moments these days, her attitudes indicated.

He admired her dress sense, her predilection for yellow which, in his opinion, not many women could wear. Suspected that he would have known she was American even if he had just spotted her swinging down the King's Road. Imagined her naked. Felt that he was beginning to know her better than her husband. Believed that his intuition was valid – that she knew nothing about Harry Quarrick's duplicity. *If* that duplicity existed . . .

I could take him out tomorrow, Collins thought, staring, pint of bitter in one hand, through the window of the pub opposite the coffee bar. Without proof of involvement. On the word of one terrified snitch. And by doing so I would be bringing myself down to the level of those who took my family from me.

So what he needed, to keep his self-respect, the respect that Judy had handed to him when she stepped down from the catwalk, was a *prima facie* case. But he no longer had access to the instruments of surveillance. What he did have was a clear perception of the one person who could nail Quarrick; his wife.

The two women rose and disappeared from view. The door of the coffee bar opened. Collins took a last swig of his beer and put it down.

His quarry began to walk swiftly towards Fulham Broadway. He gave her a couple of minutes, then followed, eyes focused on the brown headscarf.

Five minutes later she took a right towards King's Road. And disappeared.

Collins hesitated. A professional fugitive would have dived into a basement area, slipped behind a half-open door or found an escape alley. Might have hidden behind a parked truck and, if he was cocky enough, emerged and walked towards his shadow, winking as they passed face to face. But Helen Quarrick wasn't a professional. Still, did she suspect she was being followed? She had taken evasive action earlier that morning. Worse, had Quarrick warned her that she might be? Far worse, was she collaborating with her husband?

Hunching his shoulders, Collins plunged down the residential street. A hundred yards ahead of him an ice-cream van pulled up beside the kerb. Two children, a boy and a girl, materialised beside it. And a brown scarf.

Collins opened a gate, mounted three steps and shrank into a doorway. Gave it one minute thirty seconds and peered from behind the peeling portico. She stood at the gate, licking a cornet lanced with a stick of flaky chocolate.

She said: 'Looking for Helen? Sorry, you'll have to make do with me.'

'Who are you?'

'Mindy Rivers, Helen's understudy.' She took the stick of chocolate out of the ice cream and took a bite out of it.

The streets around Streatham Common lay stunned in the heat and the only visible resident was a man sitting in a deck chair on a pocket-handkerchief lawn drinking beer from a bottle and studying a girlie magazine. He was unnaturally tanned. His hair was crisply grey, his face damaged.

Hood called over the hedge. 'Good morning, Mr Toland.'

The man dropped the magazine but held onto the bottle of beer. 'Who wants Toland?'

'I do,' Hood said, crossing the patch of grass and sitting on a wooden bench opposite the deck chair. 'And you're him.'

'And who are you?'

Hood showed him his ID.

'What the hell do you want?'

'You are a police informer, right, Mr Toland?'

'Am I?'

'What sort of an answer is that?' Hood heard his voice rearing and diving in the Welsh valleys as it always did when he became emotional.

'You tell me I'm a police informer: I don't know. I don't know what I am. All I know is that someone did this to me.' He stroked the stitch marks on his face.

'That's all you remember?'

'I remember my childhood.'

'Nothing about the beating?'

'Nothing.'

'But you do know that's how you got hurt?'

'That's what I was told at the hospital.'

'Which hospital?'

'St Charles, North Kensington.'

'Why did you have to be stitched, Toland? Not normal, is it, for a run-of-the-mill beating?'

'My cheeks were torn open. Maybe he wore a ring. A wedding ring? God help his wife. Nose broken—'

'What did he want, Toland?'

'I told you, I don't remember.'

'What did he look like?'

'Ditto.'

'What did he want?'

'Ditto, for fuck's sake.'

'Names?'

'I don't know any names,' Toland said. 'I don't know anything. Can't you understand that?'

A woman with stringy blonde hair, roots in need of restoration, appeared at the front door of the small house. 'Who's this, Jim? Friend of yours?'

'If he's a friend, I don't need enemies.'

'Then you'd better be off,' the woman said to Hood.

'You his sister?'

'What if I am?'

'Great sense of humour, your brother.'

'If he has, he hasn't shared it. Off you go, mister, or I'll call the police.'

'No need,' Hood said, showing her his ID. He turned to Toland. 'Fancy a wet?'

'If you're paying.'

As he led Toland to the Capri, his sister called out: 'Don't excite yourself, Jim. Remember what the doctor said.' And an afterthought: 'Is there a reward?'

Hood turned. 'For what?' But the door had closed.

Pointing the grey nose of the Capri east, Hood stopped it a mile away.

'Which pub are we going to?' Toland demanded.

'Taking a breather on the way,' Hood said.

'Breather? It's bloody stifling in this car.'

'What did you tell him?'

'Who?'

'You know who.'

'Look, I told you—'

'What did he want?'

'I wish I could help you—'

'Oh, but you can, Toland. I can feel it in my water. Now, let's start again. What was he wearing?'

'Clothes.'

'Don't try to be funny with me, Toland. I haven't got a sense of humour.'

'I can't remember. Honest.'

'Accent?'

'I don't know.'

'Not Welsh like me?'

'Not like anything. Christ, knock it off, my head's beginning to ache again.'

'Knock it off, now there's a thought.'

'OK, OK, I remember being a snout, right? But that's all I remember. What I told him, fuck knows. If anything. Maybe sod all, which would explain why I got the shit knocked out of me.'

'You must remember what he was after.' Hood heard his voice climb a mountain.

'Names . . . I remember a voice saying "Names?" I don't know any names.'

'Why did he pick on you, Toland?'

'I wish I knew. Are we going to have that drink? Christ, I'll pay!'

'Because *he* knew *you* knew some info he desperately wanted. What was it, Toland?'

'I'm getting out of this car,' Toland said.

'Don't even try! Don't want your face readjusted again, do you?'

Suddenly Toland began to cry. 'You don't understand, I can't help you.' He knuckled his eyes.

'Are you a member of the IRA, Toland?'

'I'm not a mick, I'm English.'

'Are you?'

'I don't give a shit about Ireland. Ireland, where's Ireland?' A note of hysteria in his voice.

A knock on the window beside Hood. He lowered the window. The young policeman said: 'Anything the matter, sir?'

'Nothing that you need to know about.'

He showed the young policeman his ID.

'Can we be of any assistance, sir?'

'Yes,' Hood said. 'You can piss off.'

'Sorry, sir—'

'Don't be. You're doing a grand job.'

Leaving the window open, Hood switched on the ignition and drove Toland back to his sister.

The City of London, the square mile of the capital devoted to finance and commerce, once contained by Roman and medieval walls, is a quiet and haunted place at night, its reverie disturbed only by trenchermen leaving a banquet (at one of the ninety-six livery companies, perhaps – Fishmongers, Skinners, Goldsmiths, Spectacle Makers), a patrolling squad car, cats doing the rounds of the kitchens, a bag lady or two snoring beneath pink sheets of the *Financial Times*, and the rumble of the last Underground train in its vaults.

Apart from the Barbican complex with its 6,000 inhabitants, so sparse are the denizens of the City at night that it is perfectly possible to explode a bomb without hurting a living soul. And that was how Harry Quarrick hoped it would be in the early hours of an August morning, moon riding high over the Guildhall and the Mansion House and the Stock Exchange and the Old Bailey and St Paul's Cathedral, over chop houses and the churches that brought a touch of piety to the frenzy of finance.

The bomb was contained in a car parked on a diagonal line between the bronze doors of the Bank of England, set in blind, sand-coloured walls, and the equestrian statue of the Duke of Wellington. Behind the statue, moonlight dispatched the ghosts at the back of the eight Corinthian columns of the Royal Exchange.

The bomb was conventional – Semtex made with penta-tetroether nitrate, RDX (cyclonite) and plastic, complete with a pulse receiver, detonated by a remote-control transmitter. The car was not conventional. It was a police car, or so it seemed, a white Ford Granada with a yellow, red-bordered stripe and the City crest – two dragons beneath a dragon's wing, and a shield bearing the Cross of St George and, in its first quarter, the sword of St Paul, the City's patron saint.

At 1.33 am on this Friday night to Saturday morning, four people were observing the car. Harry Quarrick, sharing the portals of the Royal Exchange with the ghosts; two policemen on foot patrol, uniforms bearing the distinctive gold buttons of the City force; and a fourteen-year-old girl named Penny Mountain.

Penny lived in the Barbican, the city within a city built in the 1970s on land laid waste by the Luftwaffe during the Blitz. She hated her opulent confinement. She was bored by talk of interest rates and inflation and infrastructure. She preferred discos to the London Symphony Orchestra and the Royal Shakespeare Company, both residents of the complex. And she was tragically in love with a young man whose only asset was a gold earring, and who played with a rap group in the East End when he wasn't too stoned.

She had decided to make her break at night when her parents were in deep post-banquet sleep. As she let herself out of the apartment, wearing jeans, blouse and denim waistcoat, suitcase in her hand, she heard her father snore.

From the Barbican she made her way to London Wall, the street that follows the northern boundary of the ancient wall. It seemed much more spacious than it did by day, office blocks looming ominously. As she turned into Moorgate, a rat scampered across the street. She stifled a scream.

From behind the portico of the Royal Exchange, Quarrick checked out the bogus police car resprayed at the Feltham workshop, number plate corresponding to a squad car being serviced in the City of London police garage. His thumb caressed the button of the transmitter: he was due to blow it at 0135 hours. When the police foot patrol had passed.

What would she do for money? Penny Mountain wondered. Gary would help her out but she would have to get a job of some sort. Lie about her age. She didn't know much about the East End, only that it was real life – Gary had told her that.

She remembered that she had a riding lesson in the morning in Epping Forest. The name of the horse, a chestnut, was Rufus. She hoped someone would explain to Rufus. Except that no one would know. Unless she called her mother. 'Sorry, I just had to do it.' Her parents had spent a lot on her upbringing; she had to acknowledge that – they had told her so many times.

Suppose Gary was at a gig? She turned into Moorgate and stopped at a call box.

The two policemen on foot patrol paused on the corner of King William Street. One of them, Police Constable Culbert, pointed in the direction of the Iron Duke on his horse and the Bank beyond.

Culbert, a boxer with a dented nose, said: 'Funny, I could have sworn Jock Heald said his car was in for a service.'

His colleague, PC Muirhead, adjusted his helmet over his carroty hair. 'Give the great arsebound a yell then.'

Culbert spoke into his radio set.

Quarrick steadied his thumb on the button of the transmitter. The bomb wasn't a big one but it was powerful enough to blow the doors of the Bank and knock Wellington off his saddle. Should he detonate it prematurely? Risk upsetting the fine timing of escape? He watched the two policemen.

Penny Mountain pressed 10p into the slot in the call box. 'Hello,' she said. 'Gary?'

A long, exaggerated yawn. 'No, it's Andrew Lloyd Webber.' His voice sounded rubbery.

'It's me, Gary – I've done it.'

Another yawn. 'Done what?'

'Left home. You know, like we agreed.'

Silence. Then: 'Shit, do you know what time it is?'

'About one thirty.' She could feel a terrible emptiness expanding inside her. 'Does it matter?'

'Got any dosh with you?'

'Two pounds fifty,' she said. 'No,' she corrected herself, 'two pounds forty. I put ten pence in the phone ...' She stopped: she was babbling.

'Then sod off home. And next time you do a runner, make it lunchtime.'

Click.

Penny, still holding her suitcase, made her way down Moorgate towards the Bank of England. As she passed the Bank's Prince's Street wall, she was assailed by anger – that *they* could have allowed this to happen to her! Sleeping, snoring, while she was humiliated alone in the centre of a deserted City.

Rounding the corner of the Bank, she spotted the empty police car. 'Come on, Mountain, it's peak time!' Make a stir. Driven home in a police car. Just like a scene from *The Bill*. Tears, forgiveness, her mother's arms round her, a few gruff words from her father.

She opened a door and climbed in.

The incident was destined to occupy a place in the lore of the City police at Old Jewry, Wood Street, Snow Hill and Bishopsgate.

The girl appearing from nowhere at the dead of a moonlit night. Climbing into the back of a police car which wasn't a police car. Message coming over the radio: 'Squad car with said registration still undergoing repairs.' Sotto voce: 'Are you pissed?'

Cloud covering the moon. Figure emerging from the shadows of the Royal Exchange's Corinthian columns like a demented ghost, shouting: 'Get her out! For Christ's sake, get her out!'

Bundling her away under the unrelenting gaze of the Iron Duke. Waiting for an explosion.

Nothing. No ghost either.

Arrival of bomb squad.

Enough Semtex to blast the doors of the Bank and dispatch Wellington to his own bronze Waterloo.

But who was the ghost?

Part III

Chapter Ten

Collins spotted the two pickpockets as soon as he entered the Lanes, the collection of antique and curio shops in Brighton on the south coast of England.

One was the div, the partner providing the diversion – usually a collision followed by a profuse apology. The other was the dip, the thief himself. He had learned about their modus operandi from a regional crime sergeant during his anti-terrorist stint.

'If anyone bumps you on one side, use your elbow on the other,' the sergeant had advised him.

'Supposing it's an old lady?'

'They're the worst,' the sergeant said.

As they walked past the bow windows, he said to Mindy Rivers: 'It was good of you to meet me.'

They had met half an hour earlier in the pale green entrance hall of the Royal Pavilion, its columns painted with figures from Chinese mythology. This rendezvous had been chosen because the female lead in *Pygmalion* in Chichester had retired hurt with a fractured temperament.

They strolled into the banqueting hall – Indian Moghul style outside, Chinese inside – originally built at the behest of the Prince of Wales, later George IV. The dinner table was laid beneath an eastern sky, feathered with palms, with Londonderry silver.

'Shouldn't you be rehearsing?'

'Nothing worse than a last-minute scramble,' Mindy said. 'You can easily get your plays mixed up.'

'How's your Cockney?'

'For Eliza Doolittle? Better than Dick van Dyke in *Mary Poppins*.'

'Couldn't be worse,' he said, remembering the movie from his childhood.

They made their way to the kitchen with its hundreds of items of copperware.

'I wonder who does the washing-up,' Mindy said. 'Why did you want to see me?'

They paused beside the Queen's bedroom, where Queen Victoria had slept before she abandoned the Pavilion in 1845, so the brochure said, because it lacked privacy.

'I've been rehearsing,' Collins said. 'How to tell you.' He took her arm. 'If it wasn't private enough for Queen Victoria, it isn't for me.'

They walked through the town, which still mingled vulgarity and sophistication. The sun was hot and Collins took off his blazer. He draped it over one arm, half expecting Mindy, being theatrical and generous with friendship, to slip her hand under the other.

She said: 'It's Helen, isn't it?'

'I'm afraid so.'

'Afraid? Why do Englishmen use ridiculous phrases like that? You're not afraid at all. Do you use words like that before you kill someone?'

'What makes you think I kill people?'

'Your eyes,' she said. 'No, that's stupid. Brown eyes for lovers, grey eyes for heroes. Just pigment.' Her voice was slippery, in search of character or dialect. 'The set of your eyes.'

They turned into the Lanes, teeming with tourists, pink-kneed weekenders, collectors, dealers and crooks. Collins pointed out the two pickpockets to Mindy.

They watched them following an elderly couple, aristocratically shabby and determined not to sweat in the heat. The man's fawn jacket was flapping open and Collins could see his wallet in the inside pocket.

'Aren't you going to do anything?' Mindy demanded.

'They haven't committed a crime.'

'If they do?'

'I'm not here.'

'I think you'd better explain.' He could hear disappointment in her voice.

The retired colonel – Collins had given him a rank – took the wallet from the pocket and, clutching it in one frail hand, led his lady into a shop decorated with horse brasses.

The div, angular and bespectacled, looked at the dip and shrugged. They vanished in the crowd.

Mindy said: 'So, explain.'

'It's a long story.'

'Good. Something to occupy my mind. This is a nervous time for me.'

'Have you played Eliza before?'

'Once in rep. Everyone waits for "not bloody likely". After that it's downhill.'

He took her arm again. 'Let's go down to the sea.'

'So you don't have to do anything about the pickpockets? Suppose they rob a pensioner?'

'They nearly did,' Collins said. 'Why don't *you* do something? Warn the police?'

The impact was on his right side. The jacketless side, three feet or so from Mindy. 'I'm so sorry—'

He jerked back his left arm, crooked to carry the blazer, classic soccer foul. Felt bone break as his elbow made contact.

The blazer fell to the ground. His wallet slipped out of an outside pocket. Turning, he stamped on it.

Blood poured from the dip's nose. He put one hand to it, withdrew it and, seeing the blood dripping from his fingers, collapsed.

As the div took off, Collins stuck out a leg. The div hit the ground, his glasses fell off, and someone's white training shoe crushed them.

The flow of humanity faltered. A child began to cry. In the distance Collins spotted two policemen in shirtsleeves thrusting their way through the crowd.

'Come on, let's get out of here!' He grabbed his blazer and wallet and propelled Mindy away.

They reached the sea front. No pounding feet. They mingled with the promenaders. In her white leggings patterned with blue, white cotton blouse and wooden beads, Mindy was part of the scene.

Small waves licked the shingle below the promenade. Anglers on the end of Palace Pier cast hooks to bored fish. The air smelled of tanning oil, ice cream and candyfloss. The English Channel shimmered with sunlight. He trod on a pink and white puddle of melted peppermint rock.

'What was your wallet doing in the outside pocket of your blazer?' She thrust her hand beneath his arm. 'Bait, right?'

He patted his trouser pocket. 'Credit cards, cash.' He was pleased that he had redeemed himself even though he had acted irresponsibly, endangering the mission.

A police car cruised by. Collins crouched behind a group of skinheads and tightened his shoelace. Assault was a serious crime, even if the victim was a thief. And he had no desire to explain himself in court.

The Jaguar was waiting in a multistorey car park. He drove out of town and headed in the direction of Chichester.

'It's getting late,' he said as they approached Arundel. 'Do you want me to drop you at the theatre? Have a chat tomorrow?'

'Not bloody likely,' she said.

'My wife is dead,' Collins said.

From the garden of the pub he gazed at England. A green field dozing with sheep, a church spire, a wooded hillside collecting the shadows of passing clouds. On a day such as this, England was the most beautiful place in the world.

'I'm sorry.' Mindy frowned at him over the rim of a glass of Chablis.

'Killed by terrorists. My daughter too.'

'You're not—'

'The Clapham bomb.'

'How terrible!' Sharp white teeth sank into her lower lip.

'Do you have strong feelings about terrorists?'

'Only that they should be given the same treatment that they hand out.'

'IRA *and* Loyalists?'

'Terrorists are terrorists. Nothing is worth the life of one child.'

'The IRA would say the British were to blame for the death of that child. That they are an occupying force; that they must go.' He observed Mindy carefully.

'Then they should fight British soldiers.'

'Who aren't allowed to fight back.'

Mindy sipped her wine. 'You're sidetracking now.'

'Do you think they have a point, the Provos?'

'I'm not the person to ask. I've never understood patriotism.'

'You're sidestepping now. What I'm asking you is this: Do they have a case?'

'To themselves, maybe. One person's freedom fighter is another's terrorist. One person's hero is another's butcher. Cowboys, Indians... a point of view, Mr Collins.'

'The ends justify the means?'

'How can they, when innocent people are killed?'

'Thank God you said that, Miss Rivers.' Collins fell silent while a waiter served smoked salmon and brown bread.

'So now you're going to tell me what this is all about?'

With meticulous care, in between bites, Collins outlined his suspicions about Harry Quarrick, trying to be objective.

She ate with great appetite, nodding every now and again as

though waiting for a cue. When he had finished the first round of tentative accusations, she said: 'How in God's name do you know all this, Mr Collins?'

Patiently Collins told her about Toland, the informant, omitting the details of how he had obtained the leads. He stared across verdant pastures, noticed a glint of the Arun River, imagined fish leaping.

Mindy pushed aside her empty plate and took a swallow of Chablis. 'How many Americans are there living in London with two kids?'

'In Chelsea,' he corrected her. 'Not so many. Anyway, he's a suspect, that's all.' Collins ordered coffee and watched a yellow butterfly fluttering from table to table.

'So what do you want me to do?'

'Arrange a meeting,' Collins said. 'She'll listen to you.'

'She's my friend.'

'All the more reason.' He paused. 'Where's he from originally?'

'I don't know.'

'Think.'

She picked up her cup and put it down again. 'I remember something about St Patrick's Day.'

'They celebrated it?'

'No. But she said, "Of course Harry's Irish, way back." Something like that.'

Collins added this intelligence to the dossier in his brain. 'Of course he may be totally innocent.'

'That's very open-minded of you, Mr Collins.'

The yellow butterfly circled the table, then fluttered away again. Looking for a mate? Collins had read somewhere that a butterfly's lifespan was fifteen days: it would have to hurry.

'Their marriage, how is it?'

'None of your business.' She sipped coffee. 'Not so good. He's very distant.' She frowned.

'Sex?'

'Absolutely none of your business.' She glanced at her watch. 'We'd better be going.'

Collins called the waiter. 'Will you ask her?'

'Why can't you ask her yourself? You do have a way with people. Especially pickpockets.'

'The man who approached her children outside their school?' Collins shook his head. 'She'd slam the door and call the police.'

'So? Let the police investigate.'

'He's got diplomatic immunity.'

'But if he's guilty...'

'He'd be quietly shipped back to the States.'

'No retribution, Mr Collins? No rough justice, no revenge?'

Collins handed the waiter his Visa card. When he had gone, he said: 'Do one thing for me. Find out if Harry was at home last night.'

'And if he wasn't?'

Collins told her about the attempt to detonate a car bomb outside the Bank of England twelve hours earlier. He didn't tell that he had learned about it through his IBM.

'OK, I'll do it. But even if he wasn't at home, that's hardly conclusive evidence, is it?'

'But you'll arrange a meeting? Pave the way?'

'I might.' She stood up. 'I'm going to call the theatre.'

Collins signed the Visa slip and slid the card and the rest of his plastic into his empty wallet.

When she returned she was sparkling, a popular actress making her entrance. 'I can do it sooner than I thought,' she said in a Joanna Lumley voice.

'Do what?'

'Your bidding.' She sat down. 'The leading lady has been to see her shrink. He told her what they tell pilots after they've crashed: get back there. She's appearing tonight.'

He looked into her eyes expecting to see tears, but they were clear and bright. 'I'm sorry.' He touched her hand. 'I'll drive you back to London.'

The yellow butterfly alighted on the table, alone.

The coffee was even worse than usual, lukewarm with traces of powdered milk floating on it.

'You're right,' Helen said, 'we've really got to find some other place.'

Mindy didn't reply. Her gloom was out of character, Helen thought. This was not the first time her friend had lost a part, and she usually surfaced like bubbles in champagne. Helen experienced a sense of foreboding.

'A lousy break, yesterday,' she said. 'You know why she changed her mind?' And when Mindy didn't respond: 'Because she knew you were better, is why.'

'Thanks. You know, like the Avis ad, we understudies try harder.' She started to say something else, but stopped.

'Anything else on your mind, Mindy?'

'How's Harry?'

'He's OK. No change, that is.'
'Did you go out last night?'
'Why, should I have done?' The foreboding intensified.
'You look tired.'
'Too much television, I guess. Harry went out.'
'Really? A stag night?'
'A banquet,' Helen said, searching in her purse for the cigarettes she knew weren't there. 'I don't care for banquets. Coupe Jacques, cigar smoke, I'll-be-brief speeches that last till next week ... Why?'
'So he knew you wouldn't be going with him?'
'What is this, Mindy?'
'In the City?'
'The banquet? Yeah, in the City of London.'
'Home late?'
'Late enough. So what?'
Behind them the geriatric coffee-making machine spat and fizzed.
Leaning across the table, Mindy told her.
When she had finished, Helen began to shiver.

Chapter Eleven

Quarrick was summoned to Washington on the Glorious Twelfth of August, the day grouse shooting begins. Why, he had no idea. His anxiety was compounded by the conspiratorial silence of the attaché for Politico-Military affairs, a honey-voiced Southerner with his sights on a job at the White House.

The summons was TOP PRIORITY and URGENT. Had he been blown? Was an accomplice on Capitol Hill spiriting him back to the United States on an official pretext?

'I'm sure it's nothing to worry about, Harry,' the attaché said, curving a smile like a scimitar.

'Short notice, isn't it?' He had been booked on United Airlines flight 6457 leaving Heathrow at 1800 hours that evening.

The attaché shut his eyes as though he were listening to his favourite symphony on the radio. He didn't know why, Quarrick realised.

Helen cooked him a cheese omelette and French fries while he packed. Would he be away for long? A few days, he guessed. The rest of his life?

They sat in the kitchen forking mouthfuls of omelette, together but apart. In the past couple of days they seemed to have grown even more remote from each other. His fault, no question, but just lately she also seemed to have been preoccupied.

Helen drove him to the airport. On the plane he sat next to a big bony man wearing heavy glasses and a grey lightweight suit that looked as though it had been tailored before he started dieting. A spook.

Quarrick said: 'You needn't have worried, I'm not going to jump out.'

'Excuse me?'

'You could have saved the fare.'

'I'm sorry...'

'Just testing,' Quarrick said, still not totally convinced that he hadn't acquired a guardian.

The man leaned away from him, opened a briefcase with a combination, shielding the numbers from the maniac beside him, and began reading a paper published by the British Numismatic Society. Quarrick fell asleep and had bad dreams.

He was picked up at 8 pm at Dulles International Airport in a snarling black Trans-Am driven by a man with big ears who was named Marchetti.

When he asked Marchetti where they were going, he said: 'You'll find out soon enough.'

'Are you always as outgoing as this?'

'Only this morning,' Marchetti said, 'I caught myself picking my own pockets.'

They drove in silence past Reston and the turn-off for Wolf Trap Farm where, in the 1980s, he and Helen had sat in the open air eating a picnic, drinking champagne and listening to jazz or the National Symphony.

'Take the George Washington,' Quarrick said.

'You figure you know where we're going?'

'I don't give a shit where we're going, just take it.' For old times' sake.

Marchetti shrugged, drove north on the Capital Beltway and south again on George Washington Memorial Parkway beside the Potomac. Past the turn-off for CIA headquarters at Langley. Quarrick glanced at Marchetti for a reaction, but the driver stared impassively ahead.

Quarrick said, 'Have you ever been to the zoo?'

Marchetti said: 'I work in one.' As he swung the wheel to overtake a dawdling Buick, Quarrick caught a glimpse of a pistol in a shoulder holster.

Theodore Roosevelt Island to the left; to the right Arlington National Cemetery. He had taken the boys there once and shown them the graves of John and Robert Kennedy but they had been more interested in the identity of those buried at the Tomb of the Unknowns. Pentagon to the right, Jefferson Memorial across the river to the left... They skirted the National Airport, by which time Quarrick knew they were heading for Alexandria.

They stopped outside an apartment hotel near Landmark shopping centre on Reynolds Street in the town, once a tobacco port, where George Washington had occupied a townhouse.

Marchetti said: 'First floor, room eight. You don't have to sign.'

The apartment was functional but comfortable, walls hung with prints of Washington, Robert E Lee and the Stabler-Leadbeater Apothecary Shop; in the corner stood a TV with a flickering image of the late Lucille Ball.

Quarrick showered, changed into slacks, loafers and a blue, open-neck shirt and went looking for a hamburger. Marchetti went with him.

'I like to dine alone,' Quarrick said.

'Me too.'

'Suppose I lost you.'

'You could try,' Marchetti said.

Quarrick sprinted round two blocks. A man who looked like Marchetti but with smaller ears held up one arm and said: 'Easy, pal.'

Marchetti joined them. 'Stupid,' he said.

They went to a hamburger joint and sat facing each other. Quarrick said between sips of Coke: 'So, who do you work for?'

Marchetti munched French fries. 'A deal?' He fingered one ear. 'I tell you and you don't try and make a break for it and we both sleep sweetly tonight?'

'OK, a deal.'

'The Secret Service,' Marchetti said, stuffing more chips into his mouth.

'Whose job is to protect the President—'

'On the button.'

'I'm a threat to the President of the United States?'

'Jerks like you are a threat to humanity,' Marchetti said.

Quarrick didn't sleep sweetly. Throughout the night he was visited by the President and when he went down to the lobby in the morning and Marchetti said: 'OK, we're going to the White House,' he thought he might still be dreaming.

This time Marchetti sat at the wheel of a Lincoln with smoked windows.

Quarrick said: 'You've had your fun. Now you can tell me.'

'Got to deliver you is all.'

As Quarrick disappeared inside the Executive Mansion, accompanied by a young, balding aide who smelled of exotic after-shave, Marchetti waved.

The President was sitting at his desk in the Oval Office flanked by the presidential flag to his left and the Stars and Stripes to his right. He signed a document with a practised flourish, looked up and smiled his boyish smile. 'Good to see you, Mr Quarrick. As you know, this is where the buck stops.' The smile lengthened. 'I though we might take a stroll,' pointing behind him at the Rose Garden. 'But first,' he said, 'I want you to meet the man behind this whole venture.'

'In fact, we've already met,' said the coin collector from the plane, rising from a seat and offering Quarrick his bony hand. 'But we haven't been formally introduced. My name's Draper.'

Despite the heat, the garden was cool as though a breeze had been specially imported. The roses behind miniature hedges were rallying for the second flowering; the lawn was as smooth as the rug in the Oval Office.

'Excuse me, Mr Draper, but who do *you* represent?'

Draper frowned, took off his heavy glasses and examined them as if he had just become aware of their existence.

The President said: 'Mr Draper represents the government.'

'CIA?'

'If you must. Lay it on the line, George.'

Replacing his spectacles and blinking, Draper told Quarrick that the President was rightly proud of his diplomatic triumphs with the Middle East factions. Another wouldn't go amiss...

The President laid one hand on Quarrick's shoulders. 'The Irish question. As you probably know, the IRA is about to announce a cease-fire. Thanks largely to the intervention of the American delegation in Dublin.'

'And you want the final agreement in the peace process to be signed on this lawn?'

The President nodded. 'Possibly the first step towards a united Ireland. Encouraged, of course, by financial and economic aid from us. Carry on, George.'

'In our opinion,' Draper said, 'the conflict has been wrongly handled from the beginning.' He spoke in the swallowed tones of a man weaned since college on duplicity. 'False values have been encouraged – polarisation of different religions, insular patriotism, the whole gamut of bigotry. Worse, the differences have been handled by the wrong people.'

'Crazy clerics,' the President said. 'Blinkered British politicians.' He gazed towards the white pillars of the colonnade outside the Oval Office.

'We've been studying your credentials,' Draper said. 'The Irish connection. Fine record at the State Department and the embassy in London.'

'What do you want me to do, work for the CIA?'

'Responsible to the head of our bureau in the embassy in London. In your section, as a matter of fact.'

'But why,' Quarrick asked, 'if a cease-fire is going to be announced?'

The President picked a rose and smelled it. 'The difficulties ahead don't even bear thinking about. What we want you to do is try and lessen them.'

'We've worked out a timetable,' Draper said.

'Let me guess,' Quarrick said. 'Handshakes on this lawn just before the next presidential election?'

'Now that,' the President said, 'would be perfect timing.'

'And if the cease-fire breaks? If negotiations fail?'

'Then this discussion never took place.'

Smiling, the President began to retrace his footsteps towards the Oval Office.

Quarrick couldn't believe what he was hearing as he and Draper walked along the Mall, the greensward between the Capitol and the Lincoln Memorial. Draper walked with the assertive stride of a man who lacked confidence, the jacket of his grey suit billowing. Tourists got themselves and their cameras out of his way; Quarrick had to hurry to catch his muted words of wisdom.

'The President is an idealist,' Draper said.

'He is?'

'Although with his schedule he doesn't always have time for realities. You and I figure we have problems when we wake up in the morning. Can you imagine what it's like for him?'

The message was reaching Quarrick: the President would not be told about some shitty deal concocted by this lanky spook who could make a conspiracy out of a fine summer day.

'It must be tough,' Quarrick said.

'I'll say.' Draper cut through a group of East Europeans tentatively paying homage to the Capitol instead of the Kremlin. 'And of course he can't be expected to concern himself with the details of the cease-fire.'

'You can?'

'I *am* a realist, Harry.'

Small white clouds lingered high above the Washington Monument.

'So what do you want me to do?'

'There is only one way the cease-fire can hold. It's got to be handled by doves, not hawks.'

'So?'

'Remove the hawks, the hard men on both sides, Provos and Loyalists, and there will be real hope.'
'Remove them?'
Draper sighed and said so softly that Quarrick barely caught the words: 'You know what I mean, Harry, take them out.'
The enormity of the proposition startled Quarrick who answered to Butler, one of the hawks Draper was suggesting he should eliminate.
'It's the only way,' Draper said. 'They are expendable in the greater scheme of things.'
'Casualties of war?'
'Of peace. You're going to ask, what's in it for you?'
'I wasn't.'
'Then you're a fool.'
'OK, what's in it for me?'
'Leapfrogging up the diplomatic ladder? First secretary, counsellor... Ambassador in, say, Switzerland, within five years. The President doesn't forget favours.'
'Supposing he isn't re-elected?'
'You help make sure he is.'
'Jesus!' Quarrick walked quicker, gaining on Draper, past the Smithsonian Institution and its museums. Turning his head, he said: 'And just how in God's name do you think I'm going to kill these people? Take a pistol out of the diplomatic bag? "Sorry about this, Paddy. Bang, you're dead!" '
'Keep your voice down, Harry.' Draper caught up with him.
'Why me?'
'Because you're credible. And you're a marksman. No one to touch you on the range at Queens, was there?'
They walked on, Draper swinging his jacket from the tab at the neck, a curiously adolescent flourish.
'Suppose I say no?'
'But you won't.'
'I won't?'
'You haven't got any love for the British, have you. Killed your father, didn't they?'
Sweat trickled down Quarrick's chest. 'How long have you known?'
'Your foster father in Queens was a fount of information. Getting on in years, not quite as bright as he was. Your real mother, she died shortly after your father, didn't she?'
'None of your fucking business.'
'So in a way the British killed her, too.'

'You haven't answered the question. Suppose I refuse?'

Draper tut-tutted. 'You got your job by false pretences. Because you knew that someone as prejudiced as you would never be allowed to work for the State Department. You could be dismissed, prosecuted or eliminated. How are the kids, Harry?'

'Keep them out of it.'

'As you please. I heard you murmur their names when you were having a bad dream on the plane.' Draper lengthened his stride. 'You'll do it?'

'I don't have any choice, do I?'

'Not really.'

Wrong, Quarrick thought.

Chapter Twelve

They met on the edge of the Royal Forest of Dean, between the Severn and Wye rivers on the border of Wales. Helen recognised Collins at once, leaning against a silver Jaguar on the banks of the Severn. The cleft in his chin, of course. No, more than that – an air of concentrated loneliness. A man who had lost everything, a man driven.

They shook hands and got into the car.

'Where are we going?' Helen asked.

'I thought we'd take a drive in the forest.'

'You sure pick your spots.'

'I don't understand.'

Helen, who had done her homework, said: 'Newnham. Where Henry II set out from for Ireland to give muscle to his puppet Strongbow.'

'The only reason I chose the forest is that it's near Hereford. I'm sorry you had to come so far.'

She wished he would stop apologising. 'SAS headquarters?'

'You know all about me?'

'Only what Mindy told me. And what I read when your family . . . I'm sorry,' she said. Now she was apologising.

They drove south along the A48, striking inland from the Severn at Lydney. He stopped the Jaguar on a narrow, unclassified road.

'Shall we walk?'

'You're not going to kill me, are you?'

'Why should I want to do that?'

'Revenge?'

'I'm not a terrorist,' Collins said. 'I don't kill the innocent.'

Centuries of leaves sank beneath their footsteps. Sunlight quivered, filtered by beech, oak, ash and birch. The air smelled of mushrooms.

A rook flapped from the canopy of leaves, depositing silence. Collins sat beside a pin cushion of moss. Helen wished she hadn't come. She sat down, arranging her skirt primly.

'So what do you want from me?'

'Didn't Mindy Rivers tell you?'

'That my husband is a terrorist?'

'What she should have told you is that he may be. Nothing more. That I need proof. Of his guilt – or his innocence.'

'You want me to spy on my husband?'

He was silent. She noticed a pulse in his wrist just behind the junction of blood vessels.

Finally he said: 'Something like that.'

'You've got a nerve, Mr Collins.'

'I know.'

'Because Harry was in the City of London the night a bomb was meant to explode?'

'More than that, Mrs Quarrick, I'm sure you understand that.'

'That some snitch has mentioned a man with an American accent with two kids who lives in Chelsea?'

A grey squirrel ran along a branch of a beech tree and disappeared in a series of loops.

'You don't know Harry,' she said. 'He's a good father.'

'Then I hope he's innocent.' Collins peeled a strip of green carpet from the mound; dark-brown ants ran from his fingers. 'I really do.' He sawed at the cleft in his chin with the index finger of his right hand.

'If you think there's a case against Harry, why don't you inform . . . the proper authorities?' Pompous!

'I explained that to Mindy Rivers. Your husband could claim diplomatic immunity and return to the United States.'

'You don't have a case, do you, Mr Collins?'

'No,' he said.

'So why are you pursuing it?'

He let the ants escape across the green cushion of moss. 'I've got some dates,' he said. 'I'd like you to check them. Do you keep a diary?'

'Sure.' She took a gold ballpoint from her bag. 'Shoot.'

He consulted a notebook and gave her dates and times of terrorist attacks. Where was Harry on those days, at those times?

'Anything else?' she asked.

'Look, listen. Prove his innocence?'

'You don't really believe that, do you?'

'Where did you tell him you were going today?'

'I didn't – Harry's in America.'
'Can you get hold of a copy of his CV?'
'I know most of it.'
'Names,' he said. 'Exact dates. Addresses.'
'I can tell you the exact time and date when he met his wife.'
'Irish connections?'
'His parents were Irish, but they were killed in a car crash. He was adopted by a couple in Queens. He's American, Mr Collins.'
'There are sixteen million Americans with Irish origins way back. At least one hundred thousand give money to NORAID.' He drummed his fingers on the moss. 'How long will he be in America?'
'I don't know. Couple of days maybe.'
'It gives you opportunities.'
'To do what? Bust his safe? Bug his study? Don't come on too hard, Mr Collins.'
'OK, a deal. If those dates I've given you correspond with his absences, you'll cooperate?'
'I'll think about it.' Harry, a terrorist? Crazy! Harry's windbreaker damp to the touch after the explosion at Victoria station... She closed her eyes.
'Do you have an answering machine in the house?'
She nodded.
'Fax?'
She nodded again.
'Do you remember any messages? Names?'
Twice he had murmured a name in his sleep. Butler. But to repeat it seemed too much of a betrayal.
Collins stood up and reached into his jacket. Was he going to shoot her now?
He took out his wallet and checked it. 'Let's take a drive.'
'You sound like a gangster.'
'We're going to a place called Muffins. Doesn't sound Mafia to me.'

The Jaguar stopped at Coleford, miniature capital of the Forest, and they went to Muffins, where the tables were dressed with flowered cloths and the waitresses wore frilly caps. He ordered tea and pastries.
'I think I should know something about the man who's recruiting me as a spy,' she said.
He told her about the military disciplines of his childhood. About his rebellion. A little about the Falklands and the Gulf War. Nothing about his marriage.

'And you?'
She sketched her old-fashioned childhood, the waking years at college, the waiting years with her father.
'Waiting for what?'
'The inevitable?'
'You can change that, you know.' He took a bite out of a Swiss roll.
'Can you? I'm not so sure. What you want me to do ... I can go for it or throw it back in your face. Whichever I do, it's inevitable.'
'I don't think so,' Collins said. 'God gave us the luxury of choice.'
'You believe in God?'
'I don't disbelieve.'
'A cowardly remark for a soldier.'
'An honest one.'
'Do terrorists believe in God?'
'You'd have to ask one.'
'Harry does. But we don't know whether he's a terrorist, do we?'
'But you're going to find out?'
'Give me one good reason why I should.'
He took out his wallet and gave her two. A photograph of his wife pushing his daughter on a swing.

Helen checked her diary for 23 January the previous year.

Ben has a cold – or bad case of not wanting to sit maths exam. Letter from Jaime Jaramillo – sounds chirpy. Refers to Colombia's borders. If there weren't any borders there wouldn't be any wars. Scarcely my most original thought – I owe it to Hesse. Coffee with Mindy, who sadly has established herself as second-best. Maybe if someone wrote a play called Understudy ... *Harry home very late, around 4 am.*

She fetched *Pears Cyclopaedia*. A bomb exploded in the City on 24 January.

24 February: *Details of appeal from Children of the Andes in post. An eighteen-year-old, Mario, who overcame drug problem in one of Jaime's homes gunned down. Also a twelve-year-old, Pulgarcito (Tom Thumb?), shot stealing to get food. Must intensify my fund raising.*

More details about Ben and Jaime and a row with a neighbour about the roots of a willow tree close to her fence. *Harry in Brussels sitting in on EC talks.*

Back to *Pears*. 'Bomb rips apart country home of secretary of state for Northern Ireland.'

Two more dates. The Victoria Station explosion and the bomb that had killed Collins's wife and daughter. She knew where Harry had claimed to be on the night of the Victoria outrage. She checked her diary for his whereabouts when Judy and Jane Collins had died. Dublin. Supposedly.

No need to check out the bomb that had allegedly failed to explode outside the Bank of England. Harry had been banqueting. In the City.

She flipped back through the diary until she came to the entry about the deaths of the three children in Bogotá.

A remark that Quico had made just before the explosion came back to her. Something about revolutionary groups collaborating. 'Not so long ago they had an IRA guy training them. An American, would you believe?'

She picked up the phone and called the headquarters of the Fundación Ninõs de los Andes in Colombia and asked for Quico. Summoned his poet's face and thinning hair as she waited for him to come on the line.

'Hi,' he said. 'How you doing?'

'Quico, that terrible night in Bogotá . . . Do you remember what you said just before the explosion?'

'All I can remember are the kids' faces. How short their lives had been. One was frowning—'

'About an IRA guy training the guerrillas?'

'An American,' Quico said. 'Sure, I remember.'

'Do you remember anything more about him? What he looked like?'

An echoing silence. Then: 'As a matter of fact I do. I've got a buddy in Los Llanos. Very macho, you know. Fringe member of FARC.'

'He knew the American?'

'Met him once.'

'And?'

'Didn't look a lot like a freedom fighter. No Fidel beard, no pistol in his belt. More like a yuppie. Brown hair, in his thirties, New York accent. He taught them the finer points of detonating Semtex. The small humanities of life, you understand. But that was a long time before the explosion in the Plaza de Bolívar.'

'When, Quico?'

'Maybe 1991.'

The year after she and Harry and the kids had arrived in London.
'Month?'
'Hey, I didn't keep notes.'
'Think, Quico – it matters.'
'May, I guess.'
'Thanks, Quico. I owe you.'
She thumbed the pages of her diary.

5 May: *Harry's first European assignment outside London. Madrid. Very vague about his brief but that's Politico-Military for you*!

Accompanying memories surfaced. A phone call from one of Harry's colleagues at the embassy who thought Harry was on sick leave. She had put this to Harry when he had returned and he had winked and said: 'In my job we sometimes have to experiment with the truth.'

And when she had been rifling the pockets of one of his suits before taking it to the cleaners, she had found a Colombian peso coin in a trouser pocket. She had put that to him too and he had said: 'Those Madrid money changers are something else.'

And she had accepted the explanations and forgotten them because they had seemed unimportant. Until now. *Bottle of Poker still clutched in the hand of a dead boy who had lived all his short life in a sewer*...

She picked up the phone in the living room and punched out the number Collins had made her memorise. 'OK, I'll do it,' she said.

She imagined him sawing away with one finger at the cleft in his chin.

'Good, I'm grateful.'
'Does the name Butler mean anything to you?'
'I don't think so.'
'I've heard Harry mention it.' She couldn't bring herself to add: 'In his sleep.'
'I'll check it out. I'll be in touch.'

She replaced the receiver. Went upstairs, found the old pack of Marlboros and, with shaking hands, lit one and inhaled deeply.

Chapter Thirteen

1 September 1994. A historic day: the cease-fire announced by the IRA had come into effect. Susan Norton's in-tray overflowed with it. Plus the everyday problems of her profession – murder, espionage, MI5's public image...

But this morning a problem outside her tray prevailed – her husband. Had he for the first time in twenty-five years of marriage forgotten that it was their anniversary? Why had he been unable to return from the plant nursery near Spalding? Why all of a sudden was he doing business with Colombia?

She took off her jacket – green today because that was his favourite colour and she had expected him to take her out to lunch. Draping it over a chair, she tackled the in-tray.

THE CEASE-FIRE. A triumph of timing for the IRA. An American presence in Dublin... the fact that the British had made the initiative already forgotten. Her views, please, on the efficacy of the cease-fire in mainland Britain – for the attention of the PM. Her overall view was that any cease-fire would be broken by the violent men on both sides, Catholics and Protestants, who mistook conciliation for weakness, which didn't mean to say it wouldn't prevail. Privately she wondered why sacrificial lambs had been led to the slaughter for twenty-five years if a cease-fire could now be so glibly declared.

CHANGES IN COMMAND STRUCTURE. An overall head of intelligence? Fine in her book. It would give the impression of a comprehensive assault on the enemies of democracy and wouldn't change a damn thing.

MURDER. Whoever had killed the two Provos Brady and Secker was still on the loose. According to an informant, an MP was going to table a question about the inadequacies of the security forces when Parliament reassembled. The Secret Service had always been a splendid target for parliamentary outrage because it attracted headlines. However, there wasn't much point in having a secret service if it wasn't secret. The MP was not really expecting an answer.

She phoned Bernard Davis at the Yard and asked him to call round and bring Hood with him if he was available.

'Any progress on the murders of Brady and Secker?' she asked them when they arrived.

Davis, still in possession of his courtroom aplomb, said: 'Not that I know of. Two dead terrorists – someone did us a favour.'

'That someone murdered them. If we condone murder, we're no better than they are.' A fragment of the Thames sparkled above her green jacket like a brooch.

Davis turned to Hood. 'Any new leads, Taff?'

The familiarity didn't quite ring true, she thought. Sensing enmity between them, she wondered why Davis had recommended the Welshman. Because he didn't give a damn whether the killers were caught? Might welcome more assassinations?

'None, sir.'

'Last time we discussed this, we agreed that the killer might be someone with a score to settle,' Susan Norton said to Davis.

Hood turned to Davis. 'Last time *we* discussed this, sir, we agreed that Jack Collins might have had a motive for killing Secker. But not Brady—'

'That was your theory,' Davis interrupted, Mancunian vowels flinty.

'When Secker was dumped outside Harrods, Collins was in Hereford. And yes, I know it doesn't take long to drive to London from Hereford. But the interrogation of Toland: that wasn't professional.'

'You SAS stick together, do you?'

'I've checked him out since.'

Davis addressed Susan Norton. 'I don't think the British public would thank us for wasting too much time investigating the deaths of two Provos. Their view is simple: if we knew who the terrorists we're, why didn't we take them out?'

'Even if the violence stops, we have a killer on the loose,' she said sternly. He doesn't strike me as someone who would take a blind bit of notice of a cease-fire. In fact, he endangers it. I think you should continue your investigation, chief inspector.'

As they left a light flashed on the intercom. She pressed a button. 'A package for you,' her secretary said. 'Special delivery.'

'Checked by security?'

'Of course, Mrs Norton.'

'Bring it in then.'
The packaging had been torn open by security and the contents were visible. An orchid and a certificate. She read it. The orchid was called Susan Norton, officially registered at the Jardin Botánico in Medellín, Colombia.
A note was attached to the certificate. *You were late for your wedding – don't be late for lunch today, Le Caprice at one.*
Staring through the window at the sparkle of bright water beyond, she found to her surprise that she was crying.

Hood acted on an impulse prompted by his references to Toland's grilling at the meeting with Susan Norton and Davis.
The curator of life and death at St Charles Hospital, North Kensington, soft grey hair fashionably cut, wearing a white housecoat, was impersonally helpful.
She gave him the admission date and time for Toland. Suffering from concussion. Admitted in case, after the lucid period, damage to a blood vessel on the surface of the brain caused compression which would require surgery.
'But it didn't, did it?'
'No, he was discharged forty-eight hours later.'
'Anything else?'
'Only specialist jargon. You wouldn't understand it.'
'You do?'
'Some of it.'
'Who was in charge of Casualty when Toland was admitted?'
'Dr Khan. From Pakistan,' she said, answering the unspoken question.
'Can I see him?'
'He's off duty.'
'Address?'
'I don't think—'
'This is a murder inquiry.'
She gave him an address at Wembley and returned to the statistics in her loving care.
Dr Khan lived in a two-storey, pre-war block of flats. Children played on narrow lawns marked KEEP OFF and small, Sunday-polished cars were parked in a courtyard.
When Hood called at his flat, number three on the ground floor, he was watching a video of an ancient George Formby film and mopping tears of laughter from the corners of his eyes with a Kleenex.
He ushered Hood to an uncomfortable armchair in the neat,

unlived-in room hung with photographs of young and venerable Khans, but left the TV on. He crossed his legs and said: 'It will be over soon,' as though he were talking to a patient. He was plump and contented with a bald scalp which seemed to smile and frown.

Hood, pitching his voice above the ukulele, said: 'This is important, Dr Khan.'

Dr Khan's scalp smiled. 'He is very funny, isn't he, this Formby?'

'A murder inquiry!'

Dr Khan's scalp frowned. 'What are you saying?'

'Murder.'

'Oh, Lord!' Dr Khan turned off the sound, leaving George strumming silently.

Hood showed him a photograph of Toland from the Yard's files on the IRA. A fuzzy picture snatched as Toland jogged in a suburban park but unmistakably him.

'Remember him? He was brought to Casualty in March. He had been badly beaten so he wouldn't have looked quite as jaunty as that.'

'Name?'

'Toland,' Hood said.

'Ah, yes, a curious case.'

'Curious, Dr Khan?'

'He had been assaulted, no doubt about that. But he had also been burned.'

'Cigarette burns?'

'Not at all. He had been left under a sun-ray lamp.'

'On purpose?'

'Oh yes, on purpose, no doubt.'

'Why no doubt?'

'Because he was telling me so.'

'Dr Khan, do you mind if I switch the TV off?'

Sighing, Dr Khan switched it off himself.

'Did he say why he had been left under a tanning lamp?'

Dr Khan smoothed a frown from his scalp with one plump hand. 'Part of the interrogation, I think. Third degree, all that stuff.'

'All what stuff, Dr Khan?' A bubble of anticipation was expanding inside him.

'You have interviewed Mr Toland? You must know, I think.'

'And *you* must know he is suffering from amnesia.'

Dr Khan spoke with dignity. 'I know no such thing.'

'He hasn't lost his memory?'

'I believe that is the meaning of amnesia. Have you lost yours, Mr Hood?'

'So he remembered what his assailant looked like?'
'I didn't ask him,' Dr Khan said, staring wistfully at the TV set.
'Police work, I am thinking.'
'Tall, short; fat, thin...?'
Dr Khan shrugged. 'I only know the manner of the interrogation. To assess his injuries, you see.'
'And?'
'Second-degree burns caused by exposure to ultraviolet rays.'
'Anything else?'
'Bruising and lacerations. Cuts,' he said to a detective who apparently didn't know the meaning of 'amnesia'. 'No brain damage, he was a lucky man.'
'A brutal, unprofessional interrogation, Dr Khan?'
'Oh, yes, apart from the sun lamp. And the preliminaries.'
Hood felt the thud of his heart. 'What preliminaries?'
'The softening-up.'
'Please be more explicit, Dr Khan.'
'Disorientation, that's what it was. He was left hooded for a long time. Subjected to flashing light that reached him inside the material. That sort of thing. And then all of a sudden a savage attack. I am not understanding that, Mr Hood. Mr Hood, are you listening to me?'
Hood's eyes were closed and he was breathing rapidly.
'Mr Hood, are you all right?'
'Fine. Wonderful.' The anticipatory bubble had burst, releasing such a surge of adrenalin that he was momentarily and sublimely stunned.
Initially a classic SAS interrogation method. I should know: Collins used it on me.
Where are you, Collins?
Hood stood up, extending his hand. 'Thank you, doctor, you've been very helpful.'
'I have?' A frown reached Dr Khan's scalp.
Hood let himself out of the apartment. As the door closed, he heard a ukulele playing.

Five miles away, Harry Quarrick prepared for war. With renewed resolution since the cease-fire: he had not sold his soul for a sellout to the British. But the cease-fire did have one bonus – as Butler envisaged it there would be no more soft hits, no more children on stretchers. Only targets so prestigious that the British would be forced to retaliate. An honourable war instead of terrorism. His strength was ideas.

Quarrick parked a rented Lada four-wheel drive and walked along Edgware Road from Marble Arch. Past newsagents displaying newspapers in Arabic, food shops selling sweet cakes made with nuts, pitta bread and sesame-seed paste. Old men with desert faces sipped murky coffee on the pavement; shop windows offered cheap flights and expensive flats.

Ahead, the traffic roared on the motorway overpass. He turned into a side street and pressed a button beside a door made with reinforced glass. The door was opened by remote control: he was expected.

The owner of the premises was a Jew named Harzani living on the border of the Edgware Road *souk* like an Israeli on the frontier with Syria. He was middle-aged with cropped hair and a pugilist's nose and he possessed only one arm. Beside him on a metal, army-issue desk lay a black felt hat – under it, Quarrick suspected, a gun.

'*Shalom*, Mr Ziman,' he said. 'Take a seat. What can I do for you?'

'You know what you can do for me.'

'Just testing.'

'A helicopter,' Quarrick said.

'Of course. May I ask why you need it?'

'No,' Quarrick said.

'I didn't think so.'

'Just testing?'

'You have the money?'

Quarrick tossed an envelope on the desk. It contained £5,000 in £10 and £20 notes. Harzani moved the black hat closer to him.

'All genuine?'

'I'm not a crook, Mr Harzani.'

'Then what are you?'

'A merchant.'

'Of death?'

'A trader, Mr Harzani. Don't we all trade in some commodity? The scientists in ideas, the preacher in souls . . .'

'You've got a bargain, five thousand pounds.'

'Second-hand.'

'Five thousand pounds for a helicopter? A bargain, I think.'

'Where is it?'

Harzani replaced the money in the envelope and slid it into the inside pocket of the jacket of his blue mohair suit. 'At the back of the building.' He flicked aside the hat with his one hand and picked up the .38 automatic beneath it. 'You first, Mr Ziman.'

Quarrick turned the key in the metal door – everything seemed to be metal inside the premises of Harzani Enterprises. The miniature helicopter stood on a table – metal – in the middle of a room cluttered with surveillance equipment.

Made by Kyosho. Graupner engine. Range 2,700 metres. Max speed 100 kilometres an hour. Weight with the 35-mm Nikon camera 4.5 kilos. Fuel: standard aviation. Colour: pristine white. Length: 1.40 metres.

'How do I know it works?' Quarrick asked.

'You don't – but you know where I am.' Harzani gestured with the .38. 'Five cans of aviation fuel thrown in.'

Quarrick glanced at the cans, each bearing a skull and crossbones to indicate they didn't contain milkshakes.

He took another envelope from his pocket and handed it to Harzani. Inside were fifty more £20 notes.

Harzani counted them. 'What's this for?'

'For forgetting this deal ever took place. Should you forget to forget . . . I think you understand.'

'The deal never took place,' Harzani said. 'When can you pick it up?'

'Ten minutes.'

When he returned he packed the surveillance helicopter into a Westinghouse container that had contained a jumbo-sized refrigerator and, with Harzani's help, loaded it into the back of the Lada parked on a yellow line, warning lights blinking.

From Edgware Road he drove south to Hounslow and manhandled the container into the dingy apartment. From there he made a call to Draper in Langley, Virginia.

A woman's voice: 'Who's calling?'

'A caller from J street' – the nonexistent street missing between I and K in Washington, their prearranged code. A pause while Draper activated the scramble. A beep. Quarrick said: 'I want a three-day clearance from tomorrow for a meeting in King's Lynn, Norfolk. That's it.'

He hung up, let himself out of the apartment and drove home to Chelsea. There was a note on the kitchen table. *Gone shopping. Clothes for kids. School starts tomorrow in case you'd forgotten.*

He had.

When he got to the embassy the following morning, Fraser, from Politico-Military, who, on Quarrick's return from the United States, had identified himself as CIA, told him that he had to report to King's Lynn in Norfolk that evening to liaise with British antiterrorist agencies about the protection of Jewish establishments. When their shared secretary had turned her back, Fraser, an unlikely spook with a basketball player's frame and black, satiny skin, winked.

Quarrick called home. The answering machine replied.

He drove to Chelsea, packed a bag and left a note on the kitchen table, increasingly the only common ground for communication. *Called to three-day meeting, King's Lynn.* Spice your lies with the truth, he had once been advised. *Only 60 more days till the end of term. Report to the Heath on Saturday for kite training.*

Then he drove north to Cambridge in the Lada and across the Fens to King's Lynn a few miles from the Queen's country home at Sandringham. There he booked into a hotel on the Tuesday Market Place under the name of Ziman and telephoned Aerial Surveys Service with the unfortunate acronym of ASS and told them he had arrived.

That evening he wandered round the town, admiring its fine old churches and guildhalls, dined at the hotel and went to bed early to make sure that he was receptive for his first lesson in remote-controlled destruction.

Although, of course, his instructor wasn't aware what he was teaching him. He was a sturdy, bearded Scot who wore a Campbell tartan kilt.

Each morning they took a tiny helicopter called the *Spirit of St Louis*, identical to Quarrick's, except that it was sky blue, into the flat countryside beside the Great Ouse River and, with a Futaba remote control, practised its eight possible movements.

Following it in the Scot's Range Rover, watching it climb and bank and hover as they followed on the road to Downham Market, Quarrick imagined it flying over the Thames at Westminster.

On the last evening Quarrick took photographs, also by remote control, of landmarks chosen by the Scot. As he guided the *Spirit of St Louis* to its pad beside the river, he said: 'We could photograph Sandringham if we wanted to.'

'Aye,' said the instructor. The idea took root. 'A royal commission. Buckingham Palace, Balmoral...' He pulled at his beard. 'Anything's possible.'

Especially, Quarrick thought, with plastic explosive in the cockpit instead of a 35-mm Nikon camera.

Helen Quarrick telephoned a locksmith the day after Harry left for Norfolk. He was small and Pickwickian with a child's hands and sly eyes.

She told him she wanted the door to Harry's study and the drawers to his desk opened. 'He's at a conference in Scotland and he's left some important papers behind – I'm sending them by courier.'

'And after I've opened them – after you've found these papers – you want them locked again?' He had a working relationship with human frailty, his expression said, and when he didn't find it he invented it.

'No,' she said, 'just make me duplicate keys.'

'Before hubby gets back?'

'By tomorrow.'

'Confidential jobs come a bit more expensive.'

'How much?'

'Two hundred and fifty pounds,' he told her.

'All right.'

She sat on the sofa and watched him tackle the door: it opened with the fourth pick he tried. Together they went into the study. 'Child's play,' he said, pointing at three of the drawers. 'But he certainly didn't want that baby opened in a hurry.' He touched the upper left-hand drawer with one small finger: it was the drawer she had opened – and closed when she heard Harry's car outside.

It took him twenty minutes to open it with his cracksman's set of tools.

'Please wait outside,' she said.

'As you wish.'

She approached the drawer warily. Touched the papers and oddments fastidiously as though they were parchment that could turn to dust.

The corner of the colour photograph protruded from beneath a legal document. She pulled it out with her thumb and forefinger because, surely, there could be nothing incriminating about a photograph.

A man and a woman smiling at the photographer. A swaggering man wearing a brocade waistcoat; a gentle woman, her eyes remote from her stage smile.

Across the photograph in Harry's writing: *Victims of War.* And Helen knew that they were his true parents.

The locksmith knocked on the door. 'Everything all right, lady? You're very quiet . . .' He opened the door and peered in. 'You look as if you're somewhere else.'

She smiled at him brightly. 'I was.' On a mountain in Vermont where, instead of sugar, the snow tasted of ashes.

Chapter Fourteen

Rain washing away the long, hot summer, thunder and lightning making a spectacle of its death.

Collins placed a single red rose on the gravel in front of the gravestone fashioned from Portland stone. He was alone in the cemetery between Wimbledon Common and the roar of the A3. He had taken off his hat and rain streamed down his face. He was not sure whether it was taking tears with it. One year ago to the minute, his wife and daughter had died.

Lightning fizzed above the sheltering suburbs of London as the day got underway, and thunder cracked. Yet he stayed until the rain had eased. When he bent down and adjusted the position of the rose, jewels of water quivered in its petals. Sunlight broke through the clouds. A last flurry of rain on his cheeks.

He felt cleansed. Released not from the past but from the vengeance that was to follow outside the brief of the peacemakers.

They met once again in the Forest of Dean, this time at St Briavels, near the remains of fortifications built long ago to repeal the Welsh.

A day like today would have been enough to repel them, Helen thought. It was still September but the wind on the hillsides was singing about winter and cold crouched in the valleys.

'Are you a killer too?' she asked.

'Too? You're acknowledging your husband is one?'

'Are you?'

'I'm a victim,' he said.

They took a footpath through woodland, acorns like bullets beneath their feet.

'This cease-fire ... That won't change anything for you, will it?'

'Nothing can change what happened to me.'

No, she thought, not what happened. But the aftermath, yes. You can't change death: life can be adjusted.

She stopped to button the collar of her long, heather-coloured coat to keep out the premature cold. 'Killing one man won't achieve anything.'

'Your husband?'

'That's what you're going to do, isn't it – kill Harry?'

He walked ahead of her, rotting sticks snapping beneath his polished black shoes.

She shouted after him: 'You can't expect me to be an accomplice.'

He turned. 'All I ask from you is proof.'

She caught up with him. 'What more proof do you want?'

'Absolute proof.'

She leaned against a silver birch; small leaves spun in the air like fragile coins. 'I can't do it.'

'Have you any idea how many innocent people he may have killed?'

'You must know I can't do it.'

'Then why are we here?'

'Because I have a better idea.' Observed by a grey squirrel high in an oak tree, she told him about it.

The threat to a cease-fire came from the hard men. Men who wanted war, not peace. Instead of killing one man, wouldn't it be more positive to confound the warmongers? To penetrate their chain of command? Wasn't that a much more practical and humane solution?

'Humane?' He tasted the word.

'If you agree, I'll help.'

'Very well.'

She breathed deeply. Took a step forward and tripped over a root. He caught her and for a moment they stared into each other's eyes, searching for truth.

Casually, she told him that she was staying at a hotel in Cirencester where Mindy Rivers was auditioning. Would he like to have lunch with her there? Her treat.

'My treat,' he said.

She led the way in her Fiesta through the Vale of Gloucester to the old country town. It was 25 September, the first day of the Cotswold Country Fair. They had lunch in her hotel, the King's Head, then went to the fair.

The wind had taken the clouds with it and gentle sunshine lit the five-mile-long avenue of chestnut trees in Cirencester Park. This was the England Helen loved – the falcons, the lurchers, the young farmers heaving in the tug of war – because some of it had been carried across the ocean and planted in Vermont. Its cosiness and its contradictions. The rural crafts marquee was crammed with saddle bags, honey, mustards, conserves and beeswax, pressed flowers, home-made fudge, apple juice and elderflower cordial. Finding her hand resting on Collins's arm, she withdrew it. They discovered they had won a bottle of champagne in a draw at the Windrush Wine stand.

When they got back to the hotel, a sixteenth-century coaching inn in the market place, there was a note for Helen at reception. She read it out. *'Whisked back to London for another audition. Maybe I'm understudying the understudy. If you can't be good, be careful. Mindy.'*

'So, let's drink the champagne,' she said. 'In my room – I was sharing it with Mindy.' Without waiting for an answer, she told the receptionist to tell room service to put it in an ice bucket.

In the airy room she took off her coat and tossed it on one of the single beds.

'We aren't subtle, are we?' she said.

'I didn't plan it this way.' He took off his jacket and hung it on a chair.

'Maybe I did. Mindy helped, I guess. But it wasn't scripted, I promise.'

Despite the ice the champagne wasn't cold but they drank it just the same. Then she went into the bathroom, took off her clothes and showered, taking care not to get her hair wet. Harlot, adulteress, proprietor of lusts that demanded to be slaked, she applied body lotion and perfume, rubbed steam from a mirror and gazed at the blurred details of her body. Firm breasts, nipples already beginning to stiffen; pubic hair darker than the hair on her head, coyly shaved for outings with her bikini. Belly flat, strong thighs . . . Not a voluptuous body but pretty damned sexy, she decided, and tried to see herself as a man would, then, realising that she was indulging in private foreplay, she wrapped a towel round herself, shoulder to thigh, and returned to the bedroom to commit her first act of infidelity.

Collins was sitting in a chair in his shirtsleeves. She stood in front of him and let the towel drop to the floor. He stood up, ran his fingers down her back and buttocks, kissed her and went into the bathroom. She lay on the bed, one hand between her legs, and waited.

When he came back he was naked, penis erect, droplets of water trickling down his body. His body was lean and spare, scars on the flat, mobile muscle on one side of his chest, a path of soft hair leading from his navel to his crotch.

'A lot of people pontificate about sex and love,' she said. 'You shouldn't have one without the other, all that stuff. They never talk about sex and hate.'

'Heady combination.' He moved towards the bed.

She reached for him. 'Screwing the wife of the man you hate. Next to killing him, what better revenge?'

They went out for drinks that evening in a pub, the Wild Duck, in the village of Ewen, and later for dinner in a sturdily ornate hotel set in parkland. By the time they had finished, it was too late for Collins to drive back to Hereford, so he stayed in the King's Head in Cirencester and they made love once more, and again in the morning.

They said goodbye in the lobby and Helen watched him stride to the exit. As he reached the door, he was accosted by a man with bowed legs and cropped hair. She noticed surprise on Collins's face. The two men shook hands and walked out together into the chiming morning.

The day that Helen drove west, the day the boys were staying with friends in Hythe, Quarrick took a trip on a pleasure boat, pleasure never further from his mind.

He boarded it beside the Tower of London, the White Tower catching snatches of fleeting sunshine. What he had to do was make a rough survey of the approaches to the target, and the view from the river was unequalled. The range of the little white helicopter was 2,700 metres so he had plenty of space for manoeuvre.

Shielding his Sony cassette recorder from the breeze, Quarrick dictated notes into it over the chatter of tourists and the bad jokes of the guide. An Australian woman next to him said: 'You're not from Oz, are you? American?'

He nodded.

'I can always tell.'

'How?'

'Your shoes,' she said mysteriously.

He looked at his shoes. Black and businesslike, a little dusty. He moved further away from her.

The dome of St Paul's drifted past to the right – starboard, Quarrick corrected himself – and they sailed under Blackfriars Bridge into King's Reach. In a whisper Quarrick told his recorder about the floating police station at Waterloo Bridge.

'Are you in love with that thing?' The Australian was back.

'It isn't like a woman: it only answers back when you press a button.'

'You a tourist too?'

He didn't reply, hoping she would go away.

'Cleopatra's Needle,' the guide said, 'brought here by sea from Egypt. One of a pair – fond of a nice pair myself – which stood in Heliopolis three thousand five hundred years ago. Its twin is in Central Park, New York.'

The boat was approaching Westminster Pier, where the excursion ended. 'Beyond Westminster Bridge,' the guide was saying, 'stands the Palace of Westminster, the House of Commons and the House of Lords, the Mother of Parliaments...' He paused, contemplating another joke, but deciding against it. 'When it was rebuilt in the nineteenth century after a fire, the Duke of Wellington said it should be kept on the banks of the river so that it could never be surrounded by a mob. And that includes you lot!'

But his audience were already collecting their belongings and preparing to leave.

Never be surrounded by a mob.

No fool, the Iron Duke. What he was saying was that the best way to attack a target on the banks of a river was from the river itself. Not from a street! Especially not on the day of the State Opening of Parliament, when traffic would be diverted.

A frisson of anticipation. The little helicopter could be controlled from a boat just as easily as a car.

Chapter Fifteen

The inn, four miles off the M4 in Berkshire, was gripped by the spirit of boisterous camaraderie and family tradition that is peculiar to country pubs at Sunday lunchtime. Young men in check shirts and sweaters still glowing from yesterday's sporting endeavours giving their girls a proprietorial squeeze after the second pint; girls in shirts and jeans, pearls swinging, snuggling amorously or shrinking according to the state of the courtship; older men buying rounds of drinks that would be buried in their weekday expense accounts.

Hood and Collins shouldered their way through the throng beneath the beamed and tobacco-fumed ceiling to the bar, where Collins ordered two pints of bitter from one of the harassed young barmen brought in from the fields to cope with the Sabbath incursion. Holding their glasses aloft, they made their way to the garden. Children were playing at war on the lawn – Brits versus Paddies? Hood swigged beer and appraised Collins. Outwardly he seemed not much changed, but inwardly... there was a seam in there now as dark as coal.

Collins, dressed for the country in tweed jacket and grey slacks, looked a little jaded – not surprisingly, from what Hood had learned at the hotel in Cirencester. 'Here's to old times,' he said, and drank deeply.

'Good times, up to a point.'

'I know what you mean,' Collins said.

'Admin, is it, these days?'

'They don't trust me with anything else.'

'Important, admin. At the heart of the matter. Knowing everything that's going on – Bosnia, Kuwait, Dublin, Belfast, London.'

'Not quite everything,' Collins said. 'You know how it is.'

'Did,' said Hood. He flicked a drop of beer from the jacket of his blue striped suit.

Horses clip-clopped past the pub. Butterflies danced in a bed of Michaelmas daisies. A boy missing a front tooth pointed a toy pistol at Hood, squeezed the trigger and, lisping through the gap, said: 'Your turn to die, mister.'

Hood said: 'Behind you.'

The boy turned, too late to avoid a burst from a plastic Armalite but, sensibly, refused to die.

'Pity they weren't playing games in southern Armagh,' Collins said.

'I never thanked you properly,' Hood said. 'If you had reported me I would have been finished. Emotionally unstable – no place in the Met for people like that.'

'Poor Bomber,' Collins said.

'Yes,' Hood said, 'poor Bomber.' He raised his glass. 'Here's to Bomber. And all the other poor sods.' He put the glass down on the rickety table. 'We could have taken them out then, you and me. SAS could now.'

'Getting close to the real reason for our meeting, are we, Taff? Nothing accidental about that chance encounter in the hotel this morning, was there? Car broken down, can you cadge a lift back to London, all that crap.'

'Getting close, yes.' Hood picked up the two empty glasses. 'I'll get a couple more in. Don't drive away and leave me.'

'How can I?' Collins said. 'You've got my car keys in your pocket.'

On his way back from the bar Hood accidentally jogged a pint held by a young man wearing a moleskin waistcoat.

'Clumsy peasant,' the young man said.

Hood stopped. 'Peasant, is it?'

'Just a jest,' the young man said, smiling.

'You want to watch those jests, boyo – I can be a very unpleasant peasant.'

Collins was still sitting at the table staring at some distant horizon. The boy who had been shot was kneeling beside the Michaelmas daisies nursing his wounds and groaning horribly.

'So, what's this all about, Taff?'

'I thought you might be able to help me.'

'If I can.'

Hood told him about the murders of the two Provos. 'Could be someone with a private score to settle.'

'And I've got one? Good thinking, Taff, but you've got the wrong man.'

'I didn't even suss you at first. You see, I went to see a snitch called Toland.' He watched Collins carefully. 'He had been interrogated and given a good thumping. Not your style. Not SAS style. So I struck you off my list.'

'A long list?'

'Not any more,' Hood said.

'What changed your mind?'

'Toland—'

'Never heard of him.'

'—claimed he had lost his memory. As Mandy Rice-Davies once said: "Well, he would, wouldn't he?" I sort of believed him – until I went back to the hospital to see if he had said anything before he conveniently forgot everything. And they said he described how he had been questioned with a hood over his head, lights flashing through it. I remember an interrogator questioning me like that. You, as a matter of fact.'

'Disorientation, a common enough technique.'

'Then something seems to have snapped inside the interrogator's mind.' Did Collins's fist on his glass tighten? Hood wasn't sure. 'He beat the shit out of him. Like a scene from The Killing House. And I wondered just what it was that had suddenly turned a civilised interrogator into an animal.'

'Animal?' Collins's knuckles shone whiter, no mistake. 'You do the animal kingdom a great disservice.'

'Could it have been a chance remark linking Toland with a personal tragedy?'

'I don't have to be Brain of Britain to see what you're getting at,' Collins said. 'But I don't know any Toland. You're telling me he was IRA, right?'

'And a grass. He was lucky the IRA didn't get to him first – they would have had his balls as well as his brains.'

'Sorry I can't help you,' Collins said. 'I really am.' He sawed at the cleft in his unshaven chin with one finger.

'So am I. You see, I don't give a shit about the identity of the man who topped the two Provos. It's bigger fish I'm after. The head of the IRA here on the mainland, irrespective of the cease-fire. How does that grab you?'

'I wish you luck,' Collins said. 'I really do.'

'Just over a year, isn't it, since your missus and your daughter were killed?'

'One year, two weeks, six days, six hours.'

'I don't have to say how I feel.'

'No,' Collins said, 'you don't.'

On the far side of the lawn the 'wounded' boy had slipped one arm inside his shirt and was stalking his assassin. Their young mothers, one drinking a spritzer, the other a shandy, watched hostilities from another table.

'A terrible time for you,' Hood said. 'Brooding, planning.'

'Just grieving,' Collins said.

'Combined forces is what I thought. The two of us, nail the bastard responsible.'

'Your job, Taff. Anti-Terrorist Squad. I'm just admin.'

'Anti-Terrorist and admin, a lethal partnership. Both SAS, Jesus! What did he tell you?'

'Toland? I told you – never heard of him.'

'Identified the commander of the troops in the field, as they like to call themselves, did he?'

'You learned well, Taff. And I say, "No he didn't", and you say "Gotcha", just like that headline in the *Sun*.'

'Well, did he?'

'Come off it, Taff.'

'I think he told you something.'

'Told someone something, maybe. Not me.'

'You won't collaborate, unofficially?'

'I'm still an officer in SAS.'

'You sound pompous. Uncharacteristic.'

'If *you* were still in SAS you'd be on a court martial.'

'For speaking my mind? In SAS I'd get a gong! OK, let's get going.' He stood up. 'Before you're over the alcohol limit. I'm a police officer, don't forget – I wouldn't want to breathalyse you. Although with all that bullshit you've been giving me I wouldn't think you've got much breath left.'

Beside the Michaelmas daisies the 'wounded' soldier swivelled, firing from the hip with his good hand. The enemy fell and lay still, wanting his lunch. One of the mothers applauded languidly.

Hood said: 'Tell me one thing.'

'Go ahead, sergeant.'

'Inspector,' Hood said.

'Go ahead, inspector.'

'Why did you screw the wife of an American diplomat last night?'

A lingering pause.

Finally Collins stood, as upright as ever, and said: 'Sad – the end of professional respect.' He walked towards the car park.

Hood caught him up and handed him the car keys. 'You don't leave me with any alternative.'

Collins took the keys. 'Alternative?'

'I'll have to go back to Toland.'

The young man in the moleskin waistcoat was loitering in the car park with two other beefy young men who looked as though they were waiting impatiently for the first rugby scrum of the season.

Moleskin said: 'Ah, the unpleasant peasant.'

'Go on to the car,' Hood said to Collins, and to the trio of muscle: 'Sorry about that.'

'So you should be, you little Welsh prick. Trying to take the piss in front of my fiancée.'

Hood glimpsed a girl in a Cherokee staring out of the window, the tip of her tongue flicking between her lips.

'I said I'm sorry.'

'So you should be. Now go and apologise to my fiancée.'

'Of course. The age of chivalry isn't dead.'

He walked over to the Cherokee and indicated to the girl to lower the window on the passenger side. It slid down and she smiled wet-lipped at him.

'Know what I think?'

'What do you think?'

'I think you and I should take a walk in the woods because your fiancé has got a bad case of brewer's droop.'

Dropping, he swung with his left elbow at moleskin's crotch and was rewarded by a cry of outrage and pain. Hurling himself backwards, he hooked one foot round another young man's ankle, bringing him thudding to the ground. Then he sprang up and butted the third in the belly.

As the second young man struggled to his feet, Hood kicked him in the shin. 'Sorry,' he said. 'Used to play rugby for the Army. Always played dirty.'

'You bastard!' Moleskin said, kneeling.

'Shouldn't have said that. Bit sensitive about my parents, see.' He kicked him in the face, blew a kiss at the girl, and walked to the Jaguar.

In Chelsea another new man entered Helen Quarrick's life. She recorded his appointments, eavesdropped on his phone calls, scavenged in his wastepaper basket, noted his moods. Harry Quarrick, stranger.

She realised she had never known the man she had married. But most wives, she supposed, were married to two men – husband and lover inside the home, breadwinner outside. What do wives really know about the life that goes on beyond the mock-Georgian door, the privet hedge? Come to that, what do redundant husbands know about their working wives as they conspire over a business breakfast at the Ritz or lunch in the factory canteen? These days being kept late at work wasn't exclusively a male preserve.

What astonished Helen since she had been promoted from snoop to spy was the distinguishing marks of her husband she hadn't previously observed – mannerisms, habits, giveaways. One crossed leg swinging, finger and thumb tugging at the lobe of his right ear, his telephone voice and his false smile – the genuine one reserved for the boys – his evasions and falsehoods which she could now pluck from bland dialogue with mental forceps. Plausible, that was what Harry had been, and she had never seen it. But he had been genuine once. Hadn't he?

With the duplicate keys made by the locksmith, she entered the extension of his secret life, his study. Read scrunched-up fax messages. Rifled the drawers, taking care to leave papers as she found them. Copied addresses and phone numbers from a black address book embossed with gold leaf. Noted the number 832410 on the first page. PIN number? Too many digits. Phone? Too few.

She noted his times of departure and arrival. Monitored his flight times, to Paris, Brussels and Berlin mostly, first with the travel agency in the King's Road, then with another in Fulham so that there would be no risk of Harry's travel agent mentioning their conversations to him.

She checked the answering machine, even listened to his dreams, but discovered nothing. Hating what she was doing, she asked Collins why official eavesdroppers could not be employed. Operatives like her husband were trained to detect surveillance, he told her. One hint of suspicion and he would be on the first Concorde to the United States and that would be the end of the matter.

They were walking on Wimbledon Common. When she had phoned his flat off the Fulham Road and asked to speak to Mr Melrose, a voice, his, had said: 'There's no Mr Melrose here.' This was the prearranged signal that *he* might be under surveillance. So, as planned, she had driven, making sure she wasn't being followed, to Wimbledon, and met him beside the restored windmill in the centre of the common.

She handed over all the information she had gathered, written in a red student's notebook, glad to be rid of it.

'Not much, I'm afraid,' she said.

'Never mind. It's all part of the final Identikit. What we really need, as we're doing it your way, is some hint of the next hit.

Because there will be one – the hard men won't recognise the cease-fire.'

It was midafternoon, exhausted grass dank beneath their feet, trees hibernating. There weren't many people around: a year or so ago a young mother had been murdered somewhere near here.

She told him about the number 832410, and he made a note of it. 'Sounds like a combination,' he said. 'Wall safe? Floor safe?'

'We haven't got either. At least not as far as I know.'

'There's only one safe worth having and that's up here.' Collins tapped the side of his head. 'But that number... If you ever have cause to use it, try reversing the last two digits. Or the first two. That's what husbands having a bit on the side do with phone numbers.'

'Is that what you did last weekend, had a bit on the side?'

He glared at her. She wanted to reach out and stroke his cheek.

'Why the secrecy?' she asked.

'The Yard's Anti-Terrorist Squad have been asking questions.'

'Shortish, bow-legged?'

'You're very observant.' He turned and headed back towards the windmill. 'We don't want them interfering.'

Because you want Harry all for yourself?

'How shall I contact you then?'

'Same arrangement. "There's no Mr Melrose here." '

They reached the windmill. She wondered if he would kiss her; he didn't. She remembered young men in the past who pretended to forget the passion of the night before, as though they were ashamed of it.

Two mornings later, as October arrived on flurries of dead leaves, Harry received a phone call so urgent and furtive that he had to return the call elsewhere.

'They've sent the wrong newspapers,' he told her. Once she would have believed him. 'I'll change them – back in twenty minutes.'

'Can't you change them on the way to the embassy?'

'I'm supposed to know what's in them when I get there – you know that.'

Preoccupied and frowning, he left his briefcase beside the magazine rack. She considered it. The children were still in bed. Why not?

She turned the tumblers on the combination to 832410. The briefcase stayed as tightly shut as the jaws of a turtle.

Reverse the first or last two digits, she remembered Collins telling her. She transposed the 1 and the 0. The briefcase remained inviolate. She glanced at her watch. He had been gone five minutes.

Change the initial 83 to 38? Nothing. She tried 38 with 01. Zilch.

A bell jangled in the kitchen and she jumped. The boys were heading for the bathroom and they wouldn't linger there. As for Harry, he had been away ten minutes. He had said twenty. Only if the secret phone call was prolonged...

She stared at the briefcase.

Another bell in the kitchen. They were in the bathroom.

If you were a really cunning adulterer, would you necessarily rearrange the obvious digits? Why not those in the middle, the heart of the matter?

834210.

The briefcase opened.

Harry had been away thirteen minutes.

Splashing and shouting from the bathroom.

Black pass book compliments of New York City police – Harry had a friend there. Chase Manhattan cheque book. The address book she had already robbed. Gold Cross ballpoint. Pack of sugar-free gum. White Sony cassette recorder, one tape half-expended...

Key in the door.

He was in the room quicker than she had anticipated. Just as she had closed the jaws of the case.

'Helen, what the hell are you doing?'

Spinning the tumblers of the combination with her thumb, she turned. 'Last time you left it here, the kids knocked it flying as they came down the stairs.'

On cue, the boys clattered down the stairs, Ben having the decency to slide across the parquet flooring and stop where the briefcase had been standing.

Harry said: 'OK, thanks,' holding out his hand for the briefcase, glancing at the tumblers, seemingly satisfied.

'Did you change the papers?'

He held a bundle aloft.

'I'll complain.'

'Don't bother,' he said. 'I made my point.'

As she poured orange juice, as the toast popped, as Harry dived into yesterday's news, Helen planned. No question of what she had to do next – get the cassette out of that Sony and copy it.

Did she suspect? Envisaging a life without his family, Quarrick tightened his grip on the wheel of the Mercedes. On the pavements, children on their way to school were trying to catch flying leaves and plastic bags.

If she did, surely she would have confronted him? Or called the police. She had done neither. And he had covered his tracks. No, she didn't suspect. How could any wife suspect her husband, the father of her children, of acts of such enormity? He was becoming paranoic. He relaxed his grip on the wheel.

Stopping at a red traffic light, he called the embassy on the cellular phone and asked his shared secretary if any crises were looming. No, she said, but Fraser wanted to talk to him.

He hadn't used the mobile to call Butler in Dundalk after the coded message to his home because they were the answer to every spook's dream. Might as well go on TV and address the nation as talk on a cellular.

Butler had said: 'A progress report, that's all I want,' and Quarrick had given him one. Butler had sounded jubilant.

'I'm glad you called,' Quarrick had said: 'I want an alibi. Where will you be on November the sixteenth?'

A pause. Rustling of paper. 'Lourdes.'

'Lourdes?' Quarrick held the receiver in the call box in Battersea away from him in disbelief.

'Are you still there?'

'Why Lourdes, for God's sake?'

'Exactly,' Butler said. 'For his sake. I'm going on a pilgrimage.'

'You?'

'I didn't tell you I was a man of the cloth because I thought it might upset your sensibilities. Now you've forced my hand.'

'A priest?'

'Ordained twenty-one years ago in Dublin.'

'You can equate religion with bloodshed?'

'I can equate it with justice. And after twenty-five years of war, a cease-fire isn't justice – it's defeat. Now, what do you want me to do?'

'Nothing. You've done enough – told me where you'll be on the sixteenth. You see, I've been told to kill you.'

He heard Butler's breathing quicken. 'Are you going to, my son?'

'How can I? You're a priest: it would be like killing God.'

Fraser was waiting for him in their office, all six foot five of him. 'I could use a coffee,' he said. 'How about you?'

Their shared secretary said: 'Shit, man, you only just got here.'

Fraser rested his long thin fingers on her shoulder. 'Cover for us, honey.' She angled her head onto his hand momentarily.

They walked past Roosevelt in the middle of the square.

'Draper's fretting,' Fraser said.

'What about?'

'He wants some action.'

So casually menacing did Fraser look that even late-for-work secretaries scurrying past found time to glance at him.

'I understood time wasn't a problem.' Quarrick said. 'Just timing before the election.'

'Draper's been thinking,' Fraser said, making it sound like the second coming. 'Figures these hard guys should be taken out gradually. No St Valentine's Day massacre, but one by one, clearing the way for triumphant handshakes on the lawns of the White House. What Draper wants, man, is a body.'

'He can have one.'

'He can?'

My day for putting the heavies on the defensive, Quarrick thought.

A pale, scampering young woman in a striped jacket cannoned into Fraser and apologised. 'He ain't worth it, baby,' Fraser said. 'Come and work for me.'

She stared at him, smiled tremulously and disappeared into the Europa Hotel. They walked along Brook Street.

Fraser said: 'What the hell you talking about, man?'

'The leader of the Provo rebels is going to be in Lourdes on November the sixteenth.'

'Where the Brits play cricket?'

Quarrick looked at Fraser to see if he was joking: he was. 'I want authorisation to go there for three days.'

'To take him out?'

'No,' Quarrick said, 'to perform a miracle.' *To establish an alibi!* Fraser turned into Davies Street. 'Now why would you, an American diplomat, be going to Lourdes?'

'You'll think of something.'

'Already have,' as they turned into Grosvenor Street and headed for the embassy. 'Unofficial negotiations about the killing of foreigners in Algeria by Muslim extremists. Present: the French Secretary of State for Foreign Affairs and a high flier from the Algerian Ministry of the Interior.'

'They're both men of God?'

'Sure they are,' Fraser said. 'They both work for the CIA.'

That evening Hood drove to Streatham to talk to Toland in case Collins got to him first.

Toland opened the door of the small house close to the common. 'You again?'

'Me again,' Hood said. 'Where's your sister?'

'Bingo. Now piss off.'

But Hood had got his foot in the door. 'Mind if I come in?'

'Yes.'

'Oh dear,' Hood said, shouldering his way into the hall and kicking the door shut behind him. 'A word?'

'If you must.'

Hood walked into the sitting room. A pornographic video was playing on the TV, girls with girls. Six cans of Whitbread, one open, stood beside a stiff-backed armchair covered with cigarette-burned plastic.

Hood picked up a can and pulled the tab. It opened with a cobra hiss. He poured lager down his throat. 'Fond of this, are we?'

'Whitbread? I can take it or leave it.'

'No, that.' Hood pointed at the TV where two naked girls were soaping each other.

'Not doing any harm, is it?'

'Good ad for hygiene,' Hood said, sitting in the scarred armchair. 'Frustrating, isn't it, when you can't remember any of it?'

'Don't know what you're getting at.'

'Losing your memory. Can't remember who interrogated you? Not what they said at the hospital . . .'

'I might have remembered *then*. Forgot everything afterwards.'

'OK,' Hood said, 'I accept that.'

'You do?'

'Of course I do. Irrelevant anyway – they told me in Casualty what you said.'

'They did?'

'The hood, the flashing lights . . .'

'Oh, that.' Toland's gaze flickered to the TV screen where one of the girls was taking her time soaping the other's crotch. 'Yeah, well . . .'

'Point is, it doesn't matter.'

'What doesn't matter?'

'The interrogation.'

'The fact that I had all sorts of shit beaten out of me doesn't matter?'

'The method matters,' Hood said. 'That's what I've come to apologise about. You see, the man who questioned you was upset—'

'Upset? Jesus Christ! What do you think I was?'

'I know, I know. Old mate of mine, he was. SAS . . .'

'SAS?'

'You've got it, boyo. Unfortunately you trod on his toes while he was questioning you. Personal bereavement, you see.'

'Down to the IRA?'

'Not the Salvation Army.'

'All I said was something about time-share. Then he went ape.'

'Memory coming back, is it?'

On the screen the girl being lathered was moaning.

Hood said: 'That's what they call a soap, is it?'

Toland smiled uncertainly and opened another can of Whitbread.

'Like I said, I've come to apologise.'

'Is that all I get, an apology?' Toland touched the stitch marks on his face.

'If you've given information that will result in a positive identification, you may get a reward.'

'All I said was he had an American accent.'

Quarrick, husband of the woman Collins was screwing!

'I know,' Hood lied.

'And that he lived in Chelsea and had two kids.'

'You did well,' Hood said. He stood up and stuck out his hand. 'No hard feelings?'

'You must be fucking joking,' Toland said.

'Wouldn't want it known that you were a snitch, would you? Wouldn't want it known that you had informed on the IRA...'

'You bastards stick together, right?'

'Right.'

On the screen one girl lying on a towel screamed. Sunday bath night in the Rhondda Valley had never been like that, Hood reflected.

He let himself out of the house, climbed into the Capri and drove away.

Toland's sister returned home later that evening, desolate after a string of near misses at bingo. As usual Toland, infused with filial affection by his intake of beer, offered to take her black and white mongrel dog, Banjo, for its nocturnal promenade.

'You don't have to.' She said that every night: it was no different to being married. 'While you're away, I'll heat something up for you.'

Banjo, who knew the routine, was waiting at the front door holding his leash. He was a bad-tempered dog with ears that looked as though they had been gnawed by a rat. Toland loathed him and the feeling was reciprocated.

Once the door had closed, Toland gave the leash a wrench and said: 'You keep to heel, you little shit!' Banjo bared his teeth and snapped at Toland's ankles.

Toland knew a pub where he could tie him up outside. He quickened his pace. What the hell was Hood's game? Had he been indiscreet in repeating the info he had given to the other murderous thug?

He turned into a tidy street of semis. The lighting was interrupted by a gap when the lamp had been vandalised. This was where he normally encouraged Banjo to defecate, where no one could see him fouling the pavement. Obediently, Banjo fell in with the scheme of things.

Toland stared at the starlit sky. Why had Hood come round again if he knew what I told the SAS sod in the camel coat?

A star fell in the sky. A birth? Or was it a death?

He felt a thin cold pressure on his neck. Strand of a spider's web floating on the night air? No, that was the beer talking. He put one hand to his neck. The thin band tightened. He dropped Banjo's leash and tore at his throat with both hands.

Screamed except that there was no sound, merely the hiss of escaping life.

As he pitched forwards, Banjo trotted importantly in the direction of his home, leash trailing behind him.

Chapter Sixteen

Ten days before the hit, Quarrick went shopping. He bought three wet suits from different stores in south London.

He deposited them in the warehouse in Feltham beside the Semtex and assorted weaponry concealed in electrical-goods packaging. Much of it had been supplied courtesy of Libya, shipped to Dublin, stripped, brought to the mainland in parts and reassembled in the warehouse. Then he checked out the baby helicopter in the Westinghouse container in the flat in Hounslow.

He also bought three white housecoats.

The three other operatives, each from different cells – Liverpool, Manchester and Birmingham – booked into small hotels in Earl's Court and West Kensington, far away from the earwigging informers in Camden Town and Kilburn, each carrying false ID.

Nine days before countdown he took a flight in a real helicopter, a Bell Jet Ranger owned by a tour company in Jermyn Street. The seventy-five minute flight along the course of the Thames provided unsurpassed views of the Tower of London, St Paul's Cathedral, the South Bank and the Houses of Parliament, and like any self-respecting tourist Quarrick photographed landmarks with video and still cameras.

From the air on this crystal autumn morning the Thames was an amiable serpent lazily nosing its way through history. It had seen it all, this river, plague, fire and Blitz, and it wasn't impressed. Quarrick was becoming quite sentimental about the Thames, his accomplice.

Taking time off work, absence cleared by Fraser, he flew to Lourdes for one day, then briefed the three operatives in the flat in Hounslow, playing back his cassette, running the video and showing them stills, giving them timetables to be memorised and destroyed. The rendezvous point was to be Putney Bridge.

Occasionally a question disturbed the surface of his calculations. Why had Draper chosen him? The Irish connection, OK. But why hadn't they briefed a trained assassin to carry out the actual hit? True, he *was* trained, but Draper didn't know that. If I screw up, he thought, if I don't frame the British, then any CIA involvement will be denied and Harry Quarrick, politico-military, will be sorely missed. Quarrick could feel the friendly clump on the back from Fraser – a knife between his slender fingers.

Six days before he was due to fly to Lourdes on *official* business, Fraser gave him a fixed confirmation of a reservation at the Vatican Hotel and a plane ticket bought at a discreet travel agency in Kensington. BA332 leaving Heathrow at 0650 arriving Paris, Orly, at 0900; departing Orly on Air Inter 5903, arriving at the airport for Tarbes and Lourdes at noon.

'Vatican Hotel,' Fraser said. 'I like it. Sort of place a Bible-thumper like you would choose.'

'Bible-thumpers aren't Catholics,' Quarrick said. 'They're Holy Rollers.'

'No one's perfect,' Fraser said. They were making another circuit of Grosvenor Square.

'Are the French bringing the gun from Paris?'

'Remington 40XB with Redfield telescopic sight. Same piece you used in Queens.'

'A good gun.'

'OK, take me through it.'

At 11.30 am, Quarrick said, Butler and his group would visit the grotto where in 1858 a fourteen-year-old shepherdess, Bernadette, claimed to have seen the Virgin Mary eighteen times, thus establishing Lourdes as one of the pilgrimage capitals of the world.

The grotto was situated at the foot of the towering basilica at the end of Esplanade des Processions. Quarrick showed Fraser the map he had obtained from the tourist office in Lourdes. 'The river Gave flows beside it. I shall be on the other side of the river, beside the Orphanage of St Bernadette, with the Remington.'

'OK, so you've shot the guy. What then?'

'Remove the telescopic sight. Slide the Remington into a canvas container. Slip it into the bag with my other fishing rods.'

'Fishing freak, wow!'

'And while all hell breaks out across the river, make my way along Rue du Docteur Bossarie.' He showed Fraser the street on the map. 'Back to the hotel – through the rear entrance – where your colleagues from Paris and Algiers will confirm I never left my room.'

appealed. Puncture a tyre so that Quarrick had to take the Mercedes to his garage across the Thames in Battersea. Friendly mechanic, made even more friendly by a gift of £500, installs child locks on the front doors as well as the rear.

A call on the car phone. 'Good day, Mr Quarrick. Did you know you've got five pounds of Semtex strapped under your car? You didn't? Oh shit, sorry. You were always so good about warnings – except when a mother and her daughter were in a car. Anyway, I'm calling to tell you that you've got forty seconds on this earth before you're blown to hell where you belong.'

Brakes squealing.

'Don't waste your last few seconds, Mr Quarrick. You can't open child locks. And don't try and crash into a tree or a parked car. Reverse vibrations will detonate... Goodbye, Mr Quarrick, see you in hell – where I belong too.'

Connection severed.

That was the most attractive option. Especially now that Quarrick's guilt was established. *Victims of War*, the dates of his absences in Helen's diary... Why should a murderer receive absolution because of a political settlement?

But it would also be an act of disloyalty to Helen. What do I care about Helen Quarrick? Sex – an act of revenge. Screwing the wife of the man who killed...

He remembered the clatter of birds in branches as they walked in the woods; the cakes at Muffins; the warmth of her breasts in his hands; the questions in her eyes. There was no doubt that her proposition was more constructive. And one proposition did not exclude the other. Break the hard men, then kill Quarrick.

The old-fashioned black telephone rang beside his bed. The switchboard. 'Sorry to disturb you. There was a call for you but the caller rang off.'

'Message?'

'Said to meet you at 1100 hours tomorrow outside the Cider Museum, at Pomona Place off Whitecross Road.'

'Name?'

'Robin,' the telephonist said.

From the camp, Collins made his way along Hoarwithy and Holme Lacy Roads, past St Martin's Church where the SAS buried their dead, and across the river Wye into the centre of town, turning left at Eign Street into Whitecross Road. A comfortable city, he thought, with its cathedral, Jacobean Old House and hint of fermenting cider apples on the air.

Hood was waiting outside the Cider Museum. He was wearing a dark, belted overcoat and, despite his size, he looked like a policeman.

'Did you know that cider brandy is being produced in the King Offa Distillery once again?' He consulted a leaflet. 'First time for two hundred and fifty years.'

'No,' Collins said, 'I didn't know that.' They began to walk. 'What do you want?'

'I thought we might take a drive.'

'Nothing has changed since I last saw you,' Collins said.

'I've seen Toland.'

Collins got into the old Capri.

They drove west, past black and white villages, towards Wales.

'I always feel better when I cross the border', Hood said. 'When we were both here, I used to walk into the Black Mountains.'

'What did Toland tell you?'

'Same as he told you.'

Collins stared out of the window at a white and mauve hot-air balloon floating prettily above green fields.

'He told me that the head of the Provos in Britain spoke with an American accent.'

'And?' There was, Collins decided, something fatalistic about the balloon drifting over the Wye.

'That he lived somewhere in Chelsea. That he had two kids.'

'Proud father?'

'He told me you interrogated him.'

'Did he now?'

'That you had gone berserk.'

'Can you imagine me going berserk?'

'When he mentioned something about time-share.'

'Maybe the interrogator had been conned by a time-share salesman.'

'Did a time-share salesman call at your house? To do a recce before—'

'Killing Judy and Jane?'

'Did he?' Hood overtook a couple on a tandem, woman at the front. 'I'm not going to turn you in.'

Yes, Collins said, forcing himself to look away from the hypnotic balloon, a time-share salesman had called at their house. And yes – surfacing from a trance – he had questioned Toland.

'Quarrick?'

Yes, Quarrick.

'So why haven't you—'

155

'Killed him?' Collins grabbed Helen's threads of logic. 'Which is better, to kill one man or break the extremists threatening peace?'
'No prizes for the answer.'
'So that's what I'm going to do.'
'Correction. That's what *we* are going to do. Through Mrs Quarrick?'
'She's helping,' Collins said. 'I can handle this myself.'
'Think of the resources I've got.'
'Why don't you do it officially then?'
'I think you know the answer to that. We're leaky. As soon as it was known that we had sussed Quarrick, he would be tipped off. The CIA, very friendly with our IBMs. And in any case this is you and me, Mr Collins. We operated together before. And we have common ground. Your wife and daughter – and Bomber.'
Collins found he had been holding his breath. He relaxed, began to breathe evenly. 'All right,' he said, 'you and me.'
'It's the only way. Keep chicken-shit politicians out of it. Do it the way we were trained to.'
' "The unrelenting pursuit of excellence" – David Stirling.' He remembered another of the founder's tenets. ' "The SAS brooks no sense of class and, particularly, not among the wives." '
'Funny thing about Toland,' Hood said as they overtook a truck loaded with rotting apples. 'The hood was the giveaway. My name ... Twenty-four hours, was it, you left me hooded? Thank God I was tougher than Toland.'
'I didn't hit you.'
'Wouldn't have done any good, would it? Counter-productive, we were taught. Still, it worked with Toland. But he won't grass any more.'
'Nothing more to grass about.'
'Difficult when you're dead.'
'Dead?'
'Head almost severed. I thought you would have known about that, Mr Collins.'
'No, I didn't.'
'One thing I always meant to ask you in SAS ... Did you have a special weapon?'
'I did.'
'Can I know what it was, if we're going to work together?'
'Discipline,' Collins said.
Hood whooped. 'We're in Wales. Home!'
Collins searched the sky for the mauve and white balloon but it was nowhere to be seen.

In the living room of her Georgian house in Henley-on-Thames, Susan Norton read Davis's report on the Toland killing and its similarities to the murders of Brady and Secker.

It was Sunday and her husband was taking his statutory two pints at the Red Lion on the banks of the river. She was sipping a glass of sherry. The roast was spitting in the oven.

According to Davis, the common denominator in the murders was the murder weapon. His insight into the obvious was a revelation. Actual time of death in all three cases was vital to compare with suspects' alibis.

Suspects plural?

But, of course, estimates of time of death weren't reliable. You had to take into consideration factors affecting the cooling of the body. Rectal thermometers... She skipped a couple of paragraphs. Lividity... Susan Norton decided not to check the roast.

So what else have we got, Davis? She reached for her glass. Empty. Just another drop. With profiling and behavioural science and genetic fingerprinting, you must have come up with something.

SUSPECT. Middle-aged. Punctilious. Clock-watcher. Medium height. Powerfully built. Working knowledge of anatomy. Sexually well disciplined. That was a flier, wasn't it?

And not much else.

One suspect, Jack Collins, the SAS officer whose wife and daughter had been killed by an IRA bomb, had been cleared by Inspector Hood.

A key in the door. Enter husband, looking hungry.

'Hello darling,' she said. 'I'm afraid I'm a bit whistled.' She remembered Davis's treatise on establishing time of death. 'Could you carve?'

Collins phoned Hood in Muswell Hill from a call box near Hereford Cathedral.

He said: 'Do you believe in miracles?'

'I believe in Father Christmas too. Why?'

'Because I want you to fly to Lourdes,' Collins said.

Chapter Seventeen

Most of the visitors to Lourdes that day talked about hope. The three men sitting in room number 230 in the Vatican Hotel on the Rue de la Grotte talked about death.

The representative of the French Secretary of State for Foreign Affairs handed Quarrick the Remington. 'Think you can handle this?' He was as Gallic as Alain Delon in middle age, with diplomatic wings of grey hair cresting his ears.

'Of course.' Quarrick, sitting on the edge of one of the two single beds, snuggled the butt into his shoulder and for a moment was back on the shooting range in Queens.

'Nice piece,' said the official from the Algerian Ministry of Defence, sturdy with brown eyes as sad as a dog's. 'We could do with some of these in my country.'

The Frenchman, sitting on a delicate white chair opposite the Algerian, said: 'We're supposed to be here to discuss putting an end to the killing in your country.' No friend of the former French colony, Quarrick decided.

'So, apart from verifying that you are in the hotel at the time of the shooting, our task is finished?' The Algerian angled his wistful gaze at Quarrick.

'What task did you ever have?' the Frenchman demanded. 'Except to provide an excuse for the three of us to meet here.'

'What task did *you* have, m'sieur? Anyone can be a gunrunner.'

Quarrick checked the snug, oiled action of the Remington. 'For Christ's sake, cool it! I'm doing the killing: you're both accessories.'

The Frenchman combed one crest of hair with his fingertips. 'Is Butler here?'

'He's here.'

'You're very well informed, M'sieur Quarrick. Forgive me, but why does Draper want Butler killed? I thought the cease-fire was holding.'

'You know why – Butler wants the war to continue. He's one of the leaders of the Liberation Army.'

'War?'

'Terrorism. There are many Butlers who don't want peace: they've got to be taken out. The security forces raided them in October but they only hit the fringe.'

'By taking them out, aren't you risking a return to terrorism?'

Quarrick shook his head. 'The high command of the IRA doesn't want a return to blood-letting. We're doing their job for them. If the Butlers of Ireland had been eliminated twenty-five years ago it would never have started.'

The Algerian said: 'So the British will be blamed and America will emerge as the peacemakers?'

'Which is what they are,' snapped Quarrick. 'If it hadn't been for the United States, the Allies would have lost two world wars. And Saddam Hussein would have trampled over the Middle East.'

'Butler and his party are due at the grotto at 1000 hours,' the Frenchman said.

'Right. They will join the queue to it beneath the basilica. Maybe fill a container with holy water from a faucet. Bathe their faces in the water from the spring and follow the advice to pray to God to cleanse their souls.'

'You believe in God, M'sieur Quarrick?'

'I don't disbelieve,' Quarrick said. 'They will probably buy a candle and light it on a stand just past the grotto. I'll take out Butler between the grotto and the stand. At 1010 hours, give or take, according to the length of the queue. I should be back at the hotel at 1020. Look out of the window and you'll see me.'

'A vision, M'sieur Quarrick?'

'Hopefully flesh and blood.'

Half an hour later Quarrick left the hotel and wandered round the town, marvelling, as he had on his previous whistle-stop visit, at the confluence of the gods of Christianity and Mammon. Sanctuaries, missions, hospices; hundreds of shops selling video cassettes, candles, prints of Bernadette kneeling in front of Our Lady, T-shirts of Christ on the Cross...

Backpackers mingled with nuns and priests. Through their midst nurses and parents pushed wheelchairs in which sat invalids with patient faces waiting for a miracle but not entirely convinced that they would be the subject of divine intervention. Whatever happened, God knew best, said their expressions, fashioned gently from suffering and trust.

From the Rue de la Grotte, Quarrick crossed the Pont St-Michel and made his way down the Esplanade des Processions to the basilicas and the grotto, moving on a tide of piety and curiosity.

At the grotto where the Virgin Mary was said to have made a spring flow beneath Bernadette's fingers, crutches and sticks hung overhead. Quarrick dabbed a little water on his forehead but he didn't have the nerve to make the sign of the cross.

He bought a candle, lit it and returned along the river to the centre of the town. Then he caught the funicular to the top of the 3,000-foot Pic du Jer to discuss the final details of an act of war with a terrorist leader.

In the distance they could see the imperturbable white crests of the Pyrenees separating France from Spain. Beneath them Lourdes lay as if scattered by a giant hand. God's?

Butler was wearing a charcoal-grey suit and a dog collar, monkish fringe a distraction from his zealot's face. They walked along a path, breathing the mountain air.

'So you see,' Quarrick said, kicking a stone, 'you've got to leave tonight. Then I have the perfect excuse for not shooting you: you're not here.'

'And you still have an alibi when the hit takes place in London?'

'You got it,' Quarrick said and explained.

'Sounds foolproof. No second thoughts? Not been influenced by defeatists who don't understand that peace at any price is defeat?'

'No second thoughts,' Quarrick said. 'My father didn't die for nothing. Nor all the others.'

'That's the spirit.' Butler began to retrace his footsteps towards the funicular terminal. 'But why the day of the State Opening of Parliament?'

'Because it's the heart of the matter. Is there any better day?'

'Not a single one in the whole calendar.' Butler put his arm round Quarrick's shoulders. 'May God be with you.'

Quarrick watched him climb into the furnicular coach and descend the hillside towards the city of miracles.

He crouched beside the orphanage, floppy hat shielding his eyes from the misty rain drifting across the town from the mountains, butt of the Remington tight into his shoulder. He wore a waxed jacket and waders, fishing rods beside him in a long canvas bag.

From time to time he wiped the lens of the telescopic sight with a tissue.

1000 hours. No sign of Butler in the queue leading to the grotto across the river. A group of Central Africans in green gowns were pushing a little girl in a wheelchair.

He stroked the trigger with his forefinger.

1005. A prayer of nuns in dove grey.

1010. A huddle of Brazilians with glossy hair.

1011. He removed the telescopic sight, thrust it and the Remington into the bag containing the fishing rods, and made his way towards the centre of the town.

At a call box near two religious gift shops, he phoned the hotel where Butler was staying.

As expected, Butler had left the night before.

Shouldering the bag containing the rods and the gun, he headed for the Vatican Hotel.

The phone in room 230 rang. The Frenchman picked it up. *'Oui?'*

'The fisherman.'

'A good catch?'

'The fish swam away last night.'

'*Merde!*'

'Didn't arrive at the fishing ground. I checked the source. Change of current.'

'Where are you?'

'Look outside the hotel in two minutes. There have been complications ... Scavenger following. I suggest you return to calmer waters immediately.'

The Frenchman told the Algerian and they both peered out of the window. There he was. Funny hat, waxed jacket, waders.

A man with slightly bowed legs was walking behind him.

Hood, baffled, crossed the crowded street. What the hell was going on? Neither Collins nor Helen Quarrick had traced any Butlers in Lourdes – hardly surprising, with the daily intake of block bookings – but even if they had it was now apparent that Quarrick wasn't here to talk: he was here to kill.

He had seen him beside the orphanage aiming a rifle across the river in the direction of the grotto. But whom did he want to take out? Then, while he was wondering whether to jump him, Quarrick had calmly stashed the rifle with his fishing rods and strolled back to the grey portals of the Vatican Hotel where his wife had said he was staying. But he hadn't gone in!

Quickening his pace, Hood glanced across the street at Quarrick. Except that it wasn't Quarrick.

Smiling gently to himself, the man named Dillon turned and walked in the opposite direction to the bow-legged man who had been following him, climbed into his rented Peugeot and drove in the direction of Toulouse.

In the apartment in Hounslow near London airport, Quarrick, who had driven overnight to Bordeaux, 120 miles north of Lourdes, and caught flight BA363 direct to Heathrow, hung up the phone after speaking to the Frenchman.

He looked at his wristwatch: in less than four hours the Queen was due to open Parliament.

The day before flying to Lourdes via Paris, Quarrick had taken the two boys and their American bald eagles across the river from Chelsea to Battersea Park.

A couple of days earlier he had found a set of *How to* cassettes in a second-hand shop in Hammersmith. *How to Grow Mushrooms, How to Scuba Dive, How to Master Macramé, How to Fly a Kite* . . . He had bought the kite cassette and taken it back to the house, where it was greeted with relief because, since buying the eagles, Quarrick had discovered there was more to flying kites than a mind attuned to diplomacy and terrorism could absorb.

In the first place he hadn't studied the catalogue adequately. Three stars beside a kite was 'difficult to assemble'. The eagle had three. And the figure three clearly printed beside it meant 'experience required'.

He had also made the mistake of showing Ben and Jaime the catalogue, and the eagles were rapidly losing out to aerobatic and stunt kites. Jaime favoured a stunt kite called Wolkensturmer XL which at £290 was the most expensive; Ben, who was older, lusted for a soft figure kite called Natalie's Legs.

But today eagles were back in favour – on polyester braid flying lines with the required light medium wind, eight to twelve miles an hour, blowing upriver and finding its way through the park, making the wild deer wrinkle their noses.

Before leaving the house, Quarrick removed the cassette describing routes and vantage points on the banks of the Thames from the pocket recorder and put it in his briefcase.

Helen stayed behind.

For two hours the three of them stayed in the park coaxing the eagles into the wind, watching them soar into low, watery clouds, closing their eyes when they dived to the grass.

On the way back across the river, Jaime asked: 'What's a kite that defies classification?'

'It means it's different,' Quarrick said.

'Well, with Christmas nearly here – well, on its way – I thought that if the Wolkensturmer was too much money, I might like Icarus the Flying Man instead. The catalogue says it defies classification.'

'How much?'

'A hundred and thirteen pounds ninety-five including VAT.'

'And if you don't want me to have Natalie's Legs, you could buy me Chorus Line,' Ben said.

'How much?'

'A little more, I guess.'

'A hundred pounds more,' Jaime said.

'Icarus,' Ben said. 'What a name for a kite! The wax on his wings melted and he drowned in the sea.'

'How do you know that, smart-ass?'

'Everyone knows it,' Ben said.

In the evening Quarrick brought back a takeaway from McDonald's and they watched an old movie on TV. They were together, the four of them, until they went to bed – and went their separate ways.

The morning panic began earlier than usual. Harry's flight to Paris en route to Lourdes took off at 6.50 and Helen was making toast and coffee at four.

He sat down, swallowed his orange juice in two gulps and said: 'What time tomorrow?'

'Time?' Helen yawned and sipped her black coffee.

'The State Opening of Parliament. You *are* going to watch the Queen going there, aren't you?'

'You know I am – the boys have never seen her in person.'

'Plenty of other opportunities, surely?'

'I promised them. Why, don't you want us to go?'

'Seems a pity to miss a day's school.'

'They've promised to work harder.'

'Where are you going to be?'

'Buckingham Palace, 10.30. The Queen and the Duke of Edinburgh leave around eleven.' It might have been her imagination but she thought he looked relieved when she said where she would be.

'So what are you going to do with the rest of the day?' he asked.

'I told the boys we might go to Hampstead Heath and fly the kites.'

'I don't advise the bald-headed eagles. Take the old box kites.'

At that point Ben and Jaime materialised in the doorway, wiping sleep from their eyes. No warning bells this time.

'What do you think you're doing up at this time?' Helen said.

'We've got to say goodbye,' Ben said. 'We always do.'

Harry stood up and ruffled their hair. 'Of course you've got to say goodbye. I'll be back in a couple of days.'

The phone rang. Harry frowned. 'At this hour?' He answered it in the living room. 'Yeah, right, I'll check.' She heard him walk into the hall, heard the snap of the locks on the briefcase. The previous day she had been unable to open it: he must have changed the combination.

'OK, you've said goodbye, now go back to bed,' she told the boys.

They trooped out of the kitchen. When their footsteps had faded she picked up Harry's voice again. 'OK, but I don't need a minder.'

'Who was it?' she asked when he returned to the kitchen.

'Fraser. Checking flights and ETA.'

'At this time in the morning?'

'No point checking later. They're laying on a limo at the other end.'

'They?'

'Yes,' he said, 'they.'

In the hall he replaced his tickets in the briefcase, shut it, put on his raincoat and picked up the briefcase and the suitcase which he had insisted on packing himself.

She kissed him perfunctorily, from habit.

Before opening the front door, he called out to the boys: 'Say hello to the Queen for me.'

From the bedroom she watched the Mercedes's headlights illuminate a fine drizzle of rain. The car took off smoothly, reached the end of the street and was gone.

She went back to bed, switched off the bedside lamp and curled up like a cat. And it wasn't until the following day that she noticed the cassette.

It lay on the table beside Ben's bed beneath a Flintstones lamp. White and shiny and little used. She touched it with one finger, wondering if its tight coil contained secrets. Harry had mentioned the *How to* cassette he had bought, but there was nothing second-hand about this tape. According to the label it ran for an hour.

The boys were in the bathroom making a lot of noise. As they weren't going to school today, they probably wouldn't emerge until she called them.

She picked up the cassette, slipped it into the pocket of her gown and walked down the stairs, heart thudding.

Having slotted the cassette into the tape recorder, she lit a cigarette before pressing the play button.

The sound of seagulls and water. A voice. Harry's. 'From the Tower of London barrack-block buildings to the right, no real access, on the opposite bank HMS *Belfast*, would you believe...' A travelogue?

She pressed fast forward. A woman's voice, Australian or New Zealand. An affair? No. She shook her head, reprimanding the cassette.

Why not, though? Harry was an attractive man. She stopped fast forward, pressed play. They were further upstream on the Thames, near Somerset House, by the sound of it.

Under Waterloo Bridge.

Cleopatra's Needle.

A note of lyricism touched the urgent snap of his voice. 'Then South Bank complex, Hungerford Bridge.'

A voice from above. 'Mom!'

'Yes, Jaime?'

'Ben's taken the only towel!'

'OK, I'll be right there.'

She stopped the tape as the boat passed the Ministry of Defence.

'Mom!'

'OK, OK!'

She rewound the tape, removed the cassette and took it upstairs to the boys' bedroom.

Casually, as they dried themselves with excessive energy, she said: 'That cassette beside your bed, Ben, where did it come from?'

'Oh, that. It's that tape about flying kites. Dad left it in his briefcase by mistake. I took it out while he was on the phone yesterday morning.'

'Have you played it back since?'

'Not since,' Jaime said. 'In any case, *we* know all there is to know about flying kites.'

'So you won't need it today?'

'Flying box kites with you? You've got to be kidding!'

Collins had warned her that, if he was becoming suspicious, Quarrick might monitor her phone calls, so she called him from a pay phone near the house.

Mr Melrose wasn't at home but if she would like to leave a message on the answering machine... She scrabbled in her purse for coins and called the camp at Hereford.

Major Collins wasn't in his quarters. The voice was courteous but with a parade-ground snap to it. Did he know where Major Collins was? No, madam, could he take a message?

'Tell him I'll call back in five minutes. It's urgent. You know, really urgent.'

'I will if I can contact him.'

Five minutes later, while Ben and Jaime were still eating breakfast, she called again.

The operator said: 'The adjutant is right beside me.'

Helen told Collins about the cassette.

'Only landmarks beside the river?'

'I guess so. It sounded as though he was on a pleasure boat or something.'

'Maybe he was.' Then: 'Jesus Christ! Know what day it is today?'

'Of course, November the sixteenth. I'm taking the boys – You don't...?'

'It's possible.'

'I'll call the police?'

'Don't! Leave everything to me.'

'But—'

'Do as I say. Where are you going to be?'

'In the Mall.'

'And then?'

'We're going to Hampstead Heath.'

'OK. Keep away from Westminster.'

'Harry's—'

'I know where Harry is. He was also out of the country when my wife and daughter were killed. Not stupid, Harry: he wouldn't be the IRA commander in London if he was.'

She began to speak again but she was talking to the dialling tone.

As she hung up she remembered Harry telling the kids that Guy Fawkes had intended to watch the Houses of Parliament disintegrate from a vantage point on Hampstead Heath.

Chapter Eighteen

The old lady was jaunty. Sturdy of spirit, more powerful than her build suggested, incisive in her movements, she put many younger contemporaries to shame.

Her name was *Jenny Chandler* and she was a tug who had spent all her working life towing barges up and down the Thames. Heavy, implacable craft loaded mostly with household rubbish – a million tons of it a year – which these days was dumped in landfill sites at Rainham in Essex.

The garbage, concealed below hatches in the two barges *Jenny Chandler* was towing this fine November morning, had been transported by truck from Westminster City Council's Gatliff Road depot near Chelsea Bridge and loaded at a wharf at Wandsworth.

At the wheel stood Michael Howarth, a middle-aged man with a weathered face. He came from a family of lightermen going back to the 1830s. His expression was worried, because the future of *Jenny Chandler* was threatened. Westminster Council had recently asked for road hauliers to submit tenders for the transport of the rubbish.

Nor was his mood lightened by the presence of strangers on board. As the tug swayed at its moorings in Wandsworth, he glanced at the stern. Two young men were busily occupied between the triangle formed by the two lines to the barges. He resented their presence but they had signed permission from the Port of London Authority, which was responsible for ninety-four miles of the Thames from its tidal limit at Teddington to the seaward boundary. They had brought a miniature helicopter to do an aerial survey of the Church Commissioners' headquarters in Millbank.

Collins called Ferris, head of the SAS anti-terrorist unit, as soon as he had cut the connection with Helen.

Ferris sounded as though he was eating breakfast. 'This had better be urgent.' Collins heard him swallow.

'Red alert.'

'Hold on. I'll take the call in another room.' Little ears flapping over the cereal? 'Well?'

'I have reason to believe that an attack may be made on the Houses of Parliament today.'

'Reason to believe? You sound like PC Plod. Why do you have reason to believe?' Collins imagined the angry blue eyes glaring from the campaign-tanned face.

'I can't give you details.' *Quarrick is mine.* 'You'll have to take my word for it.'

'Making enquiries of your own? Private vendetta?'

'Information received.'

'Come off it, Collins, you're not some Vice Squad sergeant protecting his snitch.'

'I can tell you this: they've made a survey of all approaches to the Palace of Westminster.'

'They?'

'The hard men who don't want the cease-fire to hold. The Liberation Army.'

'Why today?'

'If you wanted to blow up Parliament, when would you do it?'

'Fifth of November,' Ferris said.

'To strike at the very heart of the British tradition—'

'The State Opening of Parliament.' A sigh. 'All right, I'll alert Davis at the Yard.'

'I think Downing Street and Buckingham Palace should be told too.'

'Davis will do what he thinks best,' Ferris said. The tone of his voice changed: 'Nigel, get back to the table!' Then: 'All right, Collins. We'll discuss your reluctance to collaborate further at a later date. And Collins...'

'Sir?'

'Don't do anything stupid. Everyone sympathises with you in your bereavement. Revenge won't bring them back.'

Collins looked at his watch: 8.10. The Queen would read the 'Most Gracious Speech' in the House of Lords at approximately 11.30. He had three hours and twenty minutes.

He grabbed a mug of coffee, told his sergeant that he had been summoned urgently to London, climbed into the silver Jaguar and drove south onto the M4.

He was stopped by the police near Exit 18.

'Good morning, sir.' The policeman, standing to one side of the door, as every officer in a patrol car is taught, in case you try and ram the door into them, was red-haired and paunchy. 'Thought we were Damon Hill, did we?'

'I'm sorry. I've got urgent business in London.'

'A hundred miles an hour ... Must be a matter of life and death, sir. Would you mind stepping out of the vehicle?'

Collins, in uniform but not wearing his beret, climbed out while the other policeman circled the Jaguar looking for defects.

'What sort of urgent business would that be, sir?'

Someone's trying to blow up the Houses of Parliament.

Really, sir? A Mr Fawkes, would it be?

'A matter of national security,' Collins said.

'Nice one, Barry,' the policeman said to his colleague, slighter and darker. 'Ambitious. Wife's having a baby is more common.'

Collins showed him ID.

'Wowee, SAS. Cowboys and Indians. Indians making a run for it, sir?'

'This really is important.'

'So is driving at a hundred miles an hour. Not much time to stop if you'd come across a patch of fog with other cars stalled in it. That's the stuff of pile-ups.'

'I'm sorry,' Collins said.

'That's what they all say when they kill a kid sitting underneath a toy dog with a bobbing head in the back of a car.' He paused. 'Are you all right?'

'My daughter was killed in a car. My wife, too.'

'I'm sorry,' the policeman said.

'That's what they all say.'

The policeman named Barry said: 'I remember! Blown up by an IRA bomb, weren't they?'

Collins nodded.

'Investigating something similar?'

'I could be if I don't get to London in time.'

The first policeman said: 'All right, sir. But don't go over the ton – the nearer you get to the Smoke, the less understanding our colleagues are.'

'Thank you, officer.'

He climbed into the Jaguar, turned on the ignition and took off at a decorous speed. A hundred miles or so to central London. Three hours left. Traffic on the approaches to London congested. He put his foot down.

Susan Norton sighed. If she could have had lunch at the Caprice for every bomb alert that had come her way, she would be extremely well nourished. Not that preventive measures were her responsibility; it was her network that was needed.

Then, listening to Davis on the phone, she froze. State Opening of Parliament... the Queen... red alert... Could she put out feelers?

'Of course. How serious is this?'

'Deadly serious.'

'An informant?'

'Jack Collins of the SAS.'

Then it was deadly serious – it was the first time Davis had ever disclosed a source of information to her.

'What we always feared?'

'Afraid so, ma'am. Some bastard who wants war, not peace.'

'Provos or Loyalists? They've both declared a cease-fire.'

'Could be either,' Davis said. 'You have good contacts in Parliament – Commons and Lords. Alert them. Of course state security is primarily your responsibility...' Here comes the buck, she thought. 'I suppose it's up to you to decide whether the State Opening should be postponed.'

Susan Norton made several phone calls, the last to her husband, cancelling lunch. Then she called her driver and told him to take her to 10 Downing Street.

In the headquarters of the Metropolitan Police, Thames Division, in Wapping, Chief Detective Superintendent Tim Saunders – predictably Saunders of the River – considered his resources. His modest fleet of duty boats patrolled fifty-four miles of river from Staines to Dartford Creek in Kent. But what was relevant in today's crisis was how many of the fourteen boats upstream from Wapping could be available in the vicinity of the Houses of Parliament at midday.

He turned to his deputy, Chief Inspector Andrew Lucas, a laconic Scotsman. 'So what's the score, Andy?'

'An Underwater Search Unit is already on its way to Westminster.'

The USU was Lucas's responsibility and he was proud of it – nineteen bodies, sixteen firearms, seven knives, fourteen safes, forty-six cars and thirteen motorcycles in one year. Maybe today a limpet mine with a delayed-action underwater fuse beneath the Mother of Parliaments. Lucas only became animated when his mind was submerged.

'Other craft?' Thames statistics irritated Saunders, burly with creases like tributaries on his neck, because he believed that his division was understaffed, underpaid and did not have enough boats.

Lucas, thin with a longish nose, considered a print-out. 'From Lambeth Bridge to Waterloo Bridge, seventeen pleasure boats.'

'Barges?'

'In the same stretch, four tugs towing eight barges. One tug with an aerial surveillance team on board, taking pictures of Millbank with a baby chopper.' Heights bored Lucas and his Glaswegian accent surfaced sharply. 'Authorised by the PLA – and us.'

'Board it,' Saunders snapped. 'Alert Waterloo,' invoking *his* pride, the floating police station there. 'How many duty boats can we get to Westminster by midday?'

'Twenty-four knots an hour . . . Eight or nine. Dangerous, though, with driftwood and small boats around.'

'I know how dangerous it is,' Saunders said.

A red phone rang on his desk. He handed it to Lucas. Lucas, one hand covering the receiver, said: 'The divers are going down,' his voice wet with enthusiasm.

In the Houses of Parliament ten Yeomen of the Guard with lanterns had searched the vaults at 7 am, a tradition dating back to the Gunpowder Plot in 1605. Today another search was carried out later by anti-terrorist and bomb-disposal units. The search was the most diligent around the House of Lords because that was where the Queen would make the speech outlining the government's programme.

Before that she would don her three-pound crown and robe in the Robing Room, adorned with William Dyce's frescoes based on the Arthurian legends, and make her way through the Royal Gallery, conducted by high officers of state and heralds and flanked by Yeomen of the Guard.

Personally Bernard Davis thought that a terrorist group would have little to gain by endangering the life of the Queen. But if the Houses of Parliament had been targeted, a missile would probably be used. Accordingly, all vantage points on both sides of the river were being checked.

As Davis, thumbs in waistcoat, strode the two miles of corridor traversing the eight acres of the parliamentary fiefdom, Big Ben chimed ten. Susan Norton heard the chimes as she entered 10 Downing Street.

The Prime Minister received her in the Cabinet Room. When it wasn't in use, it had a concentrated tranquillity about it and it occurred to Susan Norton that he used it as an escape hatch.

Despite his grey hair, the Prime Minister looked boyish but in command. In Susan Norton's view, his only failing was his choice of henchmen.

He said: 'So, another bomb scare? Just like old times.'

'Or a missile.' She remembered the unsuccessful mortar attack on number 10 in February 1991.

'How seriously are you taking it?'

'We can't ignore it.'

'What sort of answer is that? You sound like one of my ministers.'

'Bernard Davis is taking it very seriously. The Palace of Westminster is crawling with police. I wonder, Prime Minister, if you think we should advise the Queen to postpone the opening.'

'Let's ask her. Excuse me a moment.'

When he returned he said: 'We are not amused.' His spectacles sparkled. 'Her Majesty points out that thousands of well-wishers are already lining the streets to see her. She also makes the point that by postponing we would be admitting the cease-fire was endangered – fodder for the extremists on either side. A wise woman, our Queen.'

'And a brave one,' Susan Norton said.

As her limousine moved away from the placid Georgian façade of numbers 10, 11 and 12 Downing Street, Susan Norton glanced at her wristwatch. It was 10.35 – fifty-five minutes until the State Opening.

Two minutes later a river-police launch pulled alongside the *Jenny Chandler*, its flamboyant wake making the two barges sway ponderously, and a sergeant bellowed through a hailer to Michael Howarth to stop.

'What's this all about?' Howarth demanded as two of the three-man crew boarded the tug. It was the first time in more than thirty years on the river that the police had stopped him.

'Some sort of scare downstream,' one of the policemen said. He had been a sailor once; Howarth could tell from his complexion and his gait – even on dry land he would roll a little. Sailors home from sea tended to patronise lightermen, but they knew nothing about the treacherous currents and vicious squalls closer to the estuary.

'Mind if we have a look-see? Make sure you haven't got any stolen plutonium in the scuppers.' He was younger, Cockney, a comedian. 'What have we here?' pointing at the miniature helicopter in the stern. Howarth and the other policeman and the two men in the surveillance team waited for the joke. 'Wow, a little chopper – just like yours, Stan,' to his colleague.

They inspected the helicopter, admired the Nikon camera in the cockpit, searched the *Jenny Chandler* and reluctantly turned their attention to the barges.

Howarth, stiff and resentful at the wheel, gazed towards the Old Swan at Battersea. The original hostelry had been used by lightermen in the thirteenth century; even now a couple of barges were moored alongside the replacement. From the chancel windows of St Mary's Church overlooking the pub, Turner had surveyed the river and transferred it to canvas.

Howarth began to calm down. The river in repose had that effect on him.

The comedian opened one of the hatches on the starboard barge and stepped smartly back, witticism stifled by the stench of garbage.

Five minutes later the launch took off in wings of spray.

The *Jenny Chandler* stopped again upstream from Battersea Bridge for another private launch to come alongside, as arranged, with replacement parts for the helicopter, which had been found to be faulty at the wharf at Wandsworth.

Howarth, entranced by the reflections of clouds bobbing on the water, streaked mauve and green by oil and petrol, watched vaguely as a man wearing a yachting cap, upturned collar of his reefer jacket obscuring his features, boarded the *Jenny Chandler* from the launch. He was carrying a package wrapped in sacking which he placed very carefully on the deck beside the little helicopter.

Howarth projected his thoughts round the next bend in the river, under Battersea and Albert bridges – Albert was his favourite, a beautiful Victorian hybrid combining cantilever and suspension – to Chelsea Reach. The launch took off and Howarth restarted the engines of *Jenny Chandler.*

As he was approaching Westminster Bridge, the needle of a hypodermic syringe plunged into the side of his neck.

Helen Quarrick arrived with the children outside Buckingham Palace, ten minutes before the Queen was due to depart. The crowds flanking the Mall leading from the Palace were thickening; small Union Jacks blossomed above them and waved like flowers in a breeze.

On one side of her stood a frail woman wearing a threadbare

coat with a moulting fox fur collar; on the other an old soldier with a breastplate of medals.

'Will the King be in the coach?' Jaime asked.

'There isn't a king,' Helen said. 'Just a duke. And he isn't in the country.'

'But if there was a king on the throne, his wife would be a queen.'

'Women's lib,' Ben said. 'Everyone knows that.'

The woman with the fox fur laughed, a distant reedy sound; the old soldier's medals jingled.

Where was Harry? Lourdes? If he wasn't, it was an elaborate alibi. A part of her hoped he was there.

The old man said: 'You a Yank?' And, when Helen nodded: 'A Yank went off with my missus in the last war.'

'I'm sorry.'

'Sorry? He should have got a medal, poor sod.'

'First time you've seen her, dear?' The woman had a regional accent that Helen couldn't place.

'The Queen? Yes.'

'Me too. And the last. I came down yesterday, spent the night in the railway station.'

'That can't have been comfortable.'

'Does it matter? Like I told you, this is the first and last time.' She coughed rustily.

Voices rose like the beating of wings. 'Here she comes.' Cheers and clapping as the Irish state coach with its gilt scrolls and huge lamps approached, drawn by four horses with a sovereign escort of the Household Cavalry. The Queen wore a long evening dress, white gloves, necklace, earrings, bracelet and diamond diadem.

'She waved at me,' Jaime said.

'At me,' Ben said.

As the coach made its way down the Mall and turned across Horse Guards Parade to pass under Horse Guards Arch into Whitehall and thence to the Palace of Westminster, Helen heard gunfire. She started. The woman wearing the fox fur tapped her on the shoulder. 'It's a forty-one gun salute. I read about it before I came here.'

Where was Harry?

As one of the two accomplices – the third had taken the launch back to the shore – took over the wheel of the tug, Quarrick, wearing gloves, ripped open the packages covered in sacking and took out the wet suits.

Then he unscrewed the Nikon in the cockpit of the helicopter, now painted black to make it more inconspicuous, replaced it with Semtex explosive and inserted an impact detonator.

So far the timing – winds and tides fed into a computer – was contained within the margins allowing for imponderables such as the police boarding party. Increase the speed of the tug and they would be opposite the target shortly before 11.30.

The pile-up on the M4 near London airport wasn't high on the scale of motorway carnage – a Ford Transit had run into the back of a lorry carrying livestock and two cars had crashed behind it.

Police cars, fire engines and ambulances squawked. An injured man and woman lay motionless on the hard shoulder. A helicopter clattered overhead. Pigs squealed.

Collins cursed behind the wheel of the Jaguar. Eventually climbed out and spoke to one of the firemen who had sealed off all eastbound lanes – lorry and Transit and pigs were slewed across them. Was there any way round? Lift the Transit, shift the barriers for a minute? He showed the fireman his ID. The fireman shook his head. 'This isn't the Gulf War,' he said.

Collins returned to the Jaguar. The hands on his wristwatch seemed to accelerate. He wasn't sure what he was going to do when he reached Westminster, only that he had to be there because it wasn't right that anyone other than himself should intercept Quarrick.

He fisted his hands and closed his eyes. Hearing shots, he looked out of the window. They were shooting the wounded pigs.

Ten minutes later one lane was opened. Traffic swarmed through, Collins's Jaguar leading. He had one hour in which to reach Westminster. The speedometer reached 140 miles and hour.

In the House of Lords the peers of the realm and its gilded servants were assembling. In a committee room with panoramic views of the Thames, tailors hooked, eyed and tied Officers of Arms into their royal coats. Tabards, wands and collars lay on tables.

Elsewhere the peers adjusted their parliamentary robes and the peeresses their tiaras, and diplomats in extravagant uniforms listened meekly while the marshal and vice-marshal of the Corps Diplomatique briefed them.

Dismounted troopers of the Household Cavalry lined the staircase which the Queen would climb, Life Guards on one side, Blues and Royals on the other. Yeomen of the Guard in Tudor uniforms took up positions in the Royal Gallery leading from the Robing Room to the chamber of the House of Lords.

The Imperial State Crown, the Sword of State – symbol of royal authority – inside a scabbard of crimson velvet, and the Cap of Maintenance, red velvet and ermine, were brought in through the Sovereign's Entrance beside the Norman Porch.

As the state coach turned into Whitehall from Horse Guards Parade, cheering could be heard gaining voice. The Lord High Chancellor in a black robe trimmed with gold and a full-bottomed wig, carrying the purse containing the Queen's speech, took up position at the foot of the staircase.

At 11.15 the Royal Standard was unfurled, replacing the Union Jack on the Victoria Tower, and the Master of the Horse, the Mistress of the Robes and a Lady and a Woman of the Bedchamber took up positions at the Norman Porch. A fanfare of trumpets. At the Sovereign's Entrance waited the Earl Marshal and the Lord Great Chamberlain, wearing scarlet court dress, golden key to the Palace of Westminster hanging from his hip. The Earl Marshal raised his baton and Her Majesty entered the Parliament building.

A few miles away, Helen Quarrick and her two sons drove towards Hampstead Heath, hoping that today the kites would fly high in the wide sky. Downstream a tiny helicopter took to the air.

Quarrick coaxed it gently, using his thumbs on the remote-control transmitter to send out radio waves. Persuading it to climb, pushing the cyclic control to tilt the rotor blades and ease it forwards, making sure he increased the throttle because the change in angle reduced lift.

He navigated it once and brought it back to base. The *Jenny Chandler* and her two barges passed under Lambeth Bridge, Lambeth Palace on the south bank, Houses of Parliament ahead on the north. Michael Howarth, bound and gagged, lay beneath a tarpaulin.

As the helicopter took off again and climbed, Quarrick shouted to the Provo at the wheel, a dour ex-seaman named O'Brien: 'Take her closer to the south bank!'

'South bank? the Houses of Parliament are over there.' He pointed to the north bank.

Quarrick said: 'Whoever said anything about the Houses of Parliament?'

Collins left the Jaguar beyond the crowds in Parliament Square and pushed his way through them. Flashing his out-of-date anti-terrorist ID at a policeman, he raced across Old Palace Yard, showed his ID again – and was inside the Palace of Westminster through the Peers' Entrance.

He veered left, then right past St Stephen's Court, left into the Central Hall. To his left in the House of Commons some two hundred and fifty Members of Parliament would be awaiting the summons from Black Rod to make their way to the Bar of the House of Lords to listen to the Queen's Most Gracious Speech. But first the Sergeant-at-Arms would slam the door in his face, keeping it shut until he had knocked three times with his rod.

Bernard Davis held out one arm. 'What the hell—'

'Follow me!' Collins shouted.

From the Central Hall he sprinted onto the terrace where on fine days MPs sat with guests. Armed police wearing flak jackets and dark-blue combat jerseys crouched there.

Davis shouted: 'I don't think—'

'Shut up!'

Collins grabbed a pair of field glasses from one of the policemen. Any attack had to come from the river, hence Quarrick's cassette. Pleasure boats... oil slicks... driftwood... a tug towing two barges...

Quarrick on the tug! Transmitter in his hands. Ahead of the tug, high and banking towards the *opposite* bank, a black object that, with the naked eye, would not have seemed bigger than a crow. With field glasses he could identify it as a miniature helicopter. Obviously primed with explosive. Aimed not at the Houses of Parliament but at the headquarters of British intelligence. The perfect strategic target, the hit to synchronise with a ceremony across the water that harked back to the first drumbeat of British colonial rule.

Collins tried to grab a rifle from a police sniper. The sniper turned the gun on him.

Collins said to Davis: 'Tell him to give it to me.'

'Why?'

'Tell him!'

'Give it to him,' Davis said.

'But—'

Collins snatched the rifle. Leaning on the parapet, he aimed the telescopic sight on the helicopter. Took first pressure on the trigger. Hit the helicopter in the cockpit and the explosive would blow. He aimed at the tail rotor.

Pulled the trigger. At exactly 11.30.

The little helicopter skewered to one side like a swatted insect, then plunged into the water.

Chapter Nineteen

Quarrick and the other two Provos, having previously dumped their clothes in weighted plastic liners into the Thames, slipped sideways into the water and, shielded by the two barges and the drifting tug, its engine cut, began to swim towards the south bank.

POLICE was printed on the back of each wet suit but, just in case, they dived like seals when a helicopter hovered overhead.

Quarrick was the first to reach the parked ambulance – bought at an auction. At the wheel was the Provo who had taken Quarrick to the *Jenny Chandler* in the launch.

Inside, Quarrick and his two companions peeled off their wet suits and put on conventional clothes, white housecoats on top of them. No one spoke; their words were choked by failure.

The Provo at the wheel drove the ambulance into St Thomas's Hospital directly opposite the Houses of Parliament and they split up, making their respective ways down the corridors of the hospital.

Quarrick, stethoscope dangling from his neck, walked briskly as though hurrying to an emergency. He smiled at a couple of nurses, and they smiled back.

Outside in Lambeth Palace Road, he hailed a taxi.

'Emergency, guv?' The driver looked at him expectantly.

'You could say that. Take me to Hounslow.'

'Long way for an emergency, isn't it?'

'Personal,' Quarrick said and winked.

While Quarrick was escaping, the Queen, now wearing the Imperial State Crown, was making her way along the Royal Gallery to the extravagant theatre of parliamentary pomp and circumstance, the chamber of the House of Lords.

There, seated on the throne beside Prince Charles to her right, she faced the peers and peeresses. The Lords Spiritual from the

Church wore their ecclesiastical robes; the Lords Temporal – dukes, marquesses, earls, viscounts and barons, in pecking order – wore scarlet. In the centre sat High Court judges, robed and bewigged.

The Queen took the speech from the kneeling Lord Chancellor, waited for the MPs from the House of Commons to arrive, traditionally taking their time to demonstrate that they weren't overawed by the 'other place', and began to read. Saying, among other things: 'The fight against terrorism in the United Kingdom and elsewhere will be maintained.'

In the flat in Hounslow Quarrick changed into a suit and sat in front of the television. Five hours to kill before leaving for the airport to catch the 8.10 pm flight to Bordeaux. The flight, BA366, was due to land at 10.50 local time. With luck he would be back at the Vatican Hotel in Lourdes by 1 am – with the hour's time difference, that would be midnight in London.

He switched on the TV to see if his failure had made the news. It hadn't. A cover-up!

He opened his briefcase and checked the contents. Something was missing – the cassette. A lurch of panic. When during the past two days of frenetic activity had he lost it? Could he have left it at home?

One side of the cassette had been downstream from Westminster; the other, made later, upstream.

Could anyone have found it? Worse, played it?

He switched off the TV and once again began to plan.

High above Hampstead Heath, nylon flight paths crossed and two red box kites fell squabbling to the ground.

'I want to go home anyway, I'm hungry,' Jaime said.

'So what's new?' Ben asked.

In the Fiesta, Helen switched on the radio and caught a newscast. It gave the salient points from the Queen's Speech. So the Houses of Parliament were still intact. Nothing about any hostile incident.

She relaxed.

But in a way it didn't change anything. Nothing had happened because Harry had been in France.

She stopped at a call box beside Regent's Park and called Collins at his London flat. The voice telling her that Mr Melrose wasn't there was his, and the message meant he wanted to see her.

'How about supper at Mindy's?' she said to the boys.

They liked Mindy because she allowed them to watch TV programmes banned at home and sent out for junk food.

'Are you going to eat there?' Ben asked.

No, she had to go to a meeting of the Children of the Andes, Helen lied.

'So what the hell,' Jaime said, *'we'll* eat there anyway.'

'You want to fly kites again?'

'Of course.'

'Then mind your tongue.'

She pulled up outside Mindy's studio flat off the Marylebone Road.

Mindy had a part in a pilot for a TV series about a country village, similar to the radio series *The Archers*, and was enthusiastically rolling cidery vowels.

A portly man with a rubicund face was standing in front of a wall hung with studio-lit portraits of stars, each bearing a scrawled message to the effect that Mindy could act the pants off them.

Mindy introduced him. 'He be the squire,' she said.

The squire gave them a harvest smile, picked up a country gentleman's raincoat and said to Mindy: 'See you in the studio tomorrow.'

'Arr,' Mindy said. And to the boys: 'We be muck-spreading on the morrow.'

'Do you mind having them?' Helen asked.

'Course not. Long as they don't mind cider and potato cakes.'

From Marylebone Road Helen drove to the new, after-dark winter rendezvous, outside the New London Theatre in Drury Lane where *Cats* was still playing. They went to the bar of the Drury Lane Hotel adorned with Osbert Lancaster cartoons, found an empty corner and conspired over whiskies, ice and water.

Collins told her that an attempt had been made to blow up the headquarters of British intelligence with Semtex explosive packed in a miniature surveillance helicopter which had been shot down over the Thames.

'Who shot it down?'

'Me. What's left of the helicopter has been fished out of the river. It was directed by remote control from a tug towing two barges.'

'Ingenious.' She jostled cubes of ice in her glass with a cocktail stick, aware that she was scruffily dressed – skirt and jersey – for evening drinks in the West End.

'The skipper of the tug was overpowered but he wasn't hurt. He's been told by MI5 to keep his mouth shut. A few people heard the shot but, thank God, a breeze was blowing upstream and they confused it with the gun salute. No one has reported the helicopter crashing. It was black, very small—'

'Why the State Opening of Parliament?'

'What better day for symbolism?' A party of smartly dressed cat lovers waiting for the 7.45 show came into the bar and ordered drinks. Collins said: 'The police are searching the tug for fingerprints, ordinary and genetic, but they won't find any – these men were pros.'

'Harry?'

'I saw him on the tug.'

'But he's in Lourdes.'

'Someone very much like him is in Lourdes. Same height, colouring, clothes...'

'How do you know?'

'I sent someone there to check him out.'

'Suppose the man on the tug was very much like Harry?'

'I'm sorry,' Collins said. 'It was your husband.' He went to the bar and ordered two more whiskies.

'How can you be sure?' she asked when he returned.

'It was him.'

'What's going to happen to you? You're supposed to be in Hereford.'

'A severe reprimand. They can't get any tougher – I did save the intelligence service!'

'So what do we do now?'

'Same as before. Surveillance. That's what you want, isn't it? Nail the extremists who want to break the cease-fire? Because they'll try again. A provocation that they calculate must bring a reprisal.'

'Such as what?'

'That,' Collins said, 'is for you to find out.'

She finished her drink. 'I've got to get back.' Not even a hint of affection or desire from him.

'You have to go right now?'

'Soon. Why?'

'Because I've booked a room in the hotel,' he said. 'And this may sound squalid but when you go, leave by the fire escape – in case I've been followed here.'

She lay in her own bed still feeling him inside her. Still hearing the quickening of his breathing, smelling and tasting him. After the first time in Cirencester she had felt guilty, but not this time. Harry had betrayed her trust and that was worse than sexual infidelity.

When she finally discarded the images of their lovemaking, doubts returned. How could Collins be so sure that it was Harry on the tug? He had been wearing a wet suit. She looked at the illuminated dial of her wristwatch. Five minutes past midnight. There was only one way to find out. She switched on the light, picked up the bedside phone and called the hotel at Lourdes.

Harry's voice!

'Helen? Is anything the matter?'

'I've been out. The kids have been at Mindy's. I thought you might have called while I was out...'

'Should I have done?'

In the old days, yes. 'I thought I'd call just in case. Everything OK?'

Everything was OK, he said. It was past one there. He had been going to make some notes but he had lost a cassette so he had just switched off the light and was going to sleep.

Cassette!

'Are you still there, Helen?'

She tried to control her voice. 'Notes? What kind of notes?'

'I had this great idea. Remember my history lesson on Hampstead Heath? How the kids enjoyed it? Well, I thought I'd take them down the Thames because, you know, the Thames *is* the history of London. So while you were away I took a trip on a pleasure boat, noted what I would have to bone up on. Cleopatra's Needle, that sort of thing. Good idea?'

'Terrific,' she said. 'They'll enjoy that.' Thoughts like moths around a lamp.

'Haven't seen the cassette, have you?'

'There's a cassette in the boys' room. They said it was a tape you bought about flying kites.'

'Wrong tape,' Harry said. 'That's in the kite bag with the bald-headed eagles.' A pause. 'They didn't play it, did they?'

'Not as far as I know.'

'Good. Do me a favour – get that cassette out of their room and put it in my study.'

'Your study's locked, Harry.'

'Well, anywhere out of their reach – I wouldn't want to spoil their history lesson. Maybe I should have been a teacher.'

'Maybe you should have been, Harry. You would have been good, no question.'

'How was the Queen?'

'She looked great.'

'The boys appreciate her?'

'She had a mellowing effect on them.' The wingbeat of her thoughts was beginning to slow down.

'How was the kite-flying?'

'The kites had an argument,' she said.

'Look, I'll be back tomorrow evening. Give my love to the boys.'

Quarrick put down the phone, took off his topcoat and placed his briefcase beside one of the single beds. His exhaustion was intensified by the sense of defeat.

Still, all was not lost, he told himself. An act of total warfare was what was now required. A provocation that would unleash retaliation that in its turn would convert terrorism into a crusade against oppression.

He heard a young man with cropped hair talking to him a long time ago. 'He's SAS, Harry, undercover. One day you'll get yours.'

And now the SAS would get theirs!

A gaping hole in the headquarters of British intelligence would not necessarily have provoked retaliation, but a raid penetrating the headquarters of the SAS would surely provoke it.

Who dares wins, he thought. Hands behind his head, he lay in the darkness planning, planning.

Part IV

Chapter Twenty

It was the nightmare that only a terrorist can experience. His own family inadvertently on their way to a location where he has planted a bomb.

The bomb was strapped to a bridge on the railway from Newport in Wales to Hereford. In the first carriage sat half a dozen Welsh guardsmen accepted into the ranks of the SAS.

Helen, Ben and Jaime were in the second carriage.

Quarrick tried to contact the remote-control operator on the phone in his car one mile from the bridge. Engaged.

He called British Railways in London. No reply.

The fault had to be with his own phone.

He ran to a call box as the train travelling north gathered speed.

The train was approaching the bridge.

He grabbed a patrolling policeman. 'Get your hands off me, sir!'

The bridge was a barracks.

He screamed: 'Stirling!'

The barracks was disintegrating. Rafters and guns and bodies flying high into the sky. Two young bodies . . .

Helen's hand on his forehead. 'There, there – another bad dream.'

Sterling. Quality? Worth? Currency? Helen Quarrick, eavesdropper on dreams, turned her head into her pillow, determined once again not to spy on the most private arena of human existence, the subconscious.

Because she was no longer absolutely convinced that Harry was guilty.

He hadn't been in London when Collins's family had been killed. He hadn't been in London when the attempt to destroy the headquarters of British intelligence had taken place. She should know:

she had spoken to him in Lourdes. And was she certain beyond all reasonable doubt that he had been in Colombia?

Sterling? Silver? Character?

Another thought occurred to her: whether Harry was innocent or not, she had swapped him for a man who was by repute a killer – a member of the SAS. A killer sworn to avenge the deaths of his wife and daughter.

She lay awake until dawn before going downstairs to find comfort in the kitchen. The fridge hummed, the coffee percolator bubbled. There was frost in the garden. In six weeks it would be Christmas.

Harry came downstairs, fetched the newspapers and, sipping coffee, read them. She glanced over his shoulder. The cease-fire was holding.

After seeing the boys onto the school bus, she drove to Regent's Park to meet Collins, who was in London attending the secret inquiry into the helicopter incident.

'I can't go on with it,' Helen said immediately.

He plunged his hands into the pockets of his camel-hair coat and began to walk. 'Can't go on with what?'

'Spying on my husband.'

'What changed your mind?'

'I'm not sure he's guilty.'

'He's guilty,' Collins said.

'He wasn't even in London when this helicopter thing happened.'

'Because you spoke to him in Lourdes twelves hours later?'

'He couldn't have got back.'

'There was a plane to Bordeaux at 2010 hours. I checked.'

'Bordeaux? He flew to Lourdes via Paris.'

'So? Nothing to stop him driving to Bordeaux and making a quick in-out visit to London. He could have been back in his hotel by midnight.'

'He sounded sleepy.'

'He had had a busy day.'

'Do you have proof?'

'That he bought a return ticket? No, I don't have proof. Only that a passenger named Dillon bought one.'

'I'm sorry,' Helen said as they circled the rose garden. 'I don't understand.'

'I think Dillon is Harry's lookalike. I think Harry borrowed his passport for the day.'

'But you can't be sure.'

'No,' Collins said. 'I can't be sure.'

'Harry wasn't in London the day—'

'My wife and daughter were killed? A master criminal doesn't have to be at the scene of the crime.'

Helen unbuttoned her heather-coloured coat to let the sunshine in. 'The cease-fire's holding.'

'Thank God!'

'What you're doing might destroy it.'

'What I'm doing will preserve it.'

'Killing the ringleader in London?' She lowered her head, shaking it. 'Because you do intend to kill Harry, don't you, Jack?'

'You made more sense the other day. Get to the hard men through Harry. Break them before they break the peace – because, believe me, that's what they aim to do.'

'You haven't answered my question. You didn't last time.'

'I agreed that nailing the extremists was more practical than killing one man.'

'And humane. The word surprised you. As though it wasn't part of your vocabulary. But it wasn't an answer, was it?'

Collins struck away from the inner circle of the park onto the Broad Walk. Still he didn't reply.

Following him, she said: 'OK, you figure he's a murderer. If he is and you kill him, you're no better than he is. Is that the man your wife and daughter would have wanted you to be? Brutalised by their deaths?'

He turned, face cold as though the sun hadn't touched it. 'What Judy and Jane might have thought is between me and their memory.'

She continued remorselessly, threatening what they shared. 'Consider my position. I am married to a man who may be innocent, screwing the man who's planning to kill him.'

He turned again and strode towards the lake, his normally straight back hunched as though he was carrying weights in his coat pockets.

She caught up with him. 'I'm sorry, but it's true.'

'Suppose I can prove he's guilty.'

'Can you?'

'You know about genetic fingerprinting?'

'Sure. Blood and semen—'

'Not just fluids,' Collins said. 'Hair, for example. The police found a hair in one of the wet suits.'

'And you're going to tell me it was Harry's?'

'If you can get a sample we can prove his guilt – or innocence.'

'Like what? Semen?'

'A couple of hairs from a comb, or a smear of blood if he cuts himself shaving.'

'Harry uses an electric razor.'

'Hairs, then. If the DNA matches the hair in the wet suit, then the chances of it coming from another person are minute.'
'How many wet suits were there?'
'Three. But the one containing the hair was the only one that would have fitted Harry. Will you do it?'
'If they don't match?'
'I quit.'
'You mean that?'
They had reached a group of fossilised tree trunks near the lake.
'You stay happily married,' he said, 'and we stop meeting in parks and forests—'
'And hotel bedrooms?'
'Those too.'
'Just like that?'
'No,' he said, 'not just like that.'

The hunter hunted. Quarrick felt the enemy closing on him. Heard the soft footfalls of stealthy pursuit, felt the hooded gaze of covert surveillance.

Had he been blown? Had Fraser's suspicions been alerted by Butler's unscheduled departure from Lourdes? Had the IRA, now seeking political recognition on the coat-tails of Sinn Féin, shopped him? Was the Anti-Terrorist Squad staking him out?

If none of these contingencies was valid, how was it that the security forces had anticipated the hit on 16 November even if they had initially believed that the Palace of Westminster was the target?

The cassette?

No, Ben and Jaime had admitted taking it from his briefcase because they thought it was the kite-flying tape. And they hadn't bothered to play it.

Did Helen suspect? Possibly that he was working for the CIA. How could you work for Politico-Military and not work for the Company? Maybe she believed that he was involved in some debilitating exercise that had made him impotent. Which he most certainly was. Sometimes the desire to confide in her was almost irresistible.

The sense that he was under observation only sharpened the blade of his intent. Surely his father and mother and all the others hadn't died just so that politicians could sit round a table – they could have done that in 1969.

Any day now, he thought, I will have to go to Hereford.

Collins faced Ferris across his desk in the Duke of York's barracks in Chelsea.

'I warned you.' The lines on Ferris's forehead tightened.

'About what?'

'You know about what. Pursuing a personal vendetta. You have disobeyed orders.'

'I stopped terrorists demolishing the headquarters of British Intelligence. That was wrong?'

'Your tip was sufficient.'

'And you told Bernard Davis? He didn't even realise what was happening. When I got to the terrace at Westminster, the missile was airborne.'

'You recognised the man controlling it?'

'A man in a wet suit in charge of a surveillance helicopter on the day of the State Opening of Parliament? I recognised danger.'

'I think you recognised someone. Who?'

'Just a frogman in a wet suit.'

'Bit of a risk, wasn't it, shooting down a surveillance chopper? Could have been one of ours.'

'*We* don't have any. I should know, admin—'

'Is just a front. You know that. To keep the nosy parkers happy.'

'The helicopter *was* heading towards the intelligence building.'

'You're right, of course. At that altitude it would probably have hit the fourth floor, Susan Norton's territory. You showed great initiative. Who was the man in the wet suit?'

'A man.'

'I could have you court-martialled for disobeying an order.'

'You could. But you won't. Courts martial are open to the press. All that evidence about a plot to destroy the British intelligence machine.'

'But we don't encourage courts martial in SAS. Executions are more in our line.' He laughed.

Collins waited, standing not quite to attention.

'I met your old commanding officer in the Green Jackets the other day,' Ferris said. 'Spoke very highly of you.' Collins stiffened. 'Wants you back. An overseas posting.'

'*You* contacted *him*?'

'I met him is all that matters. I told him I didn't want to lose you.'

'But you were willing to make the sacrifice?'

'I'll be sorry to see you go.'

'Suppose I don't want to go?'

'In the Army you obey orders. Or had you forgotten?'

Collins remembered his forebears staring at him from the walls of the ancestral dining room. 'I'm entitled to finish my term of service.'

'You're entitled to nothing.' Ferris picked up a document and tossed it on the desk. 'Your marching orders. Don't think I'm unsympathetic – I know what you've been through. Best for you to rejoin your old regiment. Too much licence here for an officer with an old war wound that keeps aching.'

His tone, Collins realised, was supposed to convey gruff compassion. But it was insincerity that triumphed.

'How long?'

'Three weeks,' Ferris told him.

Something wrong there. If you were posted you weren't allowed to hang around, disgruntled and disruptive.

Ferris said: 'That will be all.'

Striding round Sloane Square, Collins pondered the three-week delay in execution. It could only be for one reason – so that Ferris and Bernard Davis could keep tabs on him. Hoping he would lead them to his suspect.

He quickened his pace past the Royal Court Theatre, dived into the tube station and dived out; then stopped to allow any pursuer to emerge.

He was an old-time hippy with a Jesus beard, long hair, a poet's face and a silver earring. He was also a pro. Glancing casually from left to right, sighting Collins but suppressing any flicker of recognition.

He must know he's been sussed, so he'll wait until I turn my back and then alert his partner. Collins walked straight past him, into a cab, and told the driver to take him to St Pancras Station. Glancing behind, he picked out the motorcycle in pursuit. Tricky to park a bike and follow someone into the crowded concourse of St Pancras. Having paid the driver prematurely and over the top, Collins leaped out of the taxi and into the concourse.

When the motorcyclist appeared, helmet in one hand, Collins slipped out of the exit, sprinted along Euston Road into King's Cross Station next to St Pancras and caught a BR train to Wood Green in north London.

From there he walked through the ascending pastures of Alexandra Park to its brooding palace, twice risen from the ashes of fires, seat of Britain's first TV transmission in 1936, and made his way to Hood's home in a somnolent Victorian terrace.

Hood was sorting his collection of postcards, dealing local views like a croupier. Belgian refugees in Alexandra Palace in 1914,

Muswell Hill Broadway with Parkes chemists to the foreground, circa 1937...

He handed Collins a can of Fosters and said: 'Dodgy, wasn't it, coming here?'

'Why?' Collins sat down at the gate-legged table covered with a damask cloth and picked up a 1911 card of Muswell Hill police station, Keystone cops paraded outside it. 'Only natural we old campaigners should have a get-together.'

'I was asked to investigate you.'

'You cleared me.'

'They're having second thoughts.'

'About the murders?'

'They, the Anti-Terrorist Squad, can't forget you suffered a personal tragedy. That you might be going it alone. That you might lead them to the leader of the Provos or the Liberation Army here. Only natural, isn't it?' He pulled the tab on the can of beer and it hissed at him.

'We've got three weeks,' Collins said.

'Three, is it?' Hood dealt a rogue card – a Nuremberg rally in the 1930s – and separated it from cosy pre-war Muswell Hill. 'Why three?'

'That's when they're putting me out to grass.'

'Break the hardliners in three weeks? Tall order, that.'

'There's worse,' Collins told him. 'Quarrick's wife is refusing to cooperate. Unless I can prove that Harry is guilty.'

'Can you do that?'

Collins told him about asking her for a couple of her husband's hairs.

'You want me to get them tested?'

'You have access to the Metropolitan Police Forensic Science Laboratory.'

Another misplaced postcard skimmed from Hood's hand: a Cecil Beaton photograph of Churchill. With a caption: '... Victory however long and hard the road may be.'

Hood said: 'Suppose the two samples don't match?'

Collins stood up, made a chink in the lace curtains and stared down the tranquil street. 'Taff,' he said, 'do I have to spell it out? We both know Harry Quarrick is as guilty as hell.'

'So?'

'If you've got two of his hairs from Helen Quarrick, then they'll match, won't they?'

*

'So you outrank me,' Fraser said as they made another circuit of Grosvenor Square.

'No substitute for class,' Quarrick said. He had just been promoted to Anglo-Irish-American affairs.

'But in the Company I outrank you.'

'You have ranks in the CIA?'

'Sure we do: you're a rookie.'

'Rookies kill people?'

'In the CIA everyone kills people. Which reminds me, you didn't do so good in France.'

'Shooting phantoms *is* a challenge.'

'Why did Butler pull out?'

'Ask him,' Quarrick said.

'*You* ask him. You're the Irish-American with the contacts. Draper's man.'

'Maybe he saw a vision.'

'And the following day we have all this shit on the Thames beside the Houses of Parliament. But you were in Lourdes, right?'

'Right.'

'Sometimes I worry about you, Harry. You being Irish, you know. Maybe not all the Irish want the war to end.'

'Anyone who wants the bloodshed to continue has to be crazy.'

'Is what I was thinking,' Fraser said.

Later Quarrick phoned Butler in Ireland.

On the Friday he caught the 10.30 Concorde to New York for a briefing. He checked into the Carlyle on East 76th Street, where there was a message waiting for him: the Oh Ho So restaurant at 395 Broadway at one.

Draper was sitting at an antique table. His grey suit hung loosely on him; either he had lost more weight or he had bought it at a thrift store. He stood up and extended a bony hand. 'Glad you could make it.'

They sat beneath exposed beams in the SoHo loft-style restaurant. Draper ordered for both of them – orange steak and honey prawns. They drank beer.

'So what went wrong in Lourdes?'

'Fraser didn't tell you?'

'Sure he told me. You tell me.'

Quarrick told him.

'Some coincidence, leaving the day you plan to shoot him.'

'Coincidences happen every day. Why is everyone so amazed by coincidence?'

'What else have you come up with?' Draper bit into a prawn.

'I've got to set up Butler again.'
'No longer your first priority,' Draper said.
'Huh?' Quarrick sipped beer and stared warily at Draper. 'What is then?'
'The man who could abort the American initiative.'
'Butler, surely?'
Draper shook his head and attacked his orange steak. 'Your target,' he said, chewing, 'is in London.'
Quarrick picked up his glass of beer and gulped thirstily. 'Who in London?'
'We don't know.' Draper paused for effect. 'An American, we think.'
'That's ridiculous.'
'What better cover? We should have thought of it before.'
'Who did think of it?'
'Our computers, hacking into the Brits'. Apparently their spooks have been following a guy named Collins. Name mean anything to you?'
'The wife and daughter of an SAS officer named Collins were killed in an IRA bomb explosion.'
Quarrick had read somewhere that interrogators could see the beat of a guilty man's heart. He buttoned his jacket.
'That's him.' Draper ordered tea. 'The Brits figure he's got a lead. They think he'll lead them to a former IRA hit man in London – the American.'
'How do they know he's American?'
'Because Collins is screwing his wife.'
The restaurant sounds faded. A strumming in his ears.
'Are you sure you're all right?'
Quarrick heard his own voice coming from a distance. 'How do they know... Collins is... screwing his wife?'
'The Brits followed Collins to a hotel in London. Bugged his room after he had made a booking. Mostly heavy breathing and the language of love.' Draper winked lecherously. 'But they did pick up a reference to her husband and Collins's suspicions about him. As American as apple pie, Harry.'
'But you don't have any idea who she is?'
'None.'
'You figure the Brits do?' The answers to these questions were obvious but he had to ask just the same.
'No, they lost her. And now Collins is running like a fox.'
'Have you got the tape?'
'Come on, Harry. The Brits don't even know we know about it.

But can you imagine the mileage they'll make out of it if they nail him? The headlines – AMERICAN HIT MAN PRIMED TO BLAST IRISH PEACE. And underneath a load of crap about American hypocrisy. Always been jealous of our initiative in Ireland, the Brits. These days it really sticks in their craw.'

Helen with Collins? In a hotel room? No, not Helen. For her, family was everything: it was another American wife. So why had Collins discussed his suspicions with this other American wife?

'And so,' Draper was saying, 'we want you to get to this American first. Get him out of there. You're in charge of the London end of the Irish-American initiative: you have the contacts. I briefed Fraser today – all the Company's resources are at your disposal.'

'I thought you wanted to keep this low key. Wasn't that why you ordered *me* to take out the extremists? So that CIA involvement could be denied?'

'You're talking history,' Draper said, calling for the bill. 'The priorities have changed: you've got to get to the American before the Brits do.'

From the restaurant Quarrick took a cab to Sunnyside across the East River in Queens.

Helen with Collins? There was a devastating logic about it. Collins tracing me . . . seeking confirmation through Helen . . . seducing her as part of his revenge.

But had she betrayed him? Eavesdropped, spied, passed information to the enemy? Used the boys to deceive him? That surely was worse than sexual betrayal.

All unproven. He became aware of his surroundings. The cab was in Queens, approaching Sunnyside, a leafy residential neighbourhood. Butler was standing outside PJ Horgan's Bar on 42nd Street and Queens Boulevard, dog collar, if he was wearing one, hidden beneath a green scarf.

Quarrick paid off the taxi and they walked.

'So what went wrong?' Butler asked.

'On the Thames? Someone blew it.'

'Any idea who?'

My wife? 'Could be anyone. In London or Ireland.'

'Bit of a fuck-up all round, huh, Harry?'

'Fine language for a man of God.'

'I'm one of those man-to-man priests. You know, the ones who drink with the boys in the pubs but never put their hands in their pockets.' He turned into Skillman Avenue. 'It's almost last-chance time, Harry.'

First Draper, now Butler bawling him out.
'Not almost, it *is* last-chance time.'
'And what do you mean by that?'
'They're closing on me.'
'You're blown?'
'Not quite. Not long, though.'

Through Collins, he thought. Which meant he *was* blown. So both of us are cutting it fine. I have to make the last crucial hit; he has to eliminate me. Why hasn't he done so already? Because he's playing for higher stakes – all the hardliners in one coup? Someone has persuaded him that is more laudable than a simple execution. Helen...

'Are you listening?' Butler demanded. They had turned into a tree-lined street, gardens separating pavements from parked cars. 'I said, how do you know they're closing?'

Quarrick decided not to tell him about Collins. *Collins is mine.* 'Usual signs and symptoms of surveillance.'

'Maybe I should take you out of the front line.'

'Got anyone better?'

'How about a good Catholic priest?'

'You aren't established in London. In any case I have a plan. My last chance, my last fling.'

'Better be good, my son. So what is this plan?'

When Quarrick told him, Butler said: 'Sweet Mother of God!' and crossed himself.

Chapter Twenty-One

Hood gave the hairs, two of them, to a man named Zoltan.

That was his first name, but the British had never got their tongues round his second. Zoltan was a pathologist and a hygiene freak. He hoovered his apartment in Docklands twice a day, showered three times a day; kept the laundry and car wash in Wapping in business.

'Understandable,' he would say defensively, 'when you consider the materials of my profession.' Zoltan was a specialist in genetic fingerprinting at Scotland Yard's forensic laboratory and the materials were blood from knives, semen from rapists, flesh from underneath fingernails . . .

But some of Zoltan's acquaintances – he had no friends – believed that his obsessive cleanliness stemmed from insecurity. His parents had fled from the Russian tanks in the 1956 revolution in Hungary and settled in the East End of London, where they had spent their remaining years lamenting their fate. Zoltan won a scholarship to Oxford, emerged with a first-class degree and joined the team of Home Office sleuths cracking the genetic codes of the innocent and the guilty.

When Hood handed Zoltan the two bagged hairs, he considered them with scepticism.

'On whose authority?' he asked, standing beside a laboratory bench.

'Mine.'

'Since when did you exercise such authority?'

It was not difficult, Hood thought, to understand why Zoltan had no friends. 'This is urgent. A possible terrorist murder. You know how long officialdom takes . . .'

'Just the same, I must have higher authority. In this case Davis's.'

He smoothed his silky grey hair and examined his hand for foreign bodies.

'You have to accept my authority.'

'And why is that?'

'Because Davis is a racist,' Hood said, surprised at the energy of his lies.

'What is that supposed to mean?'

'If these two hairs match genetically, a Hungarian could be eliminated from the inquiry.'

'Davis doesn't like Hungarians?'

'He prefers Englishmen.'

'What is this Hungarian's name?'

'Szabo.' That and Nagy were the only Hungarian names Hood could remember.

'Why is a Hungarian involved?'

'Davis thinks he's a contract killer, another Carlos. I don't.'

'Are you telling the truth?'

'The truth.' The most definitive lie of all, to deny you're lying.

'All right, I'll do it.'

The following morning Hood went back to the Home Office lab and watched as Zoltan placed a radio-sensitive film over the DNA isolated from the hairs on a radioactive membrane.

'They match?'

'Patience.' Zoltan washed his hands with carbolic soap. 'Come back in a couple of hours.'

When Hood returned, Zoltan led him to a room beside the lab and switched on the light in an X-ray examination unit. What Hood saw looked like the barcode on a packet of cornflakes.

'Well?'

'A unique signature,' Zoltan said. 'The autograph of one person and one person only. There you have what has determined the colour of his eyes, the size of his brain, the texture of his skin—'

'But are the hairs from the same man?'

'Wait.'

Zoltan, entrepreneur, put up another X-ray photograph. 'See for yourself.'

Hood studied the two. 'You tell me,' he said after a while.

'The hairs come from the same man.'

'Thank you, Mr Zoltan.'

'Zoltan is my first name. Will you British never understand that?'

'I doubt it – not the sort of thing that's in our genetic fingerprinting, see.'

Taking the X-ray plates with him in an envelope, Hood drove to a dismal pub near the Post Office Tower. Collins was leaning against the bar nursing a pint of beer.

'What'll you have?' Collins asked.

Hood asked for a bottle of Guinness. It was the sort of bar, he thought, where a man might drink the courage to throw himself under a bus.

Collins said: 'Well?'

'They match.'

'So they should.'

'Not necessarily.'

'What do you mean, not necessarily? They were both from the same source.'

'No, they weren't. One came from the wet suit. I couldn't do it, see. Cheat like that and you're no better than Quarrick. You wouldn't want that, would you?'

Helen knew immediately she saw him. The backward thrust of his shoulders, the parade-ground angle of his head... Convictions vindicated was what his body language spelled out.

He beckoned her under his elegant black umbrella and they became a unit in the soft rain drifting across Regents' Park.

'You don't have to tell me,' she said. 'I can tell.'

'I'm sorry.'

'No, you're not. Don't lie to me, Jack.'

'I meant sorry for you. I knew Harry was guilty.'

Her husband was a murderer. Her children had to be saved from his dangerous love. The cease-fire had to be saved.

'What do you want me to do?' She slipped her hand beneath his arm.

'He's planning something. Has to be. I want to find out what it is.'

'I'll try.'

'And time is running out – for me *and* Harry.'

'If the British have been following you, they may know about us.'

'I doubt it. If they did, they would have reacted.'

'Suppose the Americans have penetrated British intelligence..?'

'Time is running out for *all* of us.'

Gulls settled on the grass and stood motionless. An old woman began to feed them bread.

'Have you found out anything more?' Collins asked.

'He had a bad dream the other night. He screamed – well, whimpered.'

'Did he say anything?'

'One word: Sterling. Does that mean anything to you?'
A pause. The SAS barracks at Hereford had once been called Bradbury Lines. Now they were known as Stirling, after the founder.
'Only the obvious. Sterling currency, character, values...'
'Fold the umbrella, Jack.'
Puzzled, he closed the black shroud. 'Why?'
'Everyone should kiss in the rain. Just once.'

'Had a Dutch grower over on Friday,' Tom Norton said over supper. 'We're thinking of going into business together in Northern Ireland now that it seems settled over there.'
'Really?' Susan Norton always tried to simulate interest in tulip bulbs but she really appreciated only their waxy blossoms. 'There are a lot of opportunities there now.'
If the cease-fire continued to hold, she thought. The IRA and Sinn Féin were desperate to continue their bid for respectability but, according to an Ulster Unionist MP, a splinter group of extremists was poised to destroy it. 'A hit that will make retaliation inevitable,' he had said.
'Any idea what?'
He hadn't.
She regarded her husband fondly across the table: a gentle, aristocratic man who followed the seasons, hibernating in winter, flowering in summer.
'Interesting chap, the Dutchman.'
'Interesting people, the Dutch.'
'Do you think it will last?'
'What, darling?'
'The cease-fire.'
She glanced at him guardedly. Occasionally it occurred to her that he knew more about her business than he pretended.
He poured claret and sipped it. 'This Dutchman, he was in the underground during the war.'
'Good for him.'
'A brave man. Made one big mistake. Blew up a bridge while a detachment of the SS elite, the *Leibstandarte*, Hitler's bodyguard, were passing over it.'
'Reprisals?' She had never known him to evince any interest in violence. If he had been old enough during the war, he would probably have worked for the Ministry of Agriculture.
'Terrible reprisals.'
'Why are you telling me this?'

'Because if I wanted to break the cease-fire, to provoke inevitable retribution, I would attack an elite force. In this instance the SAS.'

'There's going to be another hit, right?'

'Right,' Bernard Davis said. He walked to the window and contemplated Susan Norton's view of the Thames.

'Any ideas?'

'We've intensified surveillance on Collins.'

'Who is having an affair with an American woman.'

'Right,' Davis said.

'Do you know who?'

'We'll know soon enough.'

'How soon?'

'Very soon. Collins thinks he's smart and he knows we've been following him. He shook off a motorcyclist the other day, but our back-up caught him coming out of St Pancras Station. Followed him.'

'To where?' Susan Norton asked.

'An address.'

Anti-Terrorist Squad versus MI5, she thought. Pitiful! 'I don't think Collins is going to lead you anywhere. Not if he knows you're onto him.'

'Maybe not.' Davis shrugged.

'Suppose I were to tell you I know where the hit is going to be?'

Davis turned his back on the Thames. 'Then of course you would tell me.'

'Would I? *You*'re not being very forthcoming.'

'So what do you want to know?'

'Where Collins led your backup the other day.'

'To Taff,' Davis said. 'To Hood.'

'No reason why they shouldn't meet, is there? Old comrades together . . .'

'Hood cleared Collins.'

'So?'

'He and Hood are operating together. Because they have a shared sense of grievance.'

'And they don't want to share it with us?'

'Vengeance isn't something you share.'

'You're following Hood?'

'Also with backup.' Davis's thumbs sought his waistcoat. 'You said you knew where the hit is going to be . . .'

'If you wanted to provoke reprisals to break the cease-fire, who would you target? The SAS, of course,' she said before he had time to reply. And felt proud of the sharpness of her husband's reasoning.

The stamp on the envelope was Colombian, the handwriting childish as though its author had just learned how to join letters together.

With a sense of foreboding Helen opened it. The letter inside on lined notepaper was brief.

> *Dear Missus Quarrick,*
> *I am sad to be telling you that my mother has gone God's way. I believe she will be finding it very happy there. I know you love her very much and will be looking forward to meeting her there one day. How is England? I like very much to see it one day. I send you blessings.*

It was signed Electra.

Helen folded the letter and tucked it back in the envelope. What she wanted to do was pack a bag, drive to Heathrow and catch the first plane to Bogotá.

But not yet. She still had to spy on her husband, who had once trained Colombian guerrillas.

Chapter Twenty-Two

Quarrick caught the 1.45 pm Concorde from Kennedy. Eating smoked salmon and drinking champagne as the aircraft lanced through the stratosphere, he plotted the next two days.

Tell Helen nothing. The image of her in bed with Collins surfaced. He wanted to vomit.

Time difference added, the Concorde landed on time at 10.25 pm. As soon as he was clear of the brief formalities, Quarrick called Fraser.

A pause while the scrambler was activated. He told Fraser he had picked up a lead from NORAID contacts in Sunnyside. He needed two days' leave of absence to follow it up in Liverpool and Glasgow.

Then Quarrick rented a car, a Rover, picked up the M4 and headed west.

In the early hours of the morning he booked into the Green Man Inn, a fifteenth-century black and white coaching inn at Fownhope between Hereford and Ross-on-Wye. In his bedroom he spread the books about the SAS he had bought in London and his maps and guidebooks of Hereford and its environs, including the hills of the Brecon Beacons where the SAS endurance tests were held.

In the morning he put on plain-glass spectacles, jeans, a denim jacket and a black sweater – the sort of clothes a writer investigating the SAS for an American magazine might wear. After a light breakfast, he drove the white Rover to the Stirling barracks on the Hoarwithy Road, main gate opposite Aconbury Avenue. He approached from the centre of Hereford, squadron lines just visible through trees and shrubs behind a high wire fence.

The Rover broke down outside the main gate – as it would when the ignition was switched off.

To one side of the main gate stood a red pillar box and a pole with a surveillance camera mounted on it. The gate was high wire with a pedestrian gate to one side. Fifty yards beyond these, trees on either side, another gate with another pedestrian gate and beside it a guardroom made principally from opaque glass.

Quarrick climbed out of the Rover, opened the hood and tinkered with the engine. On the other side of the Hoarwithy Road stood semidetached houses.

A young, fit-looking man with a ferocious haircut walked out of the pedestrian gate, stopped beside Quarrick and said: 'What seems to be the trouble, sir?'

Sir! SAS troopers didn't even call their officers sir.

'I reckon I've fixed it,' Quarrick said and shut the hood.

'American, sir?'

'It shows?' Quarrick remembered the Australian woman on the river boat.

'Bit of an accent, sir. Nothing to worry about.' He stared unsmilingly at Quarrick. 'Shall we see if the engine starts now?'

Quarrick climbed back into the Rover and turned the ignition key. The engine fired. He opened the window and said: 'Thanks for your help.'

'Didn't give you any, did I?' He had a broad accent but Quarrick had no idea where it originated. 'Mind me asking something?'

'Fire away,' Quarrick said.

'What are those glasses for?'

'To look through.'

'Long sight or short? You were wearing them to inspect the engine and you're still wearing them for driving.'

'Astigmatism,' Quarrick said. 'Blurring of the vision. Comes to you as you get older. You wait.'

'I'll remember that, sir.' He turned and retraced his footsteps to the gate.

Quarrick drove towards the centre of town, turned into Walnut Tree Avenue, stopped and made notes. From there he turned into Belmont Road and the A465 to Abergavenny, where you took a right on the A40 to Brecon and the Beacons below.

He stopped at an inn in the village of Ewyas Harold where they served a beer called SA, Skull Attack. Also real ales with names such as Reverend James, Morland Old Speckled Hen, Vaux Samson and Shepherd Neame Spitfire.

He sat down beside a burly man with a shaven skull, a broken nose and an air of resolute detachment. 'Can you tell me if I'm on the right road to Abergavenny?'

'You are.' The man took a pouch from his green wax jacket and began to roll a cigarette.

'Brecon Beacons?'

'Bear right.'

Quarrick gulped Skull Attack. 'Pretty cold up there, I guess.'

'You guess right.' He ran his tongue along the gummed edge of the cigarette paper, stuck it to the other flap, lit up and inhaled deeply.

'That's where the SAS have their endurance test, isn't it?'

'Who wants to know?'

'I'm writing an article about the SAS.'

'Yank?'

'You got it.'

'Name?'

'Ziman,' Quarrick said. 'You?'

'Eastwood. As in Clint.' Accent Welsh, Quarrick decided. Eastwood held up his pint glass. 'Dry old ship.'

'Skull Attack?'

'Morland,' Eastwood said. And when Quarrick brought back the brimming glass: 'So what do you want to know?'

'I'd like to watch them. Take some pictures. Maybe go along with them for a while.'

'Fat chance.' Eastwood relit his thin cigarette. 'Maybe thirty blokes up there. Tough bastards, too. They've had five weeks of blood and sweat. This is their last test, shit or bust. Sometimes not one of them gets through—'

'I would be fresh. No pack on my back.'

'No way,' Eastwood said, pouring beer down his throat.

'OK, so I could photograph them.'

'Ever had a camera shoved down your throat?'

Quarrick bought him another pint. 'When's the next Endurance?'

'Seven days. Always the same time – they leave the camp at 1330 hours in three-ton Bedford trucks.'

Quarrick took off his spectacles and polished them with a tissue. Say two hours, maybe less, to get to the Beacons. Seventeen hours for the course. So they would leave the Beacons somewhere around 8.30 the following morning – 7 December, that would be.

'Thanks,' Quarrick said. 'One thing puzzles me.'

Eastwood began to roll another cigarette. 'What would that be?'

'I thought the SAS never talked about the way they operate.'

'They don't,' Eastwood said. 'I'm Welsh Guards. I failed the Endurance.'

Quarrick drove towards Abergavenny, Black Mountains to the northwest. Then he made a U-turn. It would make sense to make the hit closer to the camp at Hereford, when bone-weary soldiers in a Bedford three-tonner might well be asleep.

Half an hour later he checked out of the Green Man and headed for London. And it wasn't until later that he heard that on 7th December the Sinn Féin leader Gerry Adams was due back from Washington for his 'historic talks' with the British two days later. What better day to wreck the cease-fire?

Susan Norton was angry. She showed her ID at the entrance to New Scotland Yard and made her way imperiously to Davis's office.

The office was smallish and, in contrast to its occupant, dishevelled. Books on a shelf leaned sideways; faxes and print-outs littered the desk. The computer itself glowed smugly.

Davis ushered her to a chair. 'What can I do for you, Mrs Norton?'

'I understand you've been making inquiries at the American embassy.'

'Discreet inquiries, Mrs Norton.'

'Joined the diplomatic corps, have we, chief inspector?'

'Superintendent,' Davis said. 'I've just been promoted.'

'Congratulations,' Susan Norton said without enthusiasm. 'All we need, isn't it, an official complaint. Picked up by the press: US ACCUSES BRITISH SNOOPS OF SOUR GRAPES OVER IRISH PEACE MOVES... Why wasn't I informed?'

'I didn't want to waste your time with dreary field work.'

'The American embassy is *my* field, superintendent.'

'Coffee, Mrs Norton?' He pressed the intercom and an assistant came in carrying two steaming cups, traces of instant coffee on the saucers.

Davis pushed sweeteners across the desk and said: 'Just supposing the *British snoops* came up with something. The Americans wouldn't protest then, would they?'

'Come up with what?' She sipped her coffee; it tasted of cardboard.

'My accomplice – ' he tapped the computer – 'and I have been doing quite a lot of dreary field work. Interested?'

'Of course I'm interested,' she said irritably.

There weren't many dealers selling surveillance helicopters, Davis said, settling comfortably in his chair. And in any case the suspect, whoever he was, wouldn't go to a recognised dealer. 'If you're a terrorist you don't buy your guns from Purdey.' His accomplice – Davis gave the computer another friendly pat – had come up with the names of three dodgy dealers who sold mostly weapons but also dealt in sophisticated electronic equipment.

First name – zilch. Second – gold. A man named Harzani, with premises off the Edgware Road. 'We threw the book at him and he coughed. Suspect's name, Ziman. Phoney, of course. Want to know what he looks like, courtesy of Mr Harzani?'

Without waiting for an answer, Davis touched the keyboard of his accomplice. *Medium height, wearing black windbreaker, brown eyes, crisp brown hair touched with grey, gold wedding ring, looked like successful executive undergoing severe stress, spoke with slight American accent.*

'Am I forgiven?' Davis asked.

'I'm impressed,' Susan Norton said.

'There's more . . .'

To manoeuvre a surveillance helicopter by remote control you had to undergo training. One company held courses in Condover in Shropshire and Stalisfield and Wye in Kent. No one remembered anyone answering Ziman's description. But a newcomer to the scene had been traced, Aerial Surveys Service run by a Scotsman in King's Lynn.

Davis touched the keyboard to summon the Scotsman's portrait of a terrorist. It tallied with Harzani's with a few more facial details.

Susan Norton said: 'Accent?'

Davis gave her his jury smile and touched a button. *American.* Deliberately delayed, she realised.

'I'm *very* impressed,' she said.

'The Scotsman gave us a bonus,' Davis said. 'He's a squirrel. Hoards everything, even the worn cassette from his answering machine. When Ziman first called, he began to leave a message on it. Then thought better of it and hung up.'

'Voice-sensor test? The suspect *is* American?'

'Irish-American,' Davis said. 'And an artist has done an Identikit. Not detailed but a start.' He opened a dossier and handed Susan Norton a coloured sketch.

'We've also got a description of his wife from a porter at the hotel where Collins stayed with her. Tallish, blonde and attractive, wearing a yellow coat – vague, but it will help. So far we've traced six Irish-Americans with American wives in London who match up with the Identikit.' He reeled off names. 'They all work for big US corporations.'

'That's only five,' Susan Norton objected.

'The sixth works at the American embassy. His name is Quarrick. So you see—'

'I do see. I just wish you'd told me.'

'We've mounted a surveillance on all of them. And now that Collins is dodging, we're hoping Hood will lead us to the right one.'

'Have you alerted the SAS in Hereford?'

'And at the Duke of York's barracks in Chelsea.'

'How did they react?'

'With scepticism,' Davis said. 'And that's putting it mildly.'

Susan Norton put down the cup of disgusting coffee and stood up. 'Suppose Hood leads you to Quarrick?'

'Over to you, Mrs Norton.'

'Who's Pearl?' Ben asked.

'Pearl?' Helen Quarrick was writing a letter to Electra to be faxed later to Jaime Jaramillo in Bogotá. She put down her pen.

'When we came in today, Daddy was on the phone. I don't think he heard us.'

'And he was talking to someone called Pearl?'

'It wasn't *someone* called Pearl,' Jaime said. 'It was *something*.'

Helen, trying to look uninterested, yawned. 'What did he say?' She picked up the pen and began to write again.

'Something like top priority for Pearl,' Ben said. 'What's priority?'

'Something boring,' Jaime said.

'Perhaps he's buying you a pearl for Christmas,' Ben said. 'It must be secret because he hung up as soon as he saw us. Don't let on we told you.'

'No,' Helen said, 'I won't.'

'We're having initiative tests at school,' Ben said.

'So are we,' Jaime said.

'No, you're not – you're too young. And in any case I bet you don't know what "initiative" means.'

'Sure I do – doing your own thing.'

Helen intervened. 'That's sort of right. But doing it with flair and being clever at the same time.'

'What's flair?' Jaime asked.

'What do they want you to do?' Helen asked Ben.

'Something original. Whoever does the most original gets a prize.'

'Initiative tests are stupid,' Jaime said.

'So what are you going to do?' Helen asked Ben.

'I thought you might have some ideas.'

'I might,' Helen said. 'I'll think about it.'

'Then it won't be your initiative,' Jaime said to Ben, 'it'll be hers.'

Helen said: 'He showed initiative asking me.'

*

No more calls to the flat off the Fulham Road, no more meetings anywhere. Surveillance, Collins had told her, was too concentrated. Instead she waited until 8 pm and called him at the number he had given her – a pub in Soho, phone out of earshot except when customers were entering or leaving the toilets.

So this is what it's come to, she thought, standing in a call box, as the phone rang in the pub. Escaping from a husband who kills the innocent to conduct a love affair with a disembodied voice.

'Hello.'
'Is that you, Jack?'
'It's me.'
'I love you.'
She waited.
'Yes,' he said.
'Yes what?'
Silence except for the murmur of voices in the background.
'Jack?'
'I'm here.'
'Did you hear what I said?'
'I heard.'
'And that's it? *I heard.* Jack, stop playing the diffident fucking tongue-tied Englishman. I know better than that. Remember?'
'You shouldn't love me.'
'You're not worthy of me? Don't give me any crap like that. Please. Please!' she shouted.

The door of the call box opened. 'You all right, lady?' A man wearing a crash helmet.
'Get lost.'
'Sorry, I—'
'Beat it.'

The door closed. Rain wept on the windows. She fed more coins into the slot. 'Are you still there?'
He was.
'Do you love me, Jack?'
A pause.
She said: 'Up yours, Jack.'
'I love you.'
'I'm some dentist. I had to drag that out of you as if I was pulling a bad tooth.'
'It's true.'
'Then why the fuck couldn't you tell me yourself?' This wasn't good, she thought.

'You said I had become brutalised by the deaths of my wife and daughter. Someone else said something similar.'

'A woman?' *Crass!*

'No, not a woman. A colleague. What I'm trying to say is ...'

'Yes, Jack?'

'That you deserve better.'

'For me to decide, Jack.'

'OK.' A pause. More voices. Laughter. 'What I said just now, I meant it.'

'That you love me?'

'Yes.'

'Say it again, Jack.'

'I love you.' She could hear him breathing. 'But you will have to decide when this is all over.'

'Decide?'

'Decide,' he said.

Two more coins in the slot. 'I may have something for you. Pearl ... Does that mean anything to you?'

'Nothing in particular, why?'

She told him what the boys had heard Harry saying on the phone. Something like 'top priority for Pearl.'

'Was that all?'

'When he noticed the boys, he hung up. Jack, are you still there?' She couldn't hear his breathing any more.

'I'm here.' Now his breathing was faster. 'How are the boys?'

'They're fine. Ben's been given an initiative test.'

'To do what?'

'Nothing specific. Just to prove he's the greatest.'

'Know what would make him the greatest?'

'An interview with Sharon Stone?'

'If he could get into SAS headquarters they'd salute him in the playground.'

'You can fix that?'

'Breaking all the rules. But, for the time being, I'm adjutant – I can fix anything. Maybe even a couple of discreet video shots to prove his claim. And he can bring his brother too.'

The money ran out and she stayed in the call box for a moment, watching the rain on the window.

Chapter Twenty-Three

Helen knew, no question. Collins had traced him and, seeking confirmation, had persuaded her to spy on him. Quarrick made some adjustments to one of the bald-headed eagles lying on a bench in the garden. So why hadn't she gone to the police? Because Collins was her lover and he was waging a private vendetta, that was why.

Quarrick pulled a thread of nylon so hard that it bit into his finger. Four days left now until 7 December, a Wednesday. And the Anti-Terrorist Squad was closing on him, surveillance around the house palpable. There had to be other suspects, or they would have busted him already.

My Helen. He wasn't angry, just infinitely sad that their life together was over. And what would the boys think of him? Every terrorist should think of his own children. Whatever his beliefs, he should never invest himself with the glamour of heroics. How would they remember him? Please God, let them remember the friendship.

What did he need after the final act had been completed? Passport in the name of Ziman, plain-glass spectacles, cash, airline tickets... He went into the house.

Helen was sitting at the kitchen table drinking coffee and reading. She was also smoking a cigarette – that should have alerted him, when she started smoking again.

He suggested driving to Hampstead Heath with the boys to give the bald-headed eagles another airing.

'As a matter of fact I'm going—'

'Please,' he said.

'This is really important?'

He nodded.

'OK, why not? I'll call Ben and Jaime.'

It was a bright morning, frost sparkling, the sky blue and empty.

He didn't bother to check the driving mirror of the Mercedes for evidence of pursuit: it was there all right.

'You're very quiet, Dad,' Jaime said.

'I'm thinking.'

'Something you wouldn't understand,' Ben said to Jaime.

'I hope you won't always argue,' Quarrick said. 'Know what they should teach you at school? That there's no glory in war.'

'We're only kidding when we argue,' Jaime said.

'Yes,' Quarrick said. 'I understand that.'

Kites were flying high and free on the Parliament Hill stretch of Hampstead Heath. Quarrick helped Ben and Jaime to coax the bald-headed eagles into the sky, then took Helen's arm.

'I know,' he said.

'I guessed.'

'I'm going now.'

'Guessed that too.'

She seemed to be struggling to speak, just as he did sometimes in his nightmares.

He said: 'We had those years before the bad dreams began. Put them in a locket, open it from time to time.'

He kissed her and ran towards the boys. Knelt between them, arms round their shoulders.

'These are the days to remember,' he said. 'The kites and the frost and the space. The four of us. The past, the present and the future are all one, you know, a parcel. Don't ever forget that.'

He squeezed them so that they moved closer to each other.

Then he stood up, took the reel from Ben's hand and said: 'Hey, let me show you how to fly that thing.' He began to bring the kite back to earth.

Jaime shouted: 'Look out, it's going to crash!'

The kite hesitated, then dived into trees and undergrowth.

'Stay there!' Quarrick ran towards the trees. Went on running.

The blue Citroën ZX that he had rented in Golders Green was waiting at the roadside, key in the ignition, driven there by the dour Provo O'Brien. He turned the key, engaged first gear and, tyres spitting gravel, drove away at speed.

For cash, no questions asked, O'Brien rented a house in Norwood, south London, and the team moved there the same day.

It was tall and dank with red bricks that had survived two world wars and small windows like suspicious eyes. Inside it smelled of distemper and mushrooms, and the furniture had been stolen from a railway-station waiting room.

But it was detached; it had front and rear access; evergreens, laurel and yew, grew thickly behind a tall privet hedge; you could park your car down the tree-lined street and make a self-effacing approach.

It was called the Laurels. Quarrick, remembering one of the books he had read about the SAS, called it the Killing House.

The three accomplices he had used in the Thames fiasco moved in; four others, hard men from south Armagh who had been trained by ETA guerrillas in the Basque region arrived by ferry from Dublin and Belfast, security being more lax since the cease-fire.

Butler flew into London from Belfast's Aldergrove airport. Somewhere on the way he had discarded his dog collar, and his piety with it.

That made nine. They needed at least three more to make Operation Pearl credible. Quarrick contacted three old hands in north London who had never believed in political accord – a contradiction in terms, according to one.

Quarrick knew that the preparations were pushed but what they hadn't got was time. He called Fraser at home and told him he was taking a week's sick leave.

'You really sick, man?'

I really am, Quarrick thought. 'Tell Draper I've traced the American.' *Me!* 'Got it?'

'Got it. You OK?'

'Sure I'm OK. Why?'

'You don't sound your old buddy-buddy self. Not like when we're walking round the square, you know. Giving Franklin Delano the wink.'

'I'm fine,' Quarrick said.

'Good. 'Cos we don't want any more miracles. None of that Lourdes stuff – certain parties disappearing.'

'I'll be in touch,' Quarrick said.

'Yeah, I'll look forward to that. You take care now.'

Quarrick walked down the creaking stairs of the house in Norwood to the second floor. Spreading an ordinance map of Hereford and its surrounds on a table furrowed by cigarette burns, he began to brief the eleven men waiting for him there.

Collins knocked on the door of Hood's house in Muswell Hill. Hood opened it as though he had been expecting him.

Collins sat at the table covered by a damask cloth and gestured round the small room. 'Safe?'

'Dry-cleaned it personally.'

'Long distance?' Collins pointed across the street.

'All taken care of.'

'I've been followed here, of course.'

'No sweat.'

'Now they'll be following you.'

'Old hands at dodging, you and me.'

'They'll be mob-handed.'

'Makes it easier to lose them. We did it all the time in south Armagh.'

'Do you remember those psychological tests we used to have? You're given a word and you have to say what you associate it with.'

Hood looked puzzled. 'News and paper, that sort of thing?'

'Pearl,' Collins said.

'Diver.'

'Try again.'

'Necklace?'

'Once more.'

'Harbor?'

'Know when it was?'

'Are we going on a quiz show?'

'Think.'

'Nineteen forty-one.'

'Month?'

'December.'

'Day?'

'Sixth?'

'Seventh,' Collins said. 'The day Quarrick is going to hit Stirling barracks.'

When he told Hood about Quarrick's phone call that his sons had overheard, Hood said: 'Why the seventh?'

'That's what I've got to find out.'

'And me?'

'You follow Quarrick.'

Collins let himself out of the house and climbed into the Jaguar. Drove at a leisurely speed because whoever was following him would only report that he had driven to Hereford, which was where he was supposed to be anyway.

From Hereford he telephoned Helen at home. No reply. Not even the answering machine.

He tried Mindy Rivers's number.

'You heard?' Mindy prompted.

'What?'
'I got the part,' she said in her regional voice.
'Congratulations! Not understudying?'
'My own character – barmaid at the Harvester's Arms. Special clause in my contract: no cold tea, real ale.'
'Is Helen there?'
'Sitting beside me drinking real champagne.'
When she came on the line, Collins said: 'Harry isn't there, is he?'
'Harry's disappeared,' Helen said.
The implications dried up his words. Hood wouldn't be able to follow him, for one thing.
Recovering, he said: 'Any idea where he might have gone?'
'None.'
Another probability occurred to him. 'You let him go?'
'I loved him once.'
His hand tightened on the receiver. He gave it a moment, then told her about the arrangements he had made for Ben and Jaime's visit to the camp at Hereford. He would meet them at the gate at 7 pm on the evening of 6 December and give them the full tour on the 7th.

So Quarrick had done a runner. Hood wasn't surprised. He fetched his book of contacts from behind a shoebox filled with saucy postcards by Donald McGill and began to phone police informers living in London to the north of Euston Road and Pentonville Road.
He got lucky on the fourth call.
'Is Mickey there?'
'Everyone in this building is Mickey.'
'Mickey Flynn.' The jokes he must have to endure, Hood thought.
'Who wants him?' Ten pounds for every time he had heard that.
'I want you, Mickey.'
'Taff, is it?'
'I want some info, Mickey.'
'I'll call you back in ten minutes.' Hood guessed that he had taken the call on a pay phone in a hallway.
'No, I'll call you.' Because there was undoubtedly a tap on his own phone. 'Give me a number.'
Flynn gave him one. 'A friend of mine down the street.' By which he probably meant a prostitute: Mickey Flynn was a small-time pimp.
When Hood phoned again from another call box, Flynn said immediately: 'What sort of info, Taff? I thought the game was over.'

'Not everyone wants it to be over, Mickey. Some people think peace is defeat.'
'So what would you be wanting?'
'Someone's planning a big one, Mickey. I want to know where that someone is. Could be someone from across the pond.'
'A Yank?'
'You don't sound too surprised.'
'Nothing surprises me, you know that.'
'Heard any whispers, Mickey?'
'If I have, Taff, they were very faint. Didn't mean anything, you know. Not until now.'
'What sort of whispers?'
'A few missing persons, you know. Disappeared the way they did in the old days before a hit. Hard men,' he added.
'Do you know where they've gone?'
'I could make some inquiries. But this one would cost you, Taff. Dodgy, dangerous...'
'How much?'
'A monkey?'
'Five hundred pounds? It would have to be the business, Mickey.'
'I'll meet you in the Cathedral at nine tonight.'
'Hennekey's Long Bar?'
'You know your pubs, Taff. And bring the dosh with you, OK?'
'And you bring the info.'

Hood went to his bank in Muswell Hill and drew £500 in twenty-pound notes. Downed a couple of pints in the Maid of Muswell and led his shadows back to his house, where he cooked himself a steak and chips, drank half a bottle of Spanish red and slept for two hours.

When he awoke he dressed in jeans, Navy jersey and reefer jacket; let himself out of the house and, in his battered Cortina, led his pursuers to a greasy back yard in nearby Hornsey.

If you want to shake off pursuit, buy a moped!

A fat man with a beer belly showed him a selection.
'All ready to go, Mr Hood.'
'Cheque all right?'
'For you, natch. It can only bounce all the way to Scotland Yard.' His belly trembled with laughter.

Hood revved a Vespino. 'I'll take this one.' He called his insurance company, bought a red second-hand crash helmet, winked and said: 'Stand back.'

He skidded out of the yard and worked his way into rush-hour traffic so thick that not even a motorcycle could follow.

At 8.55 pm he was in Hennekey's Long Bar in Holborn, known as the Cathedral because of its tall, arched ceiling. The pub, originally built in 1430, also possessed a gallery supporting hulking barrels, and cubicles where lawyers settled out of court and lovers kissed.

Flynn came in on the stroke of nine. A good omen, Hood decided. He was as he remembered him, muscular with tattoos on his hands and long blond hair dark at the roots. They ordered two bottles of Guinness and retired to a cubicle.

'Got the money, Taff?'

'Have you done the business?'

'I might have something that will interest you.'

'Such as?'

'An address. Where one of the missing boys has gone.'

'Might not be the right one.'

'Then again it might. Supposing you were to give me the dosh and if it was the right address I'd keep it and if it wasn't—'

'You'd still keep it?'

'You know me better than that.'

'Where's the address?'

'Cash?'

Hood handed him an envelope containing the £500. Flynn didn't bother to count it. 'Norwood,' he said, and wrote an address on the top of a page of the *Evening Standard* with a Biro.

'Where would we be without snitches like you?' Hood said.

'You don't despise me?' Flynn seemed surprised.

'Of course not – you're performing a public service.'

Flynn tucked the envelope in the inside pocket of his raincoat. 'Well, I'll be off then.'

'Give my regards to the girls.'

'If you want—'

'I'll bear it in mind,' Hood said.

He waited a couple of seconds and finished his Guinness before following Flynn into High Holborn. The day had sparkled: the evening drizzled.

He followed Flynn at a distance as he turned into Hatton Garden, the undistinguished centre of the diamond trade. Flynn obviously had an assignation, probably with one of his whores.

Flynn turned right at Greville Street, deserted like the other small, rainswept streets. To the right, Bleeding Heart Yard. An invitation, surely. Rubber-soled shoes padding softly on the wet pavement, Hood closed on Flynn, taking the cheese-cutting wire with the wooden handles from the right-hand pocket of his reefer jacket.

Flynn half turned. 'What the fuck – ' Words extinguished as the wire looped over his head from behind, tightened and cut.

He writhed like a fish on a hook.

Hood felt the wire sever cartilage. He pulled the two handles, positioned between the index and second fingers, tighter.

Flynn slipped.

Hood fell with him onto the pavement, still pulling. As the life went out of him, Flynn lay still, jerked, lay still again.

Hood wondered, as he had wondered before, if the wire would sever the top of the spinal column if he gave it a last tug.

He removed the wire, wiped it on Flynn's raincoat and replaced it in the pocket of his reefer jacket. With one hand he reached inside Flynn's raincoat, took out the envelope containing the £500 and slipped it into the other pocket of the reefer.

The Vespino was parked in a modest street behind Hennekey's. As he retraced his footsteps he experienced a warm sense of accomplishment. If he hated anyone more than a run-of-the-mill terrorist, it was a terrorist doubling as an informer. Secker and Toland had been terrorists *and* snitches. Brady hadn't been a snitch but he had driven the taxi on the night of the Victoria Station bombing – police in a patrol car had provided a description – and it hadn't been difficult to anticipate that he would report to the address behind King's Cross Station from which the IRA issued false documents.

Bomber had been shot five times before he had died in Belfast. Hood would take one life for every bullet. One more left; Quarrick's. He and Collins would see to that, just like old times.

Hood drove to the house in Holloway where the woman who attended to his creature comforts had agreed to put him up. When she opened the front door she was wearing a silk robe embroidered with Chinese patterns, and high-heeled mules.

She said: 'What kept you?'

'Unfinished business.'

'That's an excuse?' The robe slipped a little, unveiling the swell of her breasts. She shivered. 'Well, you'd better come in.'

Inside the hall he slid one hand inside the robe and felt her breasts.

The house smelled of home and domestic Saturday-night sensuality. He hoped it would rain soon so that, when they had finished, he could listen to it tapping on the roof and the windows.

'Mind if I take a bath first?' he said.
'Be quick.'

It should have been a zinc bath, of course, in front of a fire made with coal mined in the valley. But her pink, slippery porcelain would have to make do.

As he slid into the hot, scented water he decided to drive the moped to Norwood at dawn.

Chapter Twenty-Four

IRISHMAN KNIFED TO DEATH. His demise merited only one paragraph in the newspaper. For 'knifed' read 'throat severed'? A cease-fire cover-up by Scotland Yard's press bureau?

Susan Norton poured herself a cup of Earl Grey tea and contemplated her husband sitting on the other side of the breakfast table applying chunky marmalade to a slice of buttered toast and scanning a bulb catalogue.

She said carefully: 'If three IRA sympathisers who were also police informers were killed within a short space of time, where would you look for the murderer?'

She expected him to say, 'Within the IRA', but instead he said: 'When was the last one?'

'Could have been last night.'

'Then it's not anyone within the IRA. They're respectable these days. If Yasser Arafat can get the Nobel Peace Prize, then so can their leaders, and they wouldn't want their prospects threatened by the murder of a snitch.'

'Snitch?'

'I have been known to watch television,' her husband said, taking a bite out of a slice of toast.

'Then who do you think killed them?'

'Police informers? Has to be someone within the police force. Normally a detective keeps a snitch to himself, protects him, even. But not when terrorism is involved; then it goes on the computers. So it has to be someone with access to the database.'

'My God,' she said, 'you *have* been watching a lot of television. Maybe you should have been a detective.'

'I prefer planting bulbs to digging up evidence,' he said.

Driving to work, Susan Norton called Davis on her car phone.

He was already at his office. Putting the finishing touches to the cover-up, she surmised.

'The dead Irishman,' she said. 'Another one?'

'Yes, as it happens. I was going to tell you.'

Sometimes it was easier to detect lies on the phone than face to face: they lodged in the receiver like dying insects. 'You could have called me at home. Has it occurred to you that the killer might be a police officer with access to the names of snitches?' She smiled into the receiver.

A pause, a stage laugh. 'Now why would a policeman kill the golden goose? In any case, we've got worse problems than a dead terrorist – Quarrick's done a runner.'

'But you had him under surveillance!'

'If someone knows they're being followed, they can always shake off the tail.'

'But you had backup!'

'Quarrick was clever.'

'Hood?'

'We lost him too.'

'Congratulations, chief inspector.'

'Superintendent.'

'By the sound of it,' Susan Norton said, 'you got your promotion just in time.'

A sigh. 'You realise what this means?'

'That some sort of hit is imminent. Like now?'

'Any time,' Davis said.

'When did Quarrick disappear?'

Davis hesitated. 'Saturday.'

'The day before yesterday? Why didn't you tell me then?'

'Didn't want to spoil your weekend, Mrs Norton. There was nothing you could do.'

'So what are *you* doing?'

'I made another call to the SAS. Whoever I spoke to sounded amused. And it is a pretty remote possibility that they would be targeted. Like punching a Scud with your fist.'

'Anything else?'

'We're interviewing Quarrick's wife,' Davis said.

Hood had arrived at the street in Norwood at dawn the previous day. The street slept and, the day being Sunday, would sleep late. Damp and leafless plane trees stood sentinel.

He observed the house, number 23, at a distance because, if they were professionals inside, they would have posted a guard at one of the windows.

Cars stood at the kerbside, leaves and bird droppings on the longtime loiterers. They didn't interest Hood. He looked instead at newcomers, in particular those parked at a distance from number 23. A blue Citroën ZX attracted his attention, rented from a company in Golders Green.

Hood knocked at the door of a tall house, white paint mottled, moss growing in the basement area, and asked if he could sit in the old rust-bucket Lancia outside.

'It won't get you nowhere, mate. Been there for eighteen months.' The young man wearing a threadbare dressing gown peered from sheepdog hair and yawned.

'Doesn't matter.' Hood handed him two five-pound notes. 'There, go back to sleep. Or whatever you were doing.'

He sat in the front of the rust-bucket, sandwiches, flask of coffee, Browning 9-mm pistol and plastic bomb and detonator in a holdall beside him, and began his vigil.

From time to time he got out to stretch his bent legs. He ate some of the sandwiches the woman in Holloway had provided, drank coffee.

At lunchtime a few cars took off to the pubs, returning after two. No movement from number 23. The afternoon faded into a cruel December evening, lights burning in four rooms in number 23.

He ate the rest of his sandwiches.

The man with the sheepdog hair knocked on the window. 'Haven't you got a home to go to?'

Hood said he hadn't and gave him another five-pound note.

The lights began to go out in number 23 at eleven. Now was the time if there was going to be any movement that night. Hood took a couple of Benzedrines to keep him awake.

Midnight... 2 am, nothing. Hood settled his head on the rest and, after an hour's fight with the Benzedrine, slept.

Quarrick began his penultimate briefing on the morning of Monday 5 December.

The whole team assembled in the living room, curtains drawn, at 8.30, draping themselves over protesting armchairs and leaning against walls papered with shepherdesses and nymphs.

Quarrick stood beside the Ordnance Survey map of Hereford and its environs pinned to the cigarette-burned table. 'First a word of warning; it's going to be goddamned cold up there. Snow on the Brecon Beacons, according to the weather forecast.'

'We'll take our winter woollies,' said a Dubliner named Delaney.

'What you *will* take,' Quarrick said, ignoring him, 'is cold-weather combat hat, sweat rag to be used as a scarf, belts of 7.62-mm ammo, camouflage gear, British Army design—'

'That sticks in the gullet,' said O'Brien, the ex-seaman who had been with him on the aborted Thames operation.

' – canvas anklets and DMS boots. Riddick will take care of that.' Quarrick nodded at a lanky bank manager's son from Londonderry.

Riddick, whose father had been shot dead coming out of church, said: 'Usual source of supplies at Aldershot. Supplemented from a government-surplus store.'

Butler, still without his dog collar, said: 'Guns – general-purpose machine guns and pistols. And a Thermit incendiary bomb. All stored in the warehouse at Feltham.'

Quarrick, pointing at Butler, said: 'Of course Conor is in charge of this operation.'

Silence. O'Brien, squat and powerful, broke it. 'And why won't you be leading us, Harry boy?'

'Because I'm blown. I would jeopardise the operation.'

'Or is it because this one's too fucking dangerous for you? Because you aren't committed?'

'It's because it's going to be too cold. I can't stand the cold, you know.' He picked up O'Brien by the lapels and threw him against the wall. When O'Brien picked himself up, he hit him on the jaw; but not too hard because in two days they would need every man in the room.

Butler broke it up, pushing them apart. 'OK, Harry, you made your point. Some of the boys have never quite understood why an American should be in charge in London.'

'They can't understand that it's the best cover an IRA freedom fighter ever had? Then they're—'

'I know what they are,' Butler said. 'Now get on with it.'

Quarrick turned back to his audience. 'OK, this is how it's going to be. And this includes you,' to O'Brien. 'We make the hit at about 0830 hours. Give or take, it doesn't matter. Where?' He prodded a finger at a farmer from south Armagh built like a barn.

'On the A465.' The farmer stabbed one finger on the map.

'Right. Barrier across the road. Conor Butler steps forward waving a flashlight – in case the light is really bad – gun in hand. Wearing an SAS beret.' He turned to Riddick. 'Got it?'

Riddick held up a sand-coloured beret.

'And then?' Quarrick addressed a one-time getaway driver who had operated the length and breadth of the border separating

Northern Ireland from the Republic, a slender young man with a twist to his mouth and the watchful eyes of a pilot.

'The Bedford stops and Butler, with a forged SAS tag on his combat jacket, asks for the password. The driver of the Bedford gives it to him—'

'And then,' Quarrick said, 'he orders the soldiers in the back to get out. Which they do – to be taken prisoners by you guys at gunpoint. And they'll be so dead beat that they won't know what time of day it is.'

'Unless,' Butler said, 'they think it's another part of the test – cunning bastards, these SAS – and they resist. In which case—'

'You shoot them,' Quarrick said. 'But hopefully that won't be necessary. Just tie them up, gag them and drive them to the house we've rented on the outskirts of Hereford. What then?' to Riddick.

'Easy. We take their ID. Drive the Bedford to the guardroom. Password? We've got that from the driver. And in we go into the holy of holies, the headquarters of the invincible Special Air Services. Plant the bombs and piss off, showing the stolen ID at the guardroom. Hoof it into Hereford, off and away in rented cars as the Semtex blows.'

Butler said: 'Why 'hopefully', Harry?'

'Hopefully what?'

' "Hopefully that won't be necessary", shooting them, that is.'

'Too messy,' Quarrick said.

'Not going soft on us, are you, Harry?'

'Ask him,' Quarrick said, jerking his thumb at O'Brien.

Two men left number 23 separately, half an hour between their departures. After the second had gone, Hood called Collins in Hereford on his mobile phone.

Collins said: 'Stay put – it's Quarrick we want.'

Hood told him he thought he had located Quarrick's car. Gave him the name and phone number of the rental company in Golders Green displayed on a sticker in the rear window. 'Tell them I've lost the key – ten quid for the boyo who brings the duplicate during his lunch break. I'll be waiting up the street. Can't miss a bow-legged miner's son with a scar on top of his head, can he?'

In the house in Chelsea the interrogation was intensifying. Pacing the living-room, Davis was making an American courtroom out of it; his assistant, a sombre man with unfashionable sideburns, stood mutely in attendance, occasionally disappearing into the kitchen where he could be heard talking conspiratorially into a handset.

'So you had no idea your husband was going to make a run for it?' Davis said.

'I don't even know that he has.' Helen lit a Marlboro and sat beside the cold ashes in the fireplace.

'He didn't tell you where he was going?'

'No.'

'Bit unusual, wasn't it?'

'Not in his line of business.'

'A diplomat. They can be devious but not that bloody devious, surely? CIA, was he, Mrs Quarrick?'

'If he was, I didn't know about it.'

'Takes you and the boys to Hampstead Heath and does a runner through the woods? Come on, Mrs Quarrick, you know more about this than you're letting on.'

'I suspected that he had come to some sort of decision.'

'Why was that?'

'He was so insistent that we go to Hampstead Heath. Right out of the blue. The way he talked to the boys—'

'What did he say to them?'

'He told them kids should be taught there's no glory in war.'

'He would know, wouldn't he, Mrs Quarrick?' And when she didn't answer: 'Anything else up there on the Heath? Was it confession time? The moment of truth? You see, we know about you and Collins . . .'

Head tilted, he studied her; looking for shock, she supposed. She didn't reward him because she wasn't surprised. Through the smoke rising from her cigarette, Davis looked like a genie.

She felt quite relaxed because there was a bleak inevitability about the interrogation. She had promised Collins they would go it alone, but now the British anti-terrorists knew about Harry anyway, and he was on the run. So she answered Davis's questions as best she could.

'Harry told me he knew.'

'About you and Collins?'

'Of course.'

'Wasn't he angry? Furious? Disgusted? Most men are when they find out their wives have been cheating.'

'He was philosophical.' As though he had known for some time, she thought.

'Where do you think he went to?' Davis started pacing again. 'You must have some idea.'

'None.' She found relief in the negative truth.

'You know about the attempt to hit the headquarters of British intelligence?'
She said she did.
'Through Collins?'
She nodded.
'You were very intimate then . . . Was he good at it?'
'Get lost, superintendent.'
Davis's assistant had gone into the kitchen. She could hear him addressing his handset. What he was saying she couldn't imagine. She lit another cigarette; the smoke burned her tongue.
Davis sat opposite her, laced his hands together and cracked his knuckles. 'We believe your husband is planning one last hit to break the cease-fire. Any ideas, Mrs Quarrick?'
'None.'
'You didn't pass on any information to Collins?'
She considered what she had told Collins. 'Top priority for pearl,' overheard by Ben and Jaime. Collins hadn't reacted.
'A trade, superintendent?'
'I don't think you're in a position to trade, Mrs Quarrick. Has it occurred to you that you could be charged with being an accessory?'
'No trade, no information.'
'What's the trade?'
'If you get an address for him, tell me.'
'Why would you want to know?'
'Because I didn't say goodbye.'
'You want to say goodbye to a terrorist?'
'No,' she said. 'To the man he was.'
'OK,' Davis said. 'A deal.'
She told him about Pearl.
Davis nodded at his assistant, who returned to the kitchen.
'Does it mean anything to you, superintendent?'
'It might. Pearl sounds like a code word. And I'm a World War II buff. The Japanese attacked Pearl Harbor on 7 December, the day after tomorrow. Anything else, Mrs Quarrick?'
'Nothing.'
'You didn't see the car he got away in?'
She shook her head.
'A man answering your husband's description rented a blue Citroën ZX in Golders Green. Your husband's Mercedes in still outside this house.'
'Then find the Citroën, superintendent.'
'Don't worry, we're looking. But he must have changed the number plate by now. He's a pro, your husband.'

A pro? Harry? It sounded faintly absurd. Had she been so naive all those years?

Davis stood up. 'If you think of anything else, give me a call.' He handed her a card.

As they left, his assistant smiled and said: 'Nice kitchen that, Mrs Quarrick. My wife would like it.'

Later she remembered Harry whimpering 'Sterling' in a nightmare. Sterling area, Sterling silver... meaningless. She began to iron clothes for Ben and Jaime for their visit to the SAS barracks.

At 11 am the man with the sheepdog fringe came out to Hood's rust-bucket and gave him a mug of tea. 'You fuzz?' When Hood shrugged, he said: 'Thought as much. Number twenty-three?'

'Could be.'

'A lot of dodgy characters use that. Drugs?'

'Soft,' Hood said.

'Soft leads to hard. Want to use the bathroom?'

'If it's no trouble. What's the going rate these days for spending a penny?'

'Have this one on me. Always a pleasure to do business with the law.'

'Mum's the word, right?'

'Silence is golden. Know what I mean?'

Hood gave him two more five-pound notes.

On the morning of the Tuesday, Butler left number 23 with three men to pick up weapons, combat uniforms and equipment packaged as electrical goods at Feltham and load them into a white Transit van bearing the slogan GET SWITCHED ON and underneath FOR ALL ELECTRIC GOODS CALL LIVE WIRES followed by a non existent address and phone number in Bristol.

Two had left for Hereford the previous day; five others now left one by one to two rendezvous points to pick up two rented four-wheel drives, a Range Rover and a Suzuki. Final rendezvous: midnight at the empty house off the A465 on the outskirts of Hereford where the SAS hopefuls were to be kept prisoner. If they weren't shot, that was.

Quarrick stayed behind in the house and wrote three letters. They were short but they took him a long time. One to Helen, one each to Ben and Jaime.

At 12.30 he let himself out of the house, walked down the street and opened the door of the Citroën ZX. He put the letters, sealed in envelopes, into the glove compartment alongside his airline ticket to Amsterdam booked in the name of Ziman and a KLM flight ticket bought at a different travel agent from Amsterdam to New York.

Seeing him, Hood lowered one hand to the butt of the pistol in the holdall. No, Quarrick was Collins's target. Reluctantly he took his hand away from the Browning and picked up his crash helmet, ready to give chase on the Vespino parked behind the rust-bucket.

Quarrick closed the door of the Citroën quietly and returned to Number 23. As the front door closed, the man with the sheepdog hair handed Hood a mug of tea through the window. And a slice of cake. 'The missus made it,' he said. Chocolate, Hood's favourite.

He waited until it was quite dark before opening the door of the Citroën ZX with the duplicate key the mechanic from the rental company in Golders Green had brought him. He pulled the hood release beneath the steering wheel and attached the plastic explosive and detonator to the distributor.

Helen left Chelsea for Hereford at 4.30 pm, the boys in the back of the Fiesta chattering excitedly. Not only were they going to penetrate the headquarters of the SAS but they were going to do it tomorrow, Wednesday, during school hours.

'Don't mess with the SAS,' Ben said as they drove west.

'He must have got a lot of clout, this friend of yours,' Jaime said. 'Has he killed many people?'

'Have you forgotten what your father told you? That there's no glory in war?'

'Where is Dad?' Ben asked.

'The embassy have sent him away for a few days.'

'A secret mission?'

'Sort of, I guess.'

'I wish he was in the SAS,' Jaime said.

'I wish he was in Delta or the Rangers or the Green Berets,' Ben said.

'I wish he was home,' Jaime said.

She stopped at a service-station cafeteria for a coffee, 7-Up for the boys, arriving at the SAS camp at seven. Collins, in uniform, was waiting at the gate.

He saluted the boys and told Helen he would drive them home the following day. He wasn't particularly tall but, as they walked towards the guardroom fifty yards away, one on either side of him, the boys looked very small.

Chapter Twenty-Five

Snow had dusted the peaks of the Brecon Beacons overnight and as the SAS hopefuls took up positions in the dawn light, the hills sparkled.

Corporal Robert 'Badger' Blaydon of the Parachute Regiment, so nicknamed because his cropped hair was patched with grey, had volunteered for the SAS after a bet during a session on Newcastle brown ale in a pub in South Shields. He now wondered why the fuck he had made the bet; only one thing bothered him more, that he might lose it.

For sixteen hours and twenty-eight minutes he had been striding through the Beacons. The snow hadn't been soft flakes; it had been pellets like buckshot. After plunging into a stream tissued with ice, weighted with his Bergen loaded with bricks, he had wondered if he might succumb to hypothermia – two participants already had, according to the word reaching him through the hills and valleys.

Like a good boy he had eaten his Mars bars to sustain his energy and body heat and plunged on through the darkness, slithering down precipitous slopes, climbing hillsides studded with clumps of grass. Now here he was at the final rendezvous watching the sun rise weakly over the sugar-loaf hills. One by one, other volunteers who had never known such fatigue joined him. No one spoke: it was too much effort.

When Badger climbed into the second of the two Bedford three-tonners sent to bring the volunteers back to the camp at Hereford, to triumph or more probably humiliation, he lit a cigarette, inhaled fiercely and delivered his views on the Endurance. No one responded. Either they were too exhausted or they hadn't understood his Geordie accent.

After a few drags Badger nipped the cigarette between thumb and forefinger, stamped on the glowing tip with his boot and, head slumped forward, slept, expecting to awake at the guardroom. But when the Bedford stopped he saw open countryside through a veil of snow. When they were all ordered out he said: 'Load of bloody wankers,' and, for once, everyone understood him.

The shooting started five minutes later.

Collins took the call from Hood in his room in the camp at 8.35 am. 'He's still there,' Hood said.

'Anyone with him?'

'Not as far as I know but you'd better hurry.'

Collins, dressed in grey sports jacket and white poloneck, fetched the Jaguar and set off for London. Stone-grey clouds had covered the sun and snow was crossing the border from Wales.

The snow followed him onto the M4, flakes driving at the windscreen. That was all he needed, visibility as bad as this. But he kept in the fast lane just the same.

He arrived in the street in Norwood at 10.35 and parked the Jaguar fifty yards from number 23. He had left the snow far behind but it was bitterly cold, patches of frost glittering on the pavement. He checked the pistol beneath his jacket, a Browning like Hood's, climbed out of the Jaguar and made his way towards number 23.

Outside he signalled to Hood in the rust-bucket further down the street on the opposite side. Hood signalled back, one hand raised. Collins rang the bell beside the door of number 23.

A voice through the mottled aluminium grill above the bell. Slight American accent. Quarrick. 'Who's that?'

'Jack Collins. You murdered my wife and daughter.'

A pause. Collins slipped one hand inside his jacket and felt the butt of the Browning in its holster.

'I didn't ... What do you want?'

'I've got your kids, Quarrick.'

Another pause. 'I don't—'

'I can prove it.'

Collins glanced along the street. A man with shaggy hair was handing Hood a mug.

'Are you armed?' Quarrick's voice sounded stretched.

'Of course. But I haven't come here to shoot you: it's your kids we've got to talk about.'

'OK, come up.'

'Put your gun down,' Collins said. 'For the kids' sake.'

A click. He pushed the door. It opened.

Quarrick was waiting for him at the top of the stairs, pistol in his hand. He was wearing jeans and a grey mohair jersey. He had cut himself shaving and the hand holding the gun shook.

Collins sawed at the cleft in his chin with one finger. 'I said, put the gun down.' He began to climb the stairs.

Quarrick tossed the gun into the room behind him. 'Where are my boys?'

'All in good time.' Collins pushed past Quarrick into the shabby room beyond. Chipped cups and mugs, plates congealed with leftover food, ashtrays overflowing. Coloured drawing pins were stuck in the table as though a map had been pinned there. Quarrick's pistol lay in the middle.

'Where are they?'

'They're safe. For the moment. Unlike my wife and daughter.'

'I was in Ireland when they were killed.'

'You were the boss,' Collins said. 'You were responsible.'

He walked to the window and stared down the street. The mechanics had arrived and were attending to the Citroën ZX. Not child locks on all the doors – there wasn't time – but deft work on the existing locks so that when the doors closed they would jam. They were going to fix the windows too, so that they wouldn't open.

'What do you want?'

To see you suffer as I suffered, Collins thought.

'You're not going to harm them?'

'*You* might if you don't cooperate.'

'I don't understand. Where are they?'

'Carrying out an initiative test set at their school.'

'Where? For Christ's sake, where?'

Collins waited for his moment. Then he said: 'At SAS headquarters in Hereford.'

The blood drained from Quarrick's face, leaving it waxen white. He put one hand to his chest and collapsed in an armchair.

Superintendent Bernard Davis had two breaks that morning, the second confirming the first.

He was seated at his desk at New Scotland Yard when he received a phone call from a regional crime squad inspector in south London, a one-time friend who might also have made superintendent if he hadn't been such a tearaway himself.

'Are you up to anything in Norwood, Bernie?'

'Nothing in particular. Keeping our eye on a couple of synagogues. Why?'

'A weirdo turned up at our nick and asked if we had mounted a surveillance operation there.'

'And you hadn't?'
'Some bloke sitting in an old rust-bucket Lancia staking out a house down the street. Paid the weirdo ten quid to sit in it – even though it wasn't his!'
'A not-so-daft weirdo,' Davis said.
'We sent a car along to suss it out. But they backed off. Recognised one of your men in the rust-bucket, Bernie. Didn't want to balls anything up for you. Are you sure you aren't pulling a flanker in Norwood?'
'Who was the officer in the Lancia?'
'They didn't know his name. Just knew he was one of your mob. He got out to stretch or have a piss or something – that's how they recognised him.'
'Short, crop-haired, bow legs?'
'That's him. What are you up to, Bernie? Can't you trust your old mates any more?'
'When did this happen?'
'Monday.'
'Why wasn't it reported to me then?'
'Because I only heard about it this morning. Casual chat with the driver of the car. No reason why he should have reported it, is there? Anti-Terrorist Squad. Don't mess with them . . .'
'What number was this officer staking out?'
'Number 23, according to the weirdo.'
'Know what day it is today?'
'December the seventh. Your birthday, Bernie?'
'The day the Japanese raided Pearl Harbor.'

Davis hung up. Picking up another phone, he alerted a hit squad with a hostage negotiator, just in case.

The confirmation came five minutes later: a call from the car-rental company in Golders Green.

'We've had a phone call from the man who wanted the blue ZX. He told us he had lost the keys. I sent one of my employees with a duplicate. He was paid ten pounds.'
'Where?'
'Where what, superintendent?'
'Where did he take the keys to, for Christ's sake?'
'Norwood.'
'Street?'

The manager told him.

'Description?'
'Odd that, superintendent. Apparently he didn't sound American.'

'Welsh?'
'Yes, as a matter of fact—'
Davis cut the connection.
Before he joined the hit squad, he made three calls. The first to Susan Norton in case she started making complaints to the Home Office about lack of cooperation.

'Sounds good, Bernard.' First name – crises generated camaraderie. 'Softly, softly catchee monkey...'

Now what the hell did she mean by that? 'Of course, Susan.'

'Because the Americans are going to be as mad as hell when they hear about this. They'll invoke diplomatic immunity and fly Quarrick back to the States. But we could strike a deal. Release him in return for information about IRA involvement in NORAID. What do you think?'

'I think the best solution would be to put a bullet through his head.'

'Anything about any threat to the SAS?'
'Nothing, Susan. I'll be in touch.'

His second call was to the police in Hereford. Yes, there had been a report about a shooting incident on the A465. Some sort of SAS operation. Good neighbours, the SAS, helped out when needed, but paranoic when it came to questions about their own exploits.

Davis made his third phone call. To Helen Quarrick.

'I think we've traced your husband.'

Helen tightened her grip on the receiver. 'Where is he?'
'In south London,' Davis said.
'Where in south London?'
'We'll pick you up and take you there, just as I promised.'
'More than you promised, superintendent. I merely asked you to tell me where he was.'
'I'll be honest – you can help.'
'How?'
'Get on the hailer. Tell him to come out. We don't want a big scene, Mrs Quarrick. Not another Iranian embassy siege seen by millions on television. Will you do it?'

She thought about it. The world watching the SAS going in, Harry overcome by stun grenades – shot, maybe. Ben and Jaime witnessing the ultimate humiliation of their father. Ben's initiative test a mockery...

'OK, I'll do it. First I've got to get in touch with the kids.'
'Where are they, Mrs Quarrick?'

'With the SAS,' she said. 'In Hereford.'

Quarrick lifted his head. Colour returned to his face. 'I don't believe it.'

'That Ben and Jaime are in the camp at Hereford?' Collins shrugged. Took a video cassette from his pocket and slotted it into the VCR below the television set in the corner of the room.

The two boys were walking towards the guardroom. Collins: 'Welcome to SAS headquarters.' Small voices: 'Wow!' and 'I can't believe it!' Pan to the guardroom. Beyond: troopers wearing sand-coloured berets.

Collins switched off the VCR, leaving the TV flickering.

Quarrick said. 'It's a trick. They wouldn't let you use a camera there.'

'Wouldn't let the adjutant use one? Come off it, Harry.'

'When was that video taken?'

'Yesterday evening. They spent the night there. Today the full treatment.'

'You've got to get them out!'

'Why? They couldn't be in a safer place than the headquarters of SAS, could they?'

'You don't understand.'

'Enlighten me.'

'There are bombs there.' Quarrick glanced at the clock on the wall. 'Primed to explode in half an hour.'

'I don't believe you.'

'There are, I tell you!' He was shouting, voice bouncing off the walls of the smoke-stale room.

Collins folded his arms. 'Come now, Harry, how could anyone have penetrated SAS headquarters? Fort Knox would be an easier proposition.'

'The volunteers coming back from the Endurance test this morning... We ambushed them. They weren't volunteers who drove into the camp – they were IRA extremists, Liberation Army.'

'IRA? Come off it! Peace has broken out, didn't anyone tell you?'

'Peace? Defeat!' Quarrick pointed at the wall clock. 'Twenty-five minutes. You've got to believe me. Evacuate the camp.'

'And make ourselves a laughing stock? You're a lousy liar, Harry.'

'It's true! For God's sake, get on the phone.'

'I've often wondered how terrorists felt when they switched on the TV and saw the victims they had killed or maimed. Kids, Harry, who trusted grown-ups—'

'For God's sake make that call!'

As Quarrick lunged for the gun on the floor, Collins tripped him, snatched his own pistol from inside his jacket and pointed it at Quarrick's head.

'Did you ever wonder how the kids' parents felt, Harry? All that love and pride they had invested in them squandered because of a cause they didn't even comprehend?'

Quarrick stood up. 'Two innocent kids are going to die if you don't make that call. And a lot of soldiers...'

'OK, tell me where these *bombs* are planted.'

'The armoury, the mess, admin...'

Collins moved to the window, keeping the pistol trained on Quarrick's head. Hood was paying off the two mechanics – £250, the second instalment.

And now he was opening the bonnet of the Citroën. Priming the delayed-action detonator.

When Helen arrived in Norwood, police in flak jackets armed with rifles and sub-machine-guns were taking up positions.

Davis pointed down the street. 'Number 23, that's where your husband is. I want you to go down there with the hailer in five minutes and appeal to him to come out, hands behind his head. Tell him the house is surrounded. Tell him your sons are safe.'

She looked at him in surprise. 'Of course they're safe.'

When Hood saw the hit squad arrive, he abandoned the rust-bucket and knocked on the door of the house where the provider of tea and chocolate cake lived.

'Mind if I come indoors?'

The man with the shaggy hair pointed at a couple of armed police at the end of the street. 'Don't you want to be where the action is?'

'Undercover,' Hood said, handing him two five-pound notes. Holdall in one hand, he stood at the bay window from where he could just see number 23.

Susan Norton, wearing a long oatmeal coat, stepped out of her black limousine.

Davis said: 'What are you doing here?'

'Message from the Home Secretary. No shooting if possible.'

'We throw buns at him?'

'I'm just the messenger.'

'We don't know for sure how many men there are in that house. Supposing they all come out guns blazing?'

'What he means is no shooting without sufficient warning, no bullets in the back.'

'It's OK if one of my men gets a bullet in the back?' Davis punched the palm of one hand with his fist. 'Because he's American? Because we don't want to ruffle that Special Relationship between London and Washington? Because *you* want to do a deal with the CIA?'

'If you've got to shoot, do it.'

He took her by the arm and led her away from Helen Quarrick. 'I've got a hunch you could have been right about the SAS,' he said.

Collins took a pocket recorder from his coat and activated it. 'One more thing before I call Hereford.'

'Are you crazy? The bombs will blow in twenty minutes.'

'Semtex? Delayed-action fuses? You've told me where you've planted them. We can defuse them in five minutes.'

'You *are* crazy! What do you want to know?'

'Nice kids, Ben and Jaime, by all accounts.'

'You've got to save them! Please, for the love of God.'

'Names and addresses of all known IRA operators past and present in the United Kingdom?'

Quarrick gabbled into the recorder. 'Now get on the phone.'

'And the names of the hardliners in the UK, Northern Ireland and the Republic who want to break the peace.'

'Butler—'

'We know about him.'

Quarrick reeled off names and addresses.

'And now for the most important part,' Collins said. 'Sinn Féin has refused to say the cease-fire is permanent.'

'I don't control Sinn Féin.'

'But it would be much more permanent, wouldn't it, if the IRA laid down its arms? Or, failing that, if we knew where they were.'

'I don't know where they are.'

'In Britain? Come off it, Harry.'

Quarrick gave him addresses in Hounslow, Cricklewood in north London, Liverpool and Glasgow.

'Northern Ireland and the Republic?'

More addresses – on the outskirts of Belfast, southern Armagh and a village near Londonderry in Northern Ireland, Dundalk and a suburb of Dublin.

When he had finished, Collins stabbed the Browning at him and said: 'Now let's wait a little while.'

'But you said—'

'I'm a liar. Have to be in our business, don't we, Harry? Two of a kind, you and me.'

'I'm going to call,' Quarrick said. He moved towards the soiled, cream-coloured telephone beside the television. 'Shoot me if you want to.'

'Going to telephone a warning?'

'I'm going to call 999.'

'Judy and Jane didn't get any warnings.'

Quarrick picked up the phone. As he began to dial, Collins shot the receiver out of his hand.

'Oh, I forgot to tell you – that clock on the wall is slow. If there were any bombs, they would have exploded by now.'

Quarrick knelt, covering his face with his hands. Wept.

Collins laid the Browning on the table, crossed the room and touched Quarrick's shoulder.

'There weren't any bombs,' he said. He grasped Quarrick's arm. 'Sit at the table, I'll explain.'

Quarrick laid his arms on the table and rested his head on them.

Pearl, Collins said – that was easy, 7 December. Stirling was easy too. So there had to be a particular reason for the date and the location. Who would know better than anyone what was happening at the camp that day? The officer in charge of admin, of course, the adjutant. And he knew that the volunteers would be returning from the Endurance that morning. 'This morning,' Collins corrected himself.

Quarrick raised his head. '*You* anticipated what we were going to do?'

'We stopped the Bedford with hopefuls inside a few miles from the Brecon Beacons. Ordered them out, replaced them with SAS. The ambush took place on the A465, right?'

Right, Quarrick said.

'When the tailgate came down the SAS piled out shooting. But not necessarily to kill. One of your men did buy it, Butler. The rest were taken prisoner.'

'My kids?'

'They were nowhere near the camp. I took them away last night and booked them into a hotel in Hereford just in case anything went wrong. They're doing the grand tour this afternoon. They'll be heroes at school—'

'But *we* aren't, are we?' Quarrick took a handkerchief from his pocket and dabbed at the tears on his cheeks.

From outside they heard a voice issuing from a hailer. Helen's. They stared at each other. Sharing.

'Come on down, Harry. Before the media get here – before Ben and Jaime see you on the box. It's all over, Harry. But I want to say this. I loved you, Harry, the man you were. Can you see me?'

Quarrick peered from behind a dusty curtain.

'I don't know if you can or not. Can you see this?'

She was holding up a photograph and he knew it was the photograph of his parents. *Victims of War.*

'I want you to know I understand. But I can't forgive. Come on down, Harry. Come on down!'

Collins said: 'If I cause a distraction, you can get to the Citroën.'

'Who says I want to?'

'Anything's better than giving yourself up.'

'What are you going to do?'

'You go downstairs. Wait till you hear the sound of glass breaking, then make a run for it. Here, don't forget this.' He handed Quarrick his mobile phone.

They stared at each other for a moment. Then Quarrick picked up the gun on the table and walked out of the room. Collins heard the stairs creak. When the creaking stopped, he knocked out the nearest window with the butt of the Browning and stepped into the frame.

A shot from across the street. The bullet thudded into the wooden strut of the frame above his head.

A sniper's warning.

An authoritative voice: 'Hold your fire! Quarrick, throw your gun out of the window.'

Collins threw his gun. Heard it hit the pavement.

Helen: 'It isn't Harry! Jack...'

Quarrick was running, feet slipping on the frost. Ahead the Citroën.

Helen's voice again: 'Harry, it's no use.'

A figure loomed in front of him. Shortish, shoulders hunched, bowed legs, handgun held professionally.

The bullet hit him in the chest, stopping him, spinning him round. He felt its impact with a kind of gratitude as the blood spread warmly.

Helen was beside him, hands reaching for the wound. 'Three letters in the car,' he said. 'All about what we had, you and me and the kids, before the bad dreams started.'

The man with the bowed legs loomed over them, gun aimed at Harry. As he pulled the trigger, Helen flung herself across his body, felt the bullet shatter bone.

'Harry!'

But his eyes were open wide and she knew that there wouldn't be any more bad dreams. She took the car keys from his outstretched hand and made her way on bending legs to the Citroën because it was important that she got to the letters before anyone else.

She found them in the glove compartment and put them in her purse. But when she tried to open the door the handle jammed. And the windows wouldn't open.

Hood took off on the Vespino. Steered it between the police gathered at the end of the street. They didn't shoot: he was one of them.

Then he headed north, arriving at his house in Muswell Hill twenty minutes later.

He made a cup of tea. They would come for him. Of that he was well aware. So? He was an inspector in the Anti-Terrorist Squad. And he had killed a terrorist – realised he was dead as he fired the second shot.

Pick the bones out of that. A charge, a trial? For doing his job? He doubted it. An elaborate cover-up more likely. Both the British and the Americans had a lot to lose through publicity.

What mattered was that Bomber had been avenged.

Collins sat beside her bed in the private ward of the hospital. One of her arms was in plaster and her shoulder ached as though the bullet which had passed through her body was still lodged there.

He said: 'I brought you this.' He placed a cardboard box on the bedside table.

'Grapes?'

'Putty.'

'I'm not into putty.'

'That was what I gave Hood, doctored to look like Semtex, to attach to the distributor in the Citroën. Originally I was going to give him explosive but I changed my mind. I couldn't tell him because he wouldn't have understood.'

'Hood?'

He told her about their partnership. 'In fact only the detonator exploded while you were in the car.'

'Why did you change your mind?'

'Because I realised that if I went through with it I was no better than Harry. No better than a lot of people who believe that a cause is more important than one life.'

'And that was it? You were going to let Harry drive away with putty in the engine of the car?'

'Not quite.' Collins sawed at the cleft in his chin. 'I was going to call him on his mobile phone. Tell him there was a bomb in the car primed to explode in a few moments. "Get out of that, you bastard," is what I was going to say. "Goodbye, Harry Quarrick, murderer, child killer." '

'That would have been monstrously cruel! What you put him through in the house was cruel.'

'I know. Cruelty is infectious.' He touched the box containing the putty. 'We've won a small victory for decency, that's all. The ceasefire will be broken, there will be more bombs, more cruelty. That's chapter and verse of history – shaking hands after the slaughter of innocents instead of before. But maybe we're learning, just maybe.'

'Don't give me shit, Jack,' she said. 'You were as much a part of that history as Harry was. Now get out.'

Chapter Twenty-Six

Autumn. Snow had come early to Vermont. Three kites, blood red against the snow, competed for the polished blue sky.

A man emerged from a belt of leafless woodland. He held a yellow kite, an ordinary, diamond-shaped model, available at most toy stores.

He hesitated, listening to the cries of the children reeling the kites. Two boys and a girl named Electra. They controlled their soaring, dipping charges well. The boys were disrespectful to the girl, who looked a little Indian, but they nevertheless seemed eager to help her. To show off in front of her, even.

The man approached. 'Hi! Can anyone help me fly this thing?'

'Jack!' The two boys ran to him while the girl stood back. One of them shouted: 'Where have you been? It's been nearly a year.'

Watching, Helen Quarrick dipped one finger into the snow. Licked it, fancied it tasted of sugar.